A CANDIDATE FOR CONSPIRACY

Yesterday he was a spy. Today he's a Washington politician. Tomorrow he could be the next President of the United States. Soon he could be in control of one of the world's most powerful nations — unless a daredevil adventurer and his beautiful accomplice can stop him. But that's a big if . . .

STEVE HAYES

◆

A
CANDIDATE FOR
CONSPIRACY

Complete and Unabridged

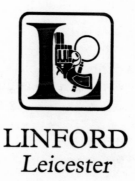

LINFORD
Leicester

First published in Great Britain

First Linford Edition
published 2014

Copyright © 2012 Steve Hayes
All rights reserved

A catalogue record for this book is available
from the British Library.

ISBN 978–1–4448–1906–9

Published by
F. A. Thorpe (Publishing)
Anstey, Leicestershire

Set by Words & Graphics Ltd.
Anstey, Leicestershire
Printed and bound in Great Britain by
T. J. International Ltd., Padstow, Cornwall

This book is printed on acid-free paper

1

Bogue Banks is a narrow offshore beach strand that hugs the North Carolina coast for some twenty-odd miles between Morehead City and Cape Carteret. The sluggish waters of Bogue Sound separate the banks from the mainland, and to drive across one must either take the Atlantic Beach Causeway near the eastern tip, or the narrow bridge that joins Cape Carteret to the western end of the banks, known as Emerald Isle.

Clare Winslow, snugly buckled in her brand-new 1980 Porsche 911s that she'd driven from Washington, D.C., buzzed across the bridge into Emerald Isle and found herself wondering if everything around her was moving in slow motion. Sunburned vacationers dozed on the beach. Dogs yawned in the shade. Sea gulls circled lazily above anchored fishing boats. Drowsy old-timers sat on front porches swapping lies, chewing Redman tobacco, and lethargically spitting into number 10 cans. *Good God*, she thought as she drove through the sleepy, sun-baked resort, *I wonder what they do around here for excitement — watch the traffic lights change?*

A short distance ahead, past a scattering of motels and beach homes on stilts, a sign indicated Coast Guard Road. Clare geared down, thrilled as always by the wonderful high-pitched whine the engine made, turned onto the paved side road, and headed west. The road ran straight for several hundred yards. Clare took advantage of it, working smoothly through the gears until she was bumping seventy. Speed exhilarated her. That was why she'd bought the Porsche. Although it wasn't new, it still had plenty of speed and hugged the corners as if it were on rails.

Outside it was a hot, blue-gold afternoon. Clare opened the throat of her stylish pink safari blouse and shook her long sun-colored hair back from her face. At twenty-eight she was a tall, willowy, graceful woman, more sultry than beautiful, who exuded the kind of smoldering elegance that smiles at you from inside another man's Rolls-Royce. Yet for all her poise and cool sophistication, she possessed a warmth that made her seem equally at home eating hot dogs at football games.

It was September, and the country was gearing up for the November 11 presidential election. The incumbent president was not in the political race, having served his maximum two consecutive terms in office, but the conventions were now over and both nominees selected by their respective parties were already 'heating up' the campaign trail with their favorite issues. Nor did it end there. The now-familiar faces of Senator James L. Cassidy and Henry 'Hank' Fontaine, ex-governor of Maryland, smiled down from billboards everywhere, while television was flooded with their political commercials.

As Clare slowed down and drove between the low scrub-covered sand dunes, her radio constantly burped out campaign messages praising the two nominees. 'This political message is paid for by the committee to elect . . . ' She knew it was useless to change stations, because every airwave and kilowatt across the country was inundated with political promises. So she listened, trying to believe that there was a genuine race going on out there; that the man she worked for, Fontaine, really did stand a chance of getting elected.

Some chance, she thought gloomily. The word around the nation's capital was Hank Fontaine couldn't win this election even with *God* as his campaign manager! Not against James L. Cassidy. 'Shining Jim,' as his devoted followers called him, was the most prohibitive, odds-on favorite to win the presidency since Ike Eisenhower. Why, it was almost un-American not to worship the Cassidys. They were America's 'royalty,' a tradition, and had been since the late 1800s. That was when the fiery old patriarch himself, Jacob Cassidy, had made his mark dealing in railroads. His only son, Julius, added more mystique and millions to the clan treasury by stock-market wizardry; while the grandsons, John and Jason, further enhanced the Cassidy legend by becoming celebrated foreign ambassadors. They were followed by Jason's sons — Jake, Julian, and Joseph — who all became World War I heroes before blossoming into United States senators. And now, finally, there was Joseph's only son, James L., perhaps the most brilliant and charismatic of all the Cassidys, about to become the next president of the United States.

It's downright sickening, that's what it is, Clare thought as she drove into the parking area fronting the Coast Guard station. Sickening and unfair. How could one family be so smiled upon, so blessed? What was worse, you couldn't even hate them for it. For other than Joseph, whose favorable leanings toward Nazism during World War II had got him into trouble with President Roosevelt, there wasn't a blemish on the whole lousy family!

Irked by her thoughts, Clare parked in the visitors' section, got out, and headed for the Administration Building. The Coast Guard station was on the westernmost tip of Bogue Banks and as Clare followed the path to the entrance, she could see beyond the chain-link security

5

fence the dock and the narrow channel connecting Bogue Sound to the ocean. A buoy-tender was tied up at the dock. Nearby, on the dirt by some oil drums, a group of enlisted men were shooting baskets into a rusty hoop.

As Clare entered the building, she found workmen redecorating the lobby. Ladders, drop-cloths and the smell of wet paint were everywhere. Worse, the air conditioning was out. Clare felt herself perspiring as she cut between two ladders and approached the information desk. The desk was unattended, so Clare stopped the first uniform she saw and asked for the operations officer.

'I'm it,' he said, smiling. 'What all can I do for you?'

'I'm Clare Winslow. I called you yesterday — from Governor Fontaine's office in Washington, remember?'

'O-Oh, sure . . . ' He shook her hand, adding: 'Public relations, wasn't it?'

'That's right.'

'Won't you come this way, please?' He led her into a tiny office. It hadn't been painted yet and all the furniture was pushed together in the middle of the room under a drop-cloth. He apologized for the mess and the lack of air conditioning, uncovered a chair for her by the open window, then lifted one edge of the drop-cloth and looked through some papers on the desk. 'On the phone, ma'am, y'all said something about needing some marine salvage work done.'

'Correct.'

'Well, I made a list of all the local companies. Ah, here it is.' He handed her a page of names. 'Some are bigger than others, but they're all reputable.'

'Which one's the best?'

'Well, I — uh . . . ' The operations officer hesitated, uncomfortable under Clare's direct green gaze. 'They're all about the same, I guess.'

'Really? Then, let's put it this way — if you needed the very best diver, which one would you recommend?'

'I can't recommend any, ma'am. It could be misconstrued as favoritism.'

'All right. Then, how about just giving me a hint — off the record?'

'Well . . . ' The operations officer

7

paused, perspiring. Clare moistened her lips. She had slightly protruding front teeth that gave her lips a desirable, sexy pout when her mouth was closed. Men wanted to kiss that pout. She knew it and kept her mouth closed now. The young officer melted. He leaned forward, smelling something behind her ears that reminded him of wet lilacs. 'Well, ma'am, the truth is, the best diver around is a guy named Ryan. He's got a place on the waterfront in Morehead City. Atlantic Salvage, it's called — '

'I don't see it here,' she interrupted, scanning the list.

'No, well — uh — you see, I figured y'all'd just be wasting your time to go see him.'

'He's that busy?'

'No, ma'am. He ain't busy. In fact, last I heard the finance company was after his boat.'

'Then . . . ?'

'Well, it's kind of hard to explain.'

'Try.'

'Well . . . you see, Ryan's sort of an unusual guy.'

'In what way?'

'Well, he's what you'd call a loner. Doesn't have any friends or anybody he's close to — 'cept maybe Mitch, the kid who works for him. Then, too, he's real independent — you know, pretends he doesn't need the business, when he really does. On top of that, he's awful moody. Girl I know who dated him once, said he acts like he's got the door closed on something that's waiting to bite him.'

'Sounds like some politicians I know,' Clare said, smiling.

The operations officer laughed. 'And a lot of admirals, too, if y'all know what I mean.'

'Only too well, I'm afraid.' She paused, frowning, then said, 'It's easy to see why he's in financial difficulty — Ryan, I mean.'

'Right. And what makes it worse, he don't like working for strangers.'

'That's encouraging. Sounds like he's deliberately trying to sabotage his business.'

'Either that, or hide something.' He wiped the sweat from his forehead. 'Now you know why I didn't include him on the list.'

She nodded, though she was more intrigued than put off. 'But he *is* the best, right?'

'Yes, ma'am. The very best. No doubt about that. *When* he wants to be, that is.'

Clare smiled. 'Well, then,' she said, rising, 'I'll just have to make sure he 'wants to be' for me, won't I?'

Leaving the Coast Guard station, Clare drove east along the two-lane blacktop that ran down the center of Bogue Banks. Both windows were open and the ocean breeze soon cooled her down. Emerald Isle fell behind her. After a few miles she passed through the tiny community of Salter Path. Then it was open road, with only an occasional beach house on stilts poking up among the sand dunes, and she began thinking about Ryan. She knew she was just being stubborn by trying to hire him, but challenges stimulated her; made her all the more determined to succeed. Besides, Governor Fontaine's campaign manager, Karl Slater, had instructed her to hire the best diver available, regardless of cost. And dammit, that's exactly what she intended to do. This was her chance to prove that Karl's faith in her as an important, integral part of Fontaine's staff wasn't misguided. Earlier that week in Washington he'd relieved her of all her PR duties so that she could fully concentrate on this unusual assignment: locating and raising a Nazi U-boat that had been sunk during World War II off the North Carolina coast.

'But I know nothing about U-boats,' she protested, 'sunken or otherwise.'

'I don't expect you to,' Slater said. 'But I know you're a competent scuba diver, and that puts you way ahead of anyone else I might ask to handle the job. Besides,' he added in a tone that insisted she obey, 'this project could be vitally important to the governor's campaign and image throughout the South. And since I can't accompany you, or influence any on-the-spot decisions, I want someone down there I can trust.'

Thinking about that conversation now, Clare realized that coming from Karl Slater, who rarely complimented anyone, it was high praise indeed. And she was determined to live up to it.

Ahead, a bright yellow sign said she was entering Atlantic Beach. It was larger than the other communities, but still small, with mostly wood-frame houses, stores, and a sprawling marina. Clare drove past the slips containing all manner of sailboats, crossed over the causeway spanning Bogue Sound, and entered Morehead City. A leathery-faced gas station attendant gave her directions to Atlantic Salvage. She followed the rusty railroad tracks through the small Confederate town, turned on 12th Street, and drove down to the waterfront.

The narrow street of clapboard houses dead-ended at the water alongside Atlantic Salvage. Derelict cars, rusted machinery, and an old bus, its axles resting on blocks, littered the area. Although it was obviously unintentional, Clare thought the abandoned objects resembled a contemporary metal sculpture that reflected an atmosphere of transiency — as if whoever lived or worked here believed that nothing was permanent, and that they were merely pausing on this spot, temporarily, while passing in and out of existence.

Amused by her thoughts, Clare parked beside a fence covered with campaign posters of the two presidential nominees. Getting out, she studied the posters for a moment. Governor Fontaine, she had to admit, was not an attractive man. His oval, sharp-featured face was noticeably lined, his brown hair thinning. His deep-set eyes had dark shadows under them, making him look older than his fifty-nine years. And his smile, although not insincere, seemed hesitant, suggesting — as his many detractors were quick to mention — a lack of confidence, as if he didn't believe in himself.

This was untrue, of course. Hank Fontaine believed avidly in everything he did or said. And beneath his hesitant, soft-spoken manner, he was a quietly confident man. He was also a brilliant statesman, similar to Adlai Stevenson. But despite these credentials, along with an economically sound domestic and foreign policy, Fontaine lacked Cassidy's key ingredient: charisma. And for the same reason that numerous people voted for Kennedy over Nixon, the public was presently being swayed by the gray-blond, blue-eyed, all-American good looks of 'Shining Jim' Cassidy.

It was too bad, too, Clare thought as she walked toward the big white barn of a building that had ATLANTIC SALVAGE painted over the entrance. For not only in her prejudiced opinion, but in the opinions of many well-respected politicians, Fontaine was better presidential material than Cassidy. But because of that damned Cassidy smile and charm, Fontaine would probably never get a chance to prove it.

The big double doors of Atlantic Salvage were open. Clare entered and found herself in a large workshop cluttered with tools, diving equipment, air tanks, and dismantled engine parts. Everything smelled of oil and grease. Crossword puzzle books were piled under the workbenches, while two signs between the rear windows caught Clare's attention. One read, DON'T EXPLAIN, DON'T COMPLAIN and the other,

14

NEVER QUIT. They added to the tough, loner image that Clare had already formed of the man she expected to meet, and wondering what would be her best approach, she picked her way through the metal obstacle course toward the rear door.

It was also open. Through it she could see some old wooden docks angling out into the murky waters of Bogue Sound. Two battered dinghies and a small white cabin cruiser were tied up to the nearest dock. The cabin cruiser, *Atlantico*, could be rigged either for salvage or sport fishing. Presently rigged for salvage, it had fine clean lines. Looking at it, Clare thought it seemed out of place in this graveyard of rusting junk.

Just then a large, muscular youth in jeans and a soiled T-shirt entered through a side-door. He staggered under the weight of an outboard motor. Unaware of Clare, he dumped it on a bench, muttering, 'Well, shitfire, why the hell won't you start?'

Then he saw Clare.

'Hey,' he said, embarrassed, 'I'm — uh

15

— sorry about that, ma'am.'

'That's okay,' she said, smiling. 'I say worse than that when some nut cuts in front of my car. Guess it's a sign of the times, huh?'

'I guess.' The youth frowned, uncertain, and ran greasy fingers through his curly red hair. 'My daddy took a belt to us if we ever cussed — me 'n my brother Virge, you know? Said cussin' was offensive to the Lord, an' them that done it was no better'n Yankees or folks who spit on Jesus. Course, daddy bein' a Bible-puncher, he was a sight more strict than some.'

'I'm sure he was. By the way, I'm Clare Winslow.'

'Bobby Mitchell, ma'am — though most everyone calls me Mitch.'

'Very well, Mitch. Now, if you'll be kind enough to tell me where Mr. Ryan is . . . '

'It's just Ryan, ma'am. He don't like to be called 'mister.' An' I think he's out on the boat.' Mitch thumbed at the *Atlantico*. 'Want me to get him for you?'

'Thanks, I'll find him.' Clare headed

16

outside. Mitch watched her walk along the narrow, weathered dock toward the cabin cruiser, envious of Ryan at that moment. Then he picked up a wrench and started dismantling the outboard motor.

Outside, before Clare reached the boat, a man jumped from the stern to the dock and began walking toward her. He carried a scuba tank, one-handed, as if it were weightless, and moved with the grace of a big cat. She guessed it was Ryan and liked what she saw: a tall, whip-lean man in sun-faded jeans and a blue denim shirt, with the shoulders of a heavyweight tapering down to cowboy hips. Under the dark unruly hair, his angular tanned face and yellow-gray hunter's eyes promised the integrity of a mountain. Despite what the Coast Guard officer had told her, Clare wanted Ryan to trust her; to call her his friend. When he was close, she said: 'Excuse me — Mr. Ryan?'

For a moment it didn't look as if he'd stop. Then, on the verge of passing her, he paused and said curtly, 'What is it?'

'I'm Clare Winslow, Mr. Ryan. I'm with

17

Governor Fontaine's office in — '

'It's Ryan,' he said softly, 'not *Mr.* Ryan. And I'm not interested in politics, so you can save the donations speech.' He moved on past and entered a shed attached to the main building. Clare hurried after him. She found him hunkered down, back to the door, tinkering with the pressure gauge of an old compressor.

'I'm sorry,' she said. 'I guess I didn't make myself clear. I'm here only as a customer. I want some salvage work done — '

'What kind of salvage work?' He spoke without turning.

'There's a submarine sunk out there.' She pointed at the ocean. 'A German U-boat. It went down in 1942, and — '

'Forget it,' he interrupted. 'Everybody's heard about that sub. Nobody knows where it's located.'

'I do.'

Surprised, he stopped tinkering and looked back at her. 'You do?'

'Yes. I have the exact location.'

'Exact location?' He repeated the words slowly, wondering as he did how the hell

18

that was possible. 'And just what do you intend on doing with that U-boat?'

'Eventually, Governor Fontaine wants it raised and brought ashore — set up in Wilmington as a war memorial for all the merchant seamen who died in battle.'

'That's noble of him.'

'He's a noble man.'

'He's a politician.'

'Can't he be both?'

'Few are.'

'Fewer become president.'

'True. Which makes me wonder if he isn't doing this to win extra votes.'

'That isn't his main purpose. But I'd be lying if I said we aren't all hoping that it'll boost his popularity around here.'

'From what I've heard,' Ryan said, still trying to repair the gauge, 'your man needs more than just a boost.'

'I agree. That's why I'm here and that's why it's so important to get the project under way. Then, even if it isn't completed by the election, at least people will know the governor's sincere — not just another politician trying to con votes out of them.'

'Good luck.'

'Does that mean you're not interested?'

'You got it.'

'Why not? You can name your own price.'

'It's not a question of money.'

'Then what *is* it a question of?'

Ryan hesitated, knowing he could never tell her the real reason, and said, 'Mostly, we're just not equipped for a job that size.'

'Couldn't you rent whatever equipment you don't have?'

'I could, yeah.'

'Then what else is stopping you?'

'Reasons.'

'I see.' She tried not to sound irritated. 'What kind of reasons?'

'Just reasons.'

''Don't Explain, Don't Complain,' right?'

'No one's said it better.' He stopped tinkering, turned everything off, and stood up, saying, 'But don't let me discourage you, lady. There are plenty of other salvage companies who'll just leap at your offer . . .'

He move dpast her, out onto the dock,

and headed for the boat.

She followed him. 'Ryan — please — wait a minute.'

He waited. 'Why?'

'I hadn't finished.'

'It doesn't matter,' he said. 'There isn't anything you can say that'd make me change my mind.' Turning, he walked to the stern of the boat, jumped aboard and disappeared below.

Clare chewed her lower lip, frustrated, and headed back inside the workshop.

Aboard the *Atlantico* Ryan removed the stern hatch covering the power plant and lowered himself into the cramped compartment. The twin engines were overdue for servicing. Without looking, he knew all the hoses needed replacing. The batteries were almost shot, too, and unless he came up with the back payments he owed Wilmington Finance, he'd lose the boat. On top of that, without money for the repairs, the boat wasn't seaworthy and he couldn't go out on a job — even if one were available. It was one of those neat, vicious circles that life enjoyed rolling at you and Ryan sighed, frustrated, knowing that the job Clare was offering would end all his financial problems and leave plenty over besides.

God, he thought suddenly, if only he didn't have a past . . . a part that was waiting like steel jaws to snap shut on him the moment his true identity was revealed.

But who was he kidding? He *did* have a past. And a job of this size and importance would bring attention his way; attention that he couldn't avoid; attention that would eventually betray his whereabouts to the government. And once that happened, he'd be imprisoned, possibly even sentenced to death. And unexciting and restricting as this life in hiding was, he wasn't ready to swap it for a shot at the electric chair. Not yet, anyway.

'Ryan? Hey, Ryan, you there?'

'Yo . . . '

Mitch boarded the *Atlantico* and hunkered down beside the engine hatch. Ryan looked up and rubbed his nose with the back of an oily hand. 'What d'you need?'

'Well, I was wonderin' . . . ' Mitch hesitated, uneasy about what he had to say. 'I mean, you're the boss an' all, but how come you turned that Clare lady down?'

'Simple. It's too big a job.'

'But all she wants is for us to dive on that U-boat.'

'That's not what she told me. Said she wanted the sub raised — brought ashore and made into some kind of museum.'

'That's eventually, she says. Right now she just wants us to bring up some souvenirs — you know, gauges, sextants, guns — anythin' that'll stir up interest an' show everyone that the U-boat's worth raisin'.'

Ryan frowned. Hell, if that was all she really wanted, maybe they could take the job after all. Then, when it came time to actually raise the sub, they could find a reason to back out and let some other salvage company take over.

'How come she didn't tell *me* that?'

'Said she tried to, but y'all wouldn't listen.'

Ryan hid a smile. 'Now I ask you,' he

deadpanned, 'does that sound like love-able ol' me?'

'If it didn't, boss, d'y'all think I'd be talkin' to you right now? How about it?' Mitch added. 'Won't you at least listen to her? We can sure use the money.'

'I know,' Ryan said, tempted.

'Not only that, but she says the sub's only down eighteen fathoms. Shoot, we can handle that with our eyes closed.'

Ryan knew Mitch was right. One hundred and eight feet was a workable depth. They wouldn't need to buy or rent any extra diving gear. And with money up front to make the boat seaworthy . . .

'Can we do it, then?' Mitch was asking. 'I told her to wait until I talked to you. She's still in the shop — '

'Not anymore,' Ryan said. He indicated the dock, where Clare and a uniformed marshal were approaching the boat.

Mitch groaned. 'Want me to stall him, while you get the boat out of here?'

'Too late, pal. Besides, I'm not sure she'll start.' Together they got off the boat and met Clare and the marshal on the dock, realizing even before they talked that this might be the end of Atlantic Salvage.

'I got a court order here,' the marshal said, showing papers. 'Wilmington Finance is repossessing your boat, the *Atlantico*.'

'That's not too smart,' Ryan said. 'They take the boat, I can't earn money to make the payments.'

'You ain't making 'em, anyway. If you were, mister, I wouldn't *be* here now.'

'How many payments are in arrears?' Clare asked.

'Three — four, including this month.'

'How much does that amount to?'

'That's none of your business,' Ryan said quietly.

'It might be,' she said. 'If you want to keep your boat.'

'Mean you'd be willin' to pay 'em off?' Mitch said excitedly.

Clare nodded and locked gazes with Ryan. 'I'm sure that could be arranged, yes. Of course, I'd have to need the boat for a very good reason.'

'That's blackmail,' Ryan said.

'No,' Clare said. 'Just good politics.' She turned to the marshal. 'If I *were* to make those back payments, would you still have to repossess the boat?'

'That ain't up to me, lady.'

'Oh? Then who is it up to?'

'Well, I — uhm . . . ' The marshal wilted under Clare's soft green gaze. 'I'd have to talk to Wilmington Finance, ma'am . . . See what they had to say.'

'But if they agreed,' put in Mitch, 'that'd make it okay, right?'

The marshal refused to make his job sound so simple. Pulling his gaze from Clare, he said stubbornly, 'I'd have to talk to Wilmington Finance.'

There was an awkward silence.

'Well?' Clare said to Ryan. 'It's up to you, Coach. Do we pass or punt?'

He stared hard at her. *All my life I've lived on the edge*, he thought, *so why should things be different now?*

'We'll pass,' he said quietly. There was the hint of a smile in his wolfish eyes. 'I never was much good at punting, anyway.'

2

The marshal used the telephone in Ryan's tiny, cluttered office to call Wilmington Finance. The credit manager was reluctant to drop the repossession action — until Clare got on the line and explained that she worked for Governor Fontaine and needed immediate use of the boat. Then he agreed to let Ryan keep the *Atlantico*, just so long as all back payments plus this month's share were paid that day to the company's branch office in Morehead City.

Clare promised to take care of it personally. She returned the phone to the marshal, then joined Ryan outside the office and told him the news. He wasn't as pleased as she had expected. He told her that he didn't accept charity, and insisted on deducting whatever money she paid the finance company from the final cost of the operation.

'That's fine with me,' she said. 'All I'm

interested in doing is getting started right away.'

'So am I,' Ryan said. 'First, though, we got to agree on a price.'

'Fair enough. What do you charge for this kind of dive?'

'Depends on if I'm working by the day or week.'

'Week.'

'Two thousand.'

'What does that include exactly?'

'The boat, gas, diving gear, Mitch's and my services — the whole nine yards.'

'Sounds reasonable. But you'd better include a rental fee for an extra wet suit, fins, tanks — '

'Don't worry about extras,' Ryan said. 'Mitch an' I got plenty.'

'Yes, but will any of them fit me?'

'You're coming along on the dive?'

'Of course. Don't worry,' she added, seeing his scowl, 'I've been cleared for open water.'

'Great. Then you must know about the buddy system?'

'Naturally. Two divers looking out for each other.'

'Right. And since you make three, that means one of us has to look out for two people.'

'So?' She shrugged. 'We'll just have to take extra care, that's all.'

'Sorry. I respect the ocean too much to take unnecessary chances.'

'No one's asking you to take unnecessary chances,' Clare said, flaring. 'I'm an experienced diver and I'm perfectly capable of looking after myself.'

'Oh,' Ryan said flatly. 'Had plenty of experience diving for U-boats, have you?'

'Well, no. But — '

'How about getting your air hose cut when you're down past a hundred feet?'

'No. But — '

'Or handling a guy twice your size who's gone goofy with nitrogen narcosis?'

'No, of course not.'

'Then, if it ain't too much to ask,' he said sweetly, 'just what the fuck *are* you experienced in?'

Clare whitened visibly. Her wide, sultry eyes blazed green.

'Listen, you,' she said, steamed. 'If you think talking tough scares me, forget it.

29

My ex-husband thought it would, too, but all it ever got him was divorce papers!'

'Lucky man.'

'He didn't think so.'

'He didn't have to dive with you.'

'He didn't *have* to, but he did — many times. That's where I acquired the experience that you don't think I have.'

'I'm impressed.'

'I don't care if you're impressed or not. All that matters to me is do you or don't you want this job?'

'I want it.'

'Even if it includes me — diving with you?'

Ryan hesitated, tempted to say no. But over the years his desire to keep a low profile had all but ruined his business, and he knew this was probably his last chance to stay afloat. So, through his teeth, he said softly: 'Yes.'

'Terrific. It's all settled then. I — ' She broke off as the marshal joined them. He craned his neck to look up at Ryan.

'Finance company says I'm to stay here, mister. Keep you off the boat till the lady makes all the payments.'

'Consider me gone,' Clare said. 'Oh, and while I'm at the bank, Ryan, how much will you need in advance?'

'Couple of hundred'll do.'

'Fine. Anything else?'

He thought a moment. 'How about if I send Mitch along — have him pick up some spare parts?'

'Terrific. He can keep me from getting lost.'

'He can also go with you to get your diving gear,' Ryan said. 'Kid ain't exactly green or anything, but I'm sure he can use your 'experience.''

He walked outside before she could find a suitable retort. But as he headed along the dock, she heard him chuckle. She knew he was starting to accept her, maybe even trust her, and it made her feel more confident that the dive would be a success.

Ryan was sitting at the end of the dock, working on a crossword puzzle, when Clare and Mitch returned from the stores. They had bought new parts for the boat engines and the compressor, and Clare had rented diving gear and a Loran-C.

She'd also paid the finance company. While she was in the office showing the receipt to the marshal, Ryan and Mitch examined the Loran-C.

The sophisticated instrument resembled a large voltmeter, contained a 12-volt battery, and displayed two rows of digital numbers. Ryan had never used a Loran-C, but he'd read about it and knew that by using signals relayed from one master station and two secondary stations located ashore, and by comparing the difference in time that it took for each one of these three signals to reach your position at sea, you could literally pinpoint whatever coordinate had been chosen as a reference.

'Now all we need,' he said, thumbing through the instruction booklet, 'is a navigation chart with a Loran-C overprint.'

'Clare's already got one,' Mitch said. 'Her boss in D.C. give it to her before she left. It's got where the U-boat went down marked on it an' everythin'.' He leaned against the cluttered workbench and admired Clare through the office window. The marshal had gone and she was now on the telephone.

Ryan made a noise that could've meant anything. Then he told Mitch to start dismantling the boat engines, and headed for the office.

Clare hung up as he entered. 'That was Karl Slater, my boss,' she explained. 'I was telling him what progress we've made.' Then, when Ryan didn't say anything: 'Did you see I've rented a Loran-C?'

'Yes.'

'What d'you think?'

'Expensive gadget.'

'I thought you'd be pleased.'

'If it helps find the sub, I will be. While you and Mitch were gone,' he continued, 'I called the Coast Guard. Weatherman says if nothing changes, we'll have perfect diving conditions tomorrow.'

'Terrific. How early do we start?'

'Depends how far out the sub is.'

'Thirty-four miles due east of Morehead City.'

'Allowing for the channel an' everything, that's about a three-hour trip.' He did some mental figuring. 'Be here at five thirty — that'll give us time to get out on the tide.'

'Five thirty?' she repeated, eyes widening. 'That's a.m., right?'

'If it's too early for a big-city girl,' Ryan said, 'you can always stay in bed and let us handle it.'

'No way,' she snapped. 'I'll just pretend I'm getting home a little later than usual.'

They locked gazes. Both realized they were getting off on the wrong foot again.

'How about we make a deal?' she said.

'What kind of deal?'

'A truce until this job's finished. Okay?'

'You make it sound like we're at war.'

'You make *me feel* like we're at war. How about it?' she said, offering her hand. 'Friends for the next seven days. Deal?'

He studied her, admiring her directness, then shook hands. 'Deal.'

'Wonderful. Well, see you in the morning then.' She stood up. 'Oh, and if you need to reach me tonight for any reason, I'll be at the Atlantis Lodge.' She started out.

'How about my two hundred?'

She gestured without stopping, 'In an envelope — middle desk drawer,' and headed outside. A few moments later Ryan heard the Porsche drive away. He opened the desk drawer and took out the unsealed envelope. Inside was three, not two hundred dollars and a note reading: 'I'm hoping that *three* will be our lucky number!'

Ryan smiled and tucked the money away. *Interesting lady*, he thought as he left the office and picked up the box of new engine parts from the bench. *A little crazy, maybe. But — definitely interesting.*

3

The next day broke cool and clear. It was five twenty-nine when Clare parked outside Atlantic Salvage, and the nude gray sky was still resisting the yellow dawn. Ryan and Mitch had already gassed up the boat, filled the scuba tanks, loaded all the diving gear aboard, and were ready to cast off.

'My God,' Clare said as she joined them on board. 'Didn't you guys sleep at all?'

'Enough,' said Ryan. He saw no reason to mention that he and Mitch had worked all night to repair the compressor, get the *Atlantico* seaworthy, install the Loran-C and its antenna, and understand the complicated operations manual. Fortunately, he'd had experience with the Loran-A, an earlier and less exotic model, and now felt secure about operating the Loran-C. So, telling Mitch to cast off, he entered the wheelhouse and pushed the self-starters.

Instantly the power plant roared alive and Ryan and Mitch exchanged grins of satisfaction.

A few minutes later the neat white cabin cruiser, twin engines throbbing smoothly, churned east along Bogue Sound. The water in the sound was oily calm. The foamy wake of the boat veed out into it, causing ever-widening swells that rocked the orange channel markers and lapped against the private docks lining the shore.

Clare had stopped for coffee and sweet rolls. By the time they'd eaten and examined her navigation chart, they had cleared the channel and Beaufort Inlet and were headed out to sea. Ryan set a course according to the chart coordinates, and locked the Loran-C onto the intermittent signals coming from the onshore Loran stations. Making himself comfortable at the wheel, he started working on a crossword puzzle.

'I was hooked on those things once,' Clare said. 'Got so bad in fact, they almost took over my life. Finally had to give them up before my boss gave up on me.'

'I like them,' Ryan said, not looking up,

'because it's something I can do by myself.'

It wasn't said nastily, but Clare took it as a hint that he wanted to be left alone and went up top to watch the sunrise.

Shortly, Mitch joined her. They sat on the flying bridge in blue canvas chairs that were bolted into position behind the dual controls. A white plastic steering wheel and chrome-plated clutch and throttle levers poked out of the dash, while streamlined grab rails with matching blue canvas side panels gave one the feeling of being in a cockpit. All about them the ocean looked hard and gray in the pale dawn light. The rising sun resembled a silvery-yellow wafer and didn't flood the stone-blue sky with its customary flaming colors. Disappointed, Clare watched a few seagulls winging inland, then turned her attention to a tanker that crawled along the distant horizon. As she watched, she felt the boat riding through the chop and could taste the salty wind-blown spray landing cool and damp on her face.

'How long have you known Ryan?' she asked Mitch.

'Almost since he first come here — to Morehead City.'

'How long ago's that?'

''Bout two and a half years.'

'Oh. That accounts for it, then. Why he doesn't have much of a local accent, I mean. D'you know where he came from — originally?'

'Up north somewheres, I think.'

'Didn't you ever ask him?'

'Once.'

'What'd he say?'

'Just that he was from 'up north' and had traveled a lot.' Mitch paused, then said sheepishly, 'Guess it was the hoping in me that stopped me from askin' any more questions.'

'Hoping?'

'That he wasn't no Yankee. See, I really liked him, an' — well, I was still livin' at home then — with my daddy, you know? An' Daddy, he hates Yankees worse'n swamp water, so just naturally I felt the same.'

'Naturally.'

'Well, anyways, as I said, I liked Ryan a lot. So I just pretended like he was from

39

around here, an' — an' pretty soon, we was real good friends an' he offered me a job. Which was kind of surprisin' really, considerin' how we first met.'

'How was that?'

'Well, truth is, Ryan caught me stealin' this rotor arm out of his shop. I needed it for my truck, you know, and since I didn't have no money — '

'You ripped it off?'

'Tried to's more like it. Ryan come in just as I was sneakin' out the back. Well, I didn't want to get arrested, so I swung on him.' Mitch chuckled as he remembered. 'Whooee, was *that* a mistake. Next thing I knowed, he had me in one of them karate holds, had flipped me down an' was tellin' me to quit or he'd bust my arm.'

'What happened then?'

'I done as he told me, an' he let me go. But instead of havin' me thrown in the can, like I expected, he asked me what I wanted the rotor arm for. And when I told him, he said for me to take it an' to pay him for it whenever I got the money. Which I done.' Mitch paused, as if still unable to believe his luck, then said,

40

'Right after that, I started hangin' around the shop an' helpin' him fix stuff, and, well, after a while he said that wasn't right — me workin' for free an' all — an' asked me if I wanted a job. I said sure, though I couldn't believe he'd asked, 'cause he never hardly spoke an' all along I figured he didn't really like me.'

'I'm not surprised,' Clare said, though she felt she was beginning to understand Ryan. 'He is kind of short on words, isn't he?'

'Yeah. But I'll tell you this — when he does say somethin', it pays to listen.'

'I'll remember that,' Clare said, smiling. 'In case he ever decides to break down and say something to me.'

Finally, they were there. Using the accuracy of the Loran-C and Clare's coordinates, Ryan stopped the *Atlantico* over the sunken U-boat and dropped the anchor. Then the three of them put on their diving gear. Ryan finished first. While he waited for the others, he double-checked all the equipment and repeated the procedures they would follow underwater. Then, satisfied, he

41

collected his underwater light, waited for Mitch to get a spear gun and Clare, her camera — and all three rolled backward off the transom into the cold gray ocean.

The icy water momentarily shocked Ryan's breath away. But once below the surface, he felt his body temperature warming the water under his wet suit and he forgot about the cold. He pinched the bottom of his mask against his nose and blew hard, clearing his nose. Exhaled bubbles rose with a tinny hollow sound on either side of his regulator. He took the lead and dived toward the ocean floor.

Ryan loved being underwater. It was the only place in which he felt truly free. The silent, calm green-blue world around him gave Ryan a sense of peaceful solitude, allowing him to enjoy what he was doing and to forget about the problems that forever dogged him on the surface.

It took them roughly five minutes to descend to the ocean floor. They were now over one hundred feet down and could feel the cold again, and the pressure of the water against them as they kicked along. The dark-blue water was clear on the bottom. But there were great jungles of seaweed, and Ryan knew it wasn't going to be easy to find the U-boat. He motioned for Clare and Mitch to fan out and kicked his way through the dense green entanglement. Streamers of seaweed tugged across his mask. Schools of curious fish swam close, some hovering there before him in mid-water. Sometimes a gleaming wall of silver. Other times a myriad of colors.

Finally, after he'd used up one air tank and had switched over to the second, he saw the U-boat. It lay on its starboard side some thirty feet ahead, leaning over at a forty-five-degree angle, heavily encrusted with barnacles and festooned with long streamers of seaweed. Ryan shone his light at it. *It looks like a giant prehistoric float*, he thought. The rusted remains of one of Hitler's war toys, a memory of Nazism at its worst had in forty years become a forgotten metal grave for the men who went down with her. Ryan felt a moment of excitement, as he always did when about to explore a new wreck. Motioning for Clare and

Mitch to follow, he kicked closer to the submarine.

When they reached the bow of the U-boat, Ryan sent up a balloon marker and tied the cord to the antenna. Then he waggled his light as a signal for Clare and Mitch to stay close, and led the way along the forward deck. The hull seemed intact. He paused over the torpedo loading hatch, located just ahead of the deck gun, and saw it was open. Here was at least one way they could enter the sub, he realized, and he gestured to the others. They nodded, smiles flashing beneath their masks. Ryan continued on, hearing his own air exhaling, and came closer to the deck gun. It was an 8.8 cm Schiffskanon c/35, and even in its encrusted form he could see it was badly damaged. He shined his light at it. The gun had been blown off its mount and its barrel was twisted upward. There was also something white clinging to the lower rung of the guardrail. Ryan moved closer and saw it was a human hand. The fleshless bones were trapped by the broken metal, and for a moment he could visualize the panicked sailor desperately trying to break loose.

Suddenly, Ryan heard a noise behind him. He turned and saw Clare and Mitch looking at the hand, Clare grimacing in horror at the gruesome sight. Then he led the way to the conning tower. The hatch was partly open. But it was encrusted with barnacles and algae, and he doubted that they could pry it open wide enough to crawl through. He shined his light around. The glare illuminated the badly damaged attack periscope. Ryan suddenly caught sight of something small wedged between the UZO or surface torpedo aiming device and the main compass housing. He swam closer. The object, even though crusted over and wrapped with seaweed, was obviously a pair of binoculars. Ryan motioned for Mitch to break it loose. Mitch used his hammer, gently tapping away the thick crusting before prying it free. They had their first souvenir and Clare and Mitch raised their thumbs in triumph as they followed Ryan aft, into the *Wintergarten*. Guardrails were missing on the round platform and there was a jagged hole in the deck by the mounted 2-cm flak gun.

Ryan shined his light into the hole and Saw a mass of twisted metal inside blocking his entry. Some kind of explosion had occurred, he realized, and it would take hours of work with a torch to cut a way through. He motioned to Clare and Mitch that the opening was blocked and motioned for them to follow him aft.

They swam along the rear deck, brushing aside the seaweed that hung from the aft antenna, then dived under the hull and paused beside the twin propellers. Curious fish came in close to investigate, but soon ducked away as Clare tried to touch them. Ryan signaled for Clare to photograph the U-boat, while he looked inside. Mitch wanted to accompany him, but Ryan gestured for him to remain with Clare. Reluctantly, Mitch obeyed. Ryan swam back alongside the hull, kicked upward, and trod water above the open torpedo loading hatch. Although the raised hatch cover was half torn from its hinges, the rim was so thickly encrusted with barnacles that it narrowed the size of the hole. Ryan slipped out of his backpack, lowered the twin tanks into the hatch ahead of him, and followed them in.

It was dark inside the U-boat. Ryan shined his light around, holding the tank harness in his other hand. The light didn't penetrate very far into the darkness, but what it did illuminate showed in its natural color. The glare seemed to hang there before him, floating in the dark water. He pushed his tanks through it, kicking gently so that he could follow without snagging against anything that might cut his hose.

When he leveled off, he found himself in the narrow aisle-way that led between the captain's cabin and the hydrophone room. Both were half-filled with mud, and Ryan kicked onward, pushing his tanks ahead of him, until he was through the watertight door and inside the control room. This area seemed spacious after where he'd been. He aimed his light around to see what condition everything was in. The numerous dials, gauges, and instrument panels were all broken beneath

47

a heavy mantle of crust. Ryan kicked gently, so as not to disturb the mud covering the deck, and shined his light over the planing equipment. He touched one of the wheels. For a moment he saw himself sitting there, receiving orders from the *kapitan*, controlling the depth and trim of the U-boat as it moved unchallenged through the silent deep.

He looked up — and at first thought he was looking in a mirror. Then, as he thrust his hand through the shiny brown reflection, he realized it was diesel oil. Apparently the fuel tanks had ruptured and the escaped oil had risen to the highest inner level. He guessed there was about a foot of it, and that it probably filled the entire sub. That was good news. Diesel oil acted as a preservative. Anything floating in it could be in salvageable condition. That reminded Ryan of why he was there. He suddenly remembered that Clare and Mitch were still outside. They were probably getting anxious. He shined his light around a final time and then swam back the way he'd entered.

Mitch was already starting down after

him. Ryan waggled his light to show he was fine, then waited for Mitch to squeeze himself and his tanks back up through the hatch. Ryan followed, and joined Clare and Mitch on the forward deck.

Clare was relieved to see him. She tapped her watch. Ryan glanced at his own watch and was surprised to see that he'd been in the sub for twenty minutes. Because of the depth, they would soon be out of air. He signaled toward the surface. Reluctantly, they all headed upward. They ascended slowly, never rising faster than their bubbles, and at the ten-foot level they paused for several minutes to decompress before surfacing and boarding the boat.

Once on board, they removed their wet suits and diving gear and toweled themselves off. It would be twelve hours before they could dive again, so Ryan collected the diving marker and headed the *Atlantico* back to Morehead City. While they drank mugs of hot chocolate that Clare made in the tiny galley, Ryan briefly described what he'd seen inside the U-boat.

'What about souvenirs?' Mitch asked when Ryan was finished. 'If everything's busted an' blown up like you say, how we gonna find anythin' worthwhile?'

'We might not,' Ryan said. He looked at Clare, who sat on the narrow bench seat with her feet tucked under her. 'Fact is, maybe you'd better call your boss — tell him what kind of condition the sub's in. He might want to call the whole thing off.'

'No way,' she said stubbornly. 'This is my chance to help the governor get in the White House and I'm not backing off now. Besides,' she added, 'both Karl and Governor Fontaine knew what to expect. Good grief, the dumb boat's been down there forty years! What's it *supposed* to look like — the U-505?'

'What's the U-505?' Mitch said.

'A U-boat in Chicago. It's been there since right after the big war. It was captured before the captain could scuttle her, and the Navy or somebody put it on display. I don't know how many thousands have been through it, but according to Karl, it's made the city a ton of money.'

'Is that where he got the idea of raisin' this sub?' Ryan asked.

Clare nodded and brushed her damp, blonde hair back from her face. 'He and the governor both. They felt Wilmington could use the extra revenue, and the governor — but we've already been through that,' she said. 'The important thing now is I don't come up empty-handed. And since the U-boat's going to be a museum anyway, the older and more beat-up it is, the better. That way, everyone will think it's more authentic and they'll get the sense of really being inside a sunken U-boat.' She paused, covered a huge yawn with her hand, and said: 'God, suddenly I'm really sleepy.'

'Divin' does that,' said Mitch, 'if you ain't used to it.'

'Or are thin on 'experience,' maybe?' Clare said, waiting for Ryan's needle.

He ignored the bait. 'Whyn't you take a nap? As head honcho of this outfit, you're entitled to some extra sack time.'

'Ho ho,' she said. 'And have you keep reminding me that I'm the weaker sex? No thanks, Cap'n Ahab.' She winked at

51

Mitch, who grinned, and then sat there trying to stay awake. It was hopeless. Although she fought it for several minutes, she couldn't keep her eyes open. Finally, she fell asleep.

'Take the wheel,' Ryan told Mitch.

Mitch obeyed. Ryan took a blanket from the cupboard, spread it over Clare and then returned to the wheel. 'What's wrong?' he asked Mitch. 'Why the look?'

'What look?'

'Like you just seen a snake grow wings.'

'You're crazy,' Mitch said. 'I wasn't givin' you no look.' He headed outside before Ryan could press him further and went up top. It was the first time he'd ever seen Ryan display any feeling toward anyone, and he wondered what it meant.

4

Early that evening they took the *Atlantico* out again and made a second dive on the U-boat. But this time all three of them entered the submarine. Each had an underwater light and a small nylon bag for souvenirs. The watertight door that led aft from the control room was corroded shut. All their efforts to open it failed. Knowing it would take an acetylene torch to burn it loose, they concentrated their search in the control room. Mitch found a barnacle-encrusted flashlight wedged behind a broken gauge panel, but before he could examine it, Clare gave a startled cry that almost blew out her mouthpiece.

Ryan and Mitch kicked over to her. Behind her mask she looked badly shaken. She pointed below her. Ryan reached under a valve wheel and came up with a human spine bone. Mitch promptly shined his light at the mud. He groped gently around and pulled out two smaller bones. Clare turned away, uneasy. Mitch touched her hand and gestured for her to go up top. She shook her head, deciding to stick it out.

Nearby, Ryan dug out a skull. He held it up. Mitch grinned and made a ghoulish face. Clare, unable to treat it lightly, swam away. Ryan watched her go, momentarily concerned, then continued searching. He dug carefully, trying not to disturb the mud, and soon found a corroded eyeglass case. He gently pried it open with his knife. Inside was a pair of rimless glasses with gold ear-frames. They were expensive-looking, and Ryan guessed they had belonged to the captain or one of the officers. He chipped away at the lid of the case and saw the initials E.R. engraved there. He wondered if E.R. and the skull he'd found were one and the same person. Ryan studied the glasses for another moment, the case-protected frames glinting brightly in the light. But his thoughts were interrupted by a noise beside him.

He turned and saw Mitch treading water on his right and holding up two objects.

One was a skeletal hand still clutching a rebreather, the other a lidless metal box containing several more rebreathers. It conjured up a grim picture as Ryan visualized the owner of the hand, somehow trapped, desperately looking for the box . . . or trying to get it open while he drowned.

'Found 'em over there!' Mitch shouted, pointing at the overturned attack-table. His voice sounded distorted in the water and air bubbled loudly from the mouthpiece in his hand. Ryan nodded to show he understood. He held up the glasses. Mitch gave him a thumbs up, stuffed his souvenirs into his 'goodie bag,' returned the mouthpiece to his mouth and swam back to the attack-table.

The kicking of his fins muddied the water. Ryan continued searching by the damaged periscope housing, but the water became too muddy and he signaled to Mitch that it was time to check on Clare. Mitch nodded and together they kicked on through the forward watertight door to the captain's quarters.

Clare's light showed inside. As Ryan and Mitch paused in the doorway, their own lights helping to illuminate the tiny quarters, they saw Clare reaching into a cabinet above a fold-down table. Ryan glimpsed something green moving in the cabinet below Clare's hand. He kicked vigorously, propelling himself close enough to grab Clare from behind and jerk her back.

Startled, she dropped her light. Then whirling around, she looked questioningly at Ryan. He aimed his light into the security cabinet. The steel door had been broken open by an explosion. Staring out of the inky interior, its open jaws exposing rows of needle-like teeth, was the head of a large moray eel.

Clare shuddered and smiled her thanks to Ryan. He indicated his watch and pointed upward: it was time to surface. Clare nodded obediently. She recovered her light and preceded him out the door. In single file the three of them headed for the forward torpedo hatch.

Later, aboard the boat, Clare thanked Ryan for saving her from the moray eel.

He shrugged, making light of it as he said, 'Morays won't bother you — not unless you bother them first. But they do take unkindly to trespassers.'

'You mean he thinks that cabin's his territory?'

Ryan nodded. 'What's more, he'll attack anything that goes in there.'

'Then we must get him out somehow. There's a gaping hole in back of that cabinet, but I saw a box wedged in the upper corner that might contain some kind of papers.'

'We can always spear him,' Mitch put in. 'I don't like killin' things when it ain't necessary, but — '

'Don't worry,' Ryan said. 'We'll find a way to get that eel out of there. We're just lucky the fuel tanks ruptured,' he added. 'Otherwise, without all that oil floating up top, anything that wasn't metal would've disintegrated years ago.'

When they were dressed, they replenished their energy with ham sandwiches, apples, and steaming hot chocolate. Then they cleared the table, intending to go over their finds. But a wind blew up and storm clouds gathered overhead. Ryan decided it was time to head home.

While he steered the *Atlantico* through the increasingly heavy chop, Clare and Mitch used their knives and hammers to gently chip away the thick crust covering their souvenirs. Their haul included binoculars, rebreathers, a flashlight, a pair of compasses with a broken point, damaged gauges, dials, and their prize possession — the rimless, gold-frame glasses.

'My God,' Clare said, impressed. 'A couple more hauls like this, and we'll need a truck to carry all our stuff.'

'Don't forget them pictures y'all took,' Mitch reminded her. 'They'll help, too.'

Clare nodded. '*If* they come out.'

At the wheel Ryan allowed himself a faint smile. Outside, he noticed, it had started raining and the seagulls were winging their way inland.

5

The rain continued through the night. It was accompanied by thunder and lightning, and in the morning heavy winds and ground swells made diving impossible.

The wind woke Ryan shortly after dawn. It was blowing between the loose sections of the corrugated roof, making them rattle. He also could hear a shutter bang-banging against the rear wall of the shop. Instinctively, he thought of the boat. Rising, he looked out of the small window facing the dock. The rain had stopped. Dark clouds blew across the gray, wind-swept sky and whitecaps dotted the sound. From his angle he couldn't see the *Atlantico* at the end of the dock, but all the smaller boats were secure at their moorings. Relieved, he threw on some clothes and went outside.

It was blowing harder than he'd thought. The wind pushed at him and tugged through his hair, cool and fresh and damp. He took a deep breath. Everything smelled of the ocean. *God*, he thought, exhilarated, *it's great to be alive!*

He hurried to the end of the dock. The *Atlantico* rocked vigorously on the swells, but its moorings were secure and the tires Ryan had cut in half and nailed along the dock prevented any damage to the hull.

Satisfied, he returned to his dingy room behind the office. There he fixed himself eggs and coffee on the battered hotplate that sat on the fold-up table beside the broken toaster and breadbox. Above the table was a shelf holding his books on diving and marine salvage. He treasured those books. They were part of what he did best, and he felt a sense of permanency, of belonging, whenever he read them.

When he'd finished eating, he showered, shaved, and dressed. Then he telephoned Clare at the motel and told her the bad news.

She'd already heard. 'I called the Coast Guard earlier,' she explained. 'The most cheerful thing the guy said was that the storm shouldn't last more than two days.'

She sounded so depressed, Ryan felt obliged to cheer her up. 'That's typical C.G. caution. They're notorious for it.'

'The storm'll end sooner, you mean?'

'Let's hope so. But if it doesn't, we can use the time to clean up the stuff we've found.'

'I've got a better idea. When I was talking to Lieutenant Ambers about the weather, I also asked him if he knew anything about the U-boat. He said he didn't personally, but that an old-timer — a retired chief petty officer named Maynard — had mentioned it on occasion, and probably knew as much about it as anyone. It's worth a try, don't you think?' she added when Ryan didn't say anything. 'I mean, the old guy doesn't live far from here. So what've we got to lose, right?'

Maybe a lot, Ryan thought. Once you start prying into the past, stirring up people's lives, you might wind up bringing attention to yourself. And attention was the last thing he needed right now.

Into the phone he said: 'When you

planning to go see this Maynard character?'

'Anytime you want.'

'What if I don't want?'

'Well,' she said, taken aback, 'then I guess I'll go alone. But I'd really like you to come with me, Ryan. Not being from around here, I probably couldn't get as much out of the man as you. Besides, if he does know about the U-boat, maybe there're some questions we should ask him — questions that only you're qualified to ask. Of course,' she added after a pause, 'I did only hire you to dive, so if you don't *want* to help me in this, don't feel obligated or anything, because I'll certainly understand.'

Like hell you will, Ryan thought. 'I'll pick you up in thirty minutes,' he growled. 'Be ready.' Hanging up, he wrote Mitch a note explaining where he'd gone.

Ryan parked his old Dodge pickup under the portico entrance of the Atlantis Lodge and waited, engine running, as Clare emerged from the lobby and climbed in beside him. She wore a fashionable shiny black vinyl raincoat and black boots, and had tied her long blonde hair back so that it fell in gentle waves about her shoulders.

'Excuse how I look,' she apologized. 'But after twisting your arm to go with me, I didn't dare be late.'

Ryan shrugged, noncommittally, and drove out of the parking lot. 'Well?' he said as they reached the highway. 'Where to now?'

'Salter Path,' Clare said. Then, reading from her notes: 'A blue and white beach house on stilts, between Ocean Drive and the restaurant, facing ocean. Lieutenant Ambers didn't know the exact address, but he said we'd have no trouble finding the house once we got there.'

Ryan drove west a few miles down the center of Bogue Banks, then gestured about him as they reached a scattering of houses dotting the sand. 'We're here,' he said. 'Start looking for a blue an' white house.'

'Better not blink,' Clare laughed. 'Or we'll miss the whole town!'

Lieutenant Ambers's directions were accurate. No sooner had they driven past

Ocean Drive, when an old sun-faded blue and white clapboard house on stilts showed among the sand dunes on their left. Ryan parked by a FOR SALE sign, and they got out. The wind had lessened but still came in sharp gusts that blew sand in their faces.

'This is definitely it,' Clare said as they passed the Maynard mailbox. 'Now, let's just hope the old boy's home.'

They walked between the scrub-covered dunes to a flight of sagging wooden steps that led up to the front porch. An old-fashioned ship's bell hung beside the steps, but before they could ring it a voice yelled down from one of the windows: 'Hold on, folks, I'll be right out.'

A few moments later the owner of the voice appeared on the porch above them. 'Come on.' He gestured. 'I been expectin' you.'

Surprised, Ryan and Clare climbed the steps and joined their host on the porch. He was a big man, as tall as Ryan but heavier, with a white beard and blue eyes. Wisps of white hair poked from under his battered captain's cap, and white paint was spattered on his navy jump suit. 'I'm Orville Maynard,' he said, smiling. 'But I'd sooner y'all call me Chief.'

'I'm Ryan and this is Miss Winslow,' Ryan said.

'Clare,' she corrected. 'How could you be expecting us, Chief, when we didn't tell anyone we were coming?'

'Sea gulls,' said the Chief. 'We have this deal, see. I feed 'em, an' they keep me posted on the latest scuttlebutt.'

Clare chuckled. 'Lieutenant Ambers told you we were coming, didn't he?'

'Aye. Said y'all was interested in the U-352, an' would probably be by to see me. But, where're my manners? Come on inside, please, an' we'll sit an' talk.'

They followed him inside. The house had tiny rooms, creaky floors, a brick fireplace, and old-fashioned sash windows overlooking the ocean. It had also just been painted and the furniture still was covered with dust-cloths. 'Excuse the mess, folks. But I'm sellin' the place an' the realtor thought a coat of paint might help.'

When they were comfortable on the

couch in the living room, he served them coffee in mugs bearing the Coast Guard crest. He then sat opposite them and asked what they wanted to know about the U-boat.

'Anything you can tell us,' Clare said.

'Well, I can't tell you much, 'cause there ain't that much to tell.'

'Do you know who sank it?' Ryan asked.

'Oh, Lordy yes. A Coast Guard cutter, *Daidalos* was her name. Skipper was a good pal o' mine, Doug Jeeter. Country lost a damn fine man when he went down.'

'What about the crew of the U-boat?'

'What about them?'

'Well . . . did anything special happen to them?'

'Not that I know of, no. They were interned at Charleston — kept there till the war ended. But other than that . . . ' He shrugged and scratched his beard. 'Why d'y'all want to know?' he asked. 'I mean, what's all this leadin' up to?'

Clare briefly explained her reason for being in North Carolina, but didn't mention that she or Ryan had located the U-boat. Chief Maynard listened with increasing surprise. And when Clare had finished, he said, 'Well, well, I'll be,' and, finally, 'A war memorial, eh? Well, how about that, Lavinia?' He tugged at his beard, adding: 'I'm sure sorry that I can't be of any real help. I'd like to be, count on that. But — '

'What?' Clare said as he abruptly stopped. 'Did you just think of something?'

'I don't know,' he said. 'Course, most of it's a rumor, you understand, but — well, there were a lot of folks back then who said the reason the U-boat was in these waters at all, was on account of that spy they never caught.'

'What spy?' Ryan said.

'The one who supplied all the shippin' dates an' routes to the U-boats. That's why we lost all them ships — over five hundred in the first six months of the war.'

'Can I ask a silly question?' Clare said.

'Shoot.'

'If this spy was never caught, how do

they know he even existed?'

'Oh, he existed, all right. Just ask the parents of all them poor boys who went down at sea. Graveyard of the Atlantic, they called it.' Chief Maynard grimaced and shook his head. 'Dirty business, submarines. Like trippin' a fella in the dark. Necessary evil, I suppose, but — Listen,' he said, leaning forward, 'everybody in the C.G. knew there was a spy. There was even a rumor it was one of our boys — which I never believed, of course. But for a time Naval Intelligence did.' He chuckled, remembering something. 'Should've seen 'em. All them hush-hush guys they put on the base to snoop around, I mean. Got so, you couldn't even go to the head without gettin' the feelin' you was being watched.'

'A spy?' Clare said, thinking aloud. 'Well, that would certainly add some intrigue to the project.'

Ryan nodded. But before he could say anything, the Chief exclaimed: 'Falcon! *That's* what his name was. Code name, anyway.' He grinned broadly. 'How about that, Lavinia? All these years, an' I can still remember his — ' He broke off, suddenly embarrassed, then said, 'Please forgive me, folks. I've gotten into this dumb habit of talkin' to my dear departed wife like she's still around. Crazy, I know. But — well, I guess that's what happens when you spend a whole lifetime with someone.'

They left shortly after that. It was raining hard again. As they drove east along the highway, Clare decided to fly to Washington and report her findings to her boss. She asked Ryan to accompany her, explaining that she wanted him to meet Karl Slater. 'You'd really like him, Ryan. He's a brilliant man. Very low-key yet dynamic and forceful. Governor Fontaine says he's the 'strength behind the crown.' And he's right, too. Without Karl, we'd have no chance at all of winning this election. Not against Shining Jim's steam-roller campaign.' She suddenly smiled. 'Now that I think of it, you and Karl would get along just great.'

'Why's that?'

'You could straighten out all of Washington's problems, and not say more than three words between you! Seriously, though,' she added when Ryan remained silent, 'I really would like you to come.'

'Sorry. I can't.'

'Why not? You said yourself that the storm mightn't clear up till after tomorrow.'

'Storm's got nothing to do with it.'

'What does, then?'

'I'm busy.'

'So busy you can't even take a day off to fly to Washington?'

'Yes.'

'I see. Well . . . ' She shrugged, disappointed. 'Another time, perhaps.'

'Sure,' Ryan said. 'When I'm not so busy.'

They drove back to the motel in silence. The wind blew the rain against the windshield with such force the wipers couldn't sweep all the water away. Hunched over the steering wheel, Ryan could barely see the road ahead. As he drove, he was tempted to change his mind and accompany Clare to Washington. He hadn't been out of Morehead City for almost three years, and could have used a change of scenery.

But going to Washington, where someone might recognize him, was an unnecessary risk that he wasn't willing to take.

It was still pouring when they reached the Atlantis Lodge. Ryan insisted on taking Clare to the airport. She didn't argue. She led him into her room, where Ryan worked on a crossword puzzle while Clare called the airlines and booked a reservation on the next flight to Washington, D.C.

Later, in the small but efficient New Bern Airport, Clare gave Ryan her Georgetown townhouse phone number and made him promise to call her immediately if the weather improved enough tomorrow to permit them to dive. 'I'll fly back right away,' she added. 'So, no matter what time it is, call me.'

He nodded. 'Will do,' he said, and walked off without even saying good-bye.

6

It wasn't raining when Clare landed at Washington National Airport, but the late-afternoon air was damp and chilly, so she kept her raincoat on as she left the terminal and caught one of the taxis parked outside.

'Fourteenth and L,' she told the driver. Then as he pulled out into the traffic leaving the airport, she settled back and started reading the notes she'd made on the dive. Everything was still fresh in her mind, but she wanted to make sure she hadn't forgotten anything important when she talked to her boss. Karl Slater was a fanatic when it came to details, and the only way to impress him was to be able to answer all his questions.

And she did want to impress him. He had made it clear when he'd given her the job of finding the sunken U-boat, that if she were as successful as he expected, then she'd be in line for an important

White House staff position that would be available once Governor Fontaine was elected. Clare knew that position was press secretary. And although there had never been a female White House press secretary, Karl thought this might be the ideal time to show the country how open-minded Governor Fontaine was by establishing a precedent and naming Clare for the job.

Clare was elated. Of course, she knew there wasn't much chance of her becoming press secretary, because there wasn't much chance of Governor Fontaine defeating Senator Cassidy in the election. But it was still a privilege even to be considered for the job and she intended to do all she could to earn it.

Driving across the 14th Street Bridge, Clare looked out the window at the calm gray Potomac, with the white-columned Jefferson Memorial showing among the trees on the south bank, and felt a sense of history. Great Americans had founded this city, and had governed from it. The famous buildings exuded historical greatness. The reason she'd chosen politics after her divorce was so she could be a part of this history and perhaps one day make a meaningful contribution. Becoming the first female White House press secretary would be a worthy beginning.

They had passed the Washington Monument and were downtown now. They drove past streets named after early presidents, and Clare glimpsed the white-domed Capitol Building at the end of the Mall. With hard work and the right connections she might eventually end up there, too, she thought ambitiously. Senator or congresswoman . . . nothing was impossible with the right people backing you. And if by her efforts to raise the U-boat she won Fontaine North and South Carolina, well — that wouldn't go unnoticed. Or unrewarded.

The driver interrupted her thoughts. 'What's the address, lady?'

'Just drop me off on the corner. That'll be fine.' As she noticed a passing billboard displaying a Governor Fontaine campaign slogan, she asked, 'What d'you think Fontaine's chances are — of getting elected, I mean?'

''bout the same as mine.' The driver

laughed and cracked his chewing gum. 'An' I'm a liberal, lady.'

Governor Fontaine's campaign headquarters occupied the ground floor of an old office building located on L Street a few doors from a multilevel parking garage. A huge blowup of the candidate smiled down from the front of the building. Below, draped over the entrance and above the windows on either side, was a long red, white, and blue banner with a slogan reading: 'A Vote for Fontaine Is a Vote for America.'

The taxi let Clare out on the corner, and she walked past the entrance ramp to the garage and entered the campaign office. The large, well-lit room buzzed with activity. Fontaine posters and campaign slogans covered the walls, while rows of eager young volunteers sat at desks, telephones pressed to their ears.

Clare returned their smiles and waves and collected her messages from the 'in' basket atop her desk. She saw there was nothing important and headed into the small office that was partitioned off in back.

Inside, Karl Slater sat talking on the phone at a desk littered with color-coded charts and maps depicting the density and sparseness of Fontaine supporters throughout the city. Larger, more detailed maps dotted with color-coded pins hung on the walls. Among them was a sign reading: 'Failure is not the missing of success, but the giving up of trying.'

Slater looked surprised to see Clare. He was a tall, distinguished gray-haired man whose constant handball workouts kept him fit and lean and younger-looking than his sixty-two years. He was vainly proud of his appearance and his good health. He didn't smoke and signs about his office and in his car warned others not to, either. He seldom swore, and never drank anything stronger than bottled water, feeling that alcohol made people say things that sooner or later they regretted. Naturally, none of these qualities made Slater exactly popular. But people did fear him. As a result he was invited to all the Washington social functions, and there were many powerful politicians on The Hill who went out of their way to befriend him.

Slater motioned for Clare to sit down, and continued to talk on the telephone: 'I don't care what your excuse is,' he said grimly. 'The governor needs results, not excuses. Now, either you've got the Fifteenth District in your pocket, as you've claimed all along, or you've been playing political pool with us and our financial support of your office will be withdrawn immediately.' He paused, and Clare heard a man's voice protesting vehemently out of the receiver. Slater soon cut him off, his tone low-key but firm as he said, 'I'm sorry, Jack. But there's no room for a loser on our team.' Clare heard more protesting. Then Slater said into the phone, 'Very well, Congressman. We'll do nothing until the 'fat lady' sings. But should the demographics still continue to look grim, we'll expect you to get back to basics and pound the streets, shake a lot of hands, kiss a million babies — do whatever you have to do in order to win back your constituents.' He hung up and shook his head at Clare.

'Congressman Wilcox — the local polls

show he's losing ground to his opponent.'

'That's Alan Quentin, isn't it?'

Slater nodded. 'Another Cassidy clone. God, I swear Shining Jim must be turning them out on a production line somewhere.' He picked up one of the charts, tapping his teeth with a pencil as he studied it. 'All year we've been pouring money into Jack Wilcox's treasure chest and he's been using it for his own personal pleasures.'

'Yes, and now he's paying for it,' Clare said.

'Now we're *all* paying for it,' Slater corrected. 'And at a time when we can ill afford to lose a single vote.'

'Couldn't we flood the Fifteenth District with canvassers? A door-to-door campaign might help stem the Cassidy tide, if we do it quickly enough.'

Slater smiled. 'I'm way ahead of you. The kids are already out in the field.'

'I should've known,' Clare said, admiring Slater. 'Day you wait for a congressman to tell you he's in trouble in his own district is the day this campaign is in trouble.'

'Spies,' Slater said disgustedly. 'We all hate them, but we all use them. But enough of that. Tell me, my dear Clare, what is the latest on the U-boat?'

Briefly but precisely, Clare related everything concerning the dive and their findings. Slater listened intently, his fingers forming a cathedral before his face. And when Clare was finished, he said: 'Excellent. Just excellent. You've accomplished everything I expected of you.'

'Thank you, Karl.' Clare savored the praise a moment before saying, 'There's something else, too. I'm not sure yet how it fits in, or how I can best use it to promote the U-boat museum angle, but — well, I'm sure I'll come up with something once I've checked it out more thoroughly.'

She then explained about Chief Petty Officer Maynard and the spy, Falcon. Again Slater listened without interrupting.

But this time he was smiling when she finished and she knew she'd played an ace.

'Most intriguing,' Slater said. 'The stuff movies are made of.'

'I just hope it's true. And not merely a figment of an old retired sailor's imagination.'

'Should be easy enough to verify. Have you checked the story with anyone else in the area?'

'Not yet, no.'

'Try the Coast Guard. They should have records of all espionage activity. And by now everything will be declassified, so they shouldn't mind showing it to you.'

'I'll check with them as soon as I get back there. Of course,' Clare added, smiling, 'it's probably wishful thinking, but I'm hoping that we'll find some kind of evidence aboard the U-boat that'll connect to the spy.'

'That would be the perfect solution, wouldn't it?'

'Well, it's a long shot, I know. Especially after forty years have lapsed. But — well, stranger things have happened and long shots do pay off occasionally.'

'Only to those daring enough to try them,' Slater said. He got up, adding: 'How would you like to tell all this to the governor?'

'W-well, I . . . I'd love to,' Clare said, surprised.

'Excellent.' Slater reached for the phone. 'I'll call him now. We're having dinner at Rive Gauche. I'll see if he'd be interested in hearing about all your progress.'

Slater's gleaming black Lincoln picked up Clare at her old, restored, Federal-fronted town house in Georgetown shortly after eight that evening. The driver apologized for being late. He'd arrived early, he explained, but spent ten minutes trying to find a parking place on the narrow cobblestone street.

'Don't talk about parking,' Clare laughed as they hurried to the limo. 'Thanks to the tourists, it's become a nightmare. If I didn't love my home so much, I would've moved long ago.'

She was exaggerating, of course. She loved Georgetown, and all its history, and knew it would take more than the parking problem to make her leave. She'd moved there right after coming to Washington, and had instantly felt at home. Now she couldn't imagine living anywhere else.

As they drove down the gentle hill, winding between rows of stately Federal, Victorian, and Georgian exteriors, Clare thought of how feeling as though she belonged somewhere had saved her from completely going to pieces after her divorce. And she couldn't have been more grateful. Four years ago, on arriving in Georgetown, she had desperately needed companionship. The young people she'd met were friendly and many of them had been divorced themselves, so they knew what she was going through. They were willing to listen if she wanted to talk, and willing to ignore the subject if she didn't want to discuss it.

Clare had married Harold Garnett, youngest son of the famous Philadelphia Garnetts, shortly before her twenty-first birthday and had divorced him one week after turning twenty-four. The years between had been nightmarishly restricting. Harold believed women were meant to be shadows: to stay home, have babies, and present the kind of image a wealthy, prominent lawyer could proudly display to his friends, parents, and visiting clients.

At first, Clare did her best to fit the image. But her mind was too active. She grew bored and depressed and, worst of all, felt she had lost her identity. She tried to explain how she felt to Harold. But he was always too busy with his friends or his work to listen. They argued incessantly. Then — worse — they stopped arguing, and caring, and merely went through the motions of being married for the sake of their parents. Divorce was never discussed. No Garnett had ever been divorced, and Clare knew her husband had no intentions of being the first to break the tradition. It was up to her, she realized. Upon turning twenty-four, she decided that she must do something worthwhile in order to justify her existence, and filed for divorce. It wasn't contested.

The horrified Garnetts handled the proceedings quickly and discreetly, and Clare soon left Philadelphia with her freedom and a satisfactory cash settlement. She'd decided to enter politics, and used the settlement to buy the restored Georgetown town house. She found work with a public relations firm whose clients were all politicians. It was immediately obvious that she had a flair for PR work, and during the next three years she promoted herself into a series of better positions with various prestigious companies. Then, last year, Karl Slater had invited her to supervise Governor Fontaine's public relations department. 'It's a difficult task,' he warned. 'The governor's personality is anything but charismatic and his speeches aren't exactly filled with contemporary witticisms, so you'll find it difficult to find quotable phrases. But he's an honest man, with great integrity, and it'll be up to you to make the voting public forget his plain looks and dull voice and be swayed instead by his brilliant mind, superior political platform, and by the fact that he's undoubtedly this country's finest statesman.'

The challenge appealed to Clare. And in the ensuing months, by means of carefully selected campaign posters and slogans, she and her staff had gradually upgraded Fontaine's rather uninspiring image until he was now considered a respectable opponent to the handsome, charismatic Senator Cassidy.

'We're here, madam.'

Clare looked out the window and saw they were at M and Wisconsin streets. Thanking the driver, she got out and entered Rive Gauche. The maitre d' led her to Governor Fontaine's table. It was in a corner by the draped windows, under a chandelier and flanked by the ever-present secret service agents. The governor and Slater rose to greet Clare. She apologized for being late, and tried not to feel conspicuous as she realized people at other tables were staring at her. Among them she recognized many famous political faces. Some of them she knew, and she returned their smiles.

Clare had met the governor on several occasions. He was a reserved, gracious man with a photographic memory. He thanked Clare for joining them, ordered her a gin and tonic, and said he was anxious to hear about her progress in North Carolina. But first he insisted on knowing the results of the recent state-wide polls across the country. Slater supplied the numbers, along with some surprising statistics — surprising, indeed, because for the first time since his nomination the governor showed signs of gaining on Senator Cassidy in key states like California, Texas, and New York.

'I'm not suggesting we're carrying these states by any means,' Slater said, 'but I honestly do believe it's the beginning of a trend, and a very healthy trend at that.'

Governor Fontaine agreed. 'Now, if we can only gain the same positive momentum in the South, especially throughout the Bible Belt where Cassidy's glib charisma hasn't gone over as well as expected — well, who knows, eh? We may just surprise the hell out of a few people on November eleventh!'

'I think there's a definite chance of that,' Slater said. 'Which is another reason, Hank, why I'm convinced that Clare, here, can be a small but important part of that momentum. The Bible Belt extends throughout North and South Carolina, and if by setting up the U-boat museum we can bring some much-needed extra revenue to the area, then your name will be favorably remembered when the voters go to the polls.'

'Yes, I suppose so.' The governor frowned, unconvinced. 'However, Karl, I don't feel we should place too much importance on the raising of a U-boat. After all, many of the voters weren't even born forty years ago, so they're not going to be too impressed by a ghost from the past.'

'That's possible. But don't forget, patriotism is very strong throughout the South — in fact, it's presently enjoying a fierce resurgence throughout the entire country. So the idea of a war memorial commemorating the deaths of merchant-men, many of whom were Southerners — plus the possibility of exposing the spy responsible for those deaths — can't do anything but glorify your image as a staunch patriot.'

'Spy?' the governor said, frowning. 'What spy's this?'

'Why don't you tell the governor?' Slater said to Clare.

She did. Carefully, briefly, she explained about Falcon and the spy's possible connection with the sunken U-boat.

'Interesting,' Governor Fontaine said when she'd finished. 'And this Falcon

— he was never caught, you say?'

'Not according to the Coast Guard, no, sir.'

Clare could see that the governor was more curious than impressed. 'Of course, it is a long time ago, as you say. But I agree with Karl. Exposing that spy — especially if he's still alive and in this country — will not only appeal to a lot of patriotic-minded voters, but it'll also show them that even during the heat and stress of a presidential campaign, you, as a concerned American, still had time to concern yourself with something other than your own personal issues or gratification.'

Governor Fontaine studied Clare with his pensive, deep-set brown eyes. 'You're a very eloquent and persuasive young lady, Miss Winslow, do you know that?'

For a moment Clare felt numb with pleasure. Then, as the governor and Slater began discussing another political matter, she realized that the maitre d' was standing beside their table.

'Excuse me, Governor . . . '

'Yes, Henri, what is it?'

'A phone call, sir — for the lady.'

Clare looked surprised. 'It must be my service,' she said, rising. 'I always tell them where I'll be.'

'That's because you're pure of heart,' joked the Governor.

Clare excused herself and used the telephone at the maitre d's desk. It was Ryan. Despite the crackle caused by a bad connection, Clare heard him say, ' . . . asked me to call if . . . weather cleared.'

'Yes, yes . . . has it?'

'Yeah. Mitch an' I will be diving first thing in the mornin'.'

'Not without me,' Clare said.

'What . . . you say?' Ryan said.

'I said, not without me. Soon as I hang up I'll be on the first available plane heading your way.'

'Figures.'

All she heard was crackling. 'What?'

'I said, let me know what time you're coming in, so I can pick you up.'

'I will. Right away. And Ryan — thanks for calling, huh?'

He'd already hung up.

7

Early the next morning, with the sun barely up and the pale violet sky still streaked with primrose, the three of them were at sea again.

Ryan sat in his shirt and shorts, legs tucked under him on the stern deck of the *Atlantico*, making his customary inspection of their diving gear. He felt good. *You're a lucky bastard*, he thought as he checked out the regulators and found they were functioning. *Thanks to Clare and her political money, you have no financial worries and you're out on the ocean doing what you like to do. How can you beat that?*

He looked up at Clare, who was asleep in one of the chairs on the flying bridge. Her head was leaned back, with all her blonde hair spilling over her shoulders and the rest of her tucked under an old blue blanket he'd bought last year at Clawson's Emporium.

'I'm sorry you had to come all this way,' she'd said as they drove back from the airport to Morehead City. 'But it was either Kinston or no flight until seven thirty tomorrow morning.'

'*This* mornin',' he corrected. 'In case you're not aware of it, it's almost sunup.'

'I'm aware of it,' she said, yawning. 'You couldn't possibly feel the way I do unless you'd spent the entire night in airports.' She'd fallen asleep right after that and hadn't woken up until they crossed the railroad tracks outside of Havelock. Then the sudden jarring bump startled her awake and she looked around, blinking, not recognizing where she was, asking sleepily: 'How much farther is it?'

' 'bout ten miles.'

'Not still mad at me, are you?'

'Never was.'

'Then why didn't you say hello?'

'I did.'

'Oh. That's what that grunt was.' She rolled her eyes, yawned and went back to sleep.

Now as Ryan looked at Clare on the

flying bridge, Mitch poked his head out of the wheelhouse and said they were almost over the U-boat. 'Better come'n check out the Loran-C,' he added. 'Make sure I ain't made no mistake about the coordinates.'

'Be right there,' Ryan replied. He finished inspecting the diving gear then entered the wheelhouse to verify Mitch's figures.

Ryan led the way into the dark, cramped quarters of the U-boat. He held his light and a Hawaiian spear in one hand, and dragged his tank along with the other. He'd chosen the longer-style spear over the conventional spear gun as a safety precaution: in case the bag of dead fish that Mitch carried failed to lure the moray eel out of the captain's cabin, and they had to spear it. The idea of spearing a large moray eel in such confined quarters worried Ryan. Eels died hard, he knew. They weren't much more than a floating muscle with teeth, and their brain was so small that even spearing them through the head seldom had any effect — other than to send them into a convulsive, thrashing rage.

As Ryan paused in the doorway of the captain's cabin, he hoped the storm had driven the eel away. Motioning for Clare and Mitch to stay back, he swam slowly into the captain's quarters and shined his light at the damaged security cabinet.

For a moment he saw nothing — just his light flaring in the blue-black water ahead. Then up it came, the blunt, green, almond-shaped head with its jaws slowly opening and closing and its rubbery black eyes unblinking in the light.

Damn, Ryan thought. Turning, he handed the light to Clare and motioned for Mitch to give him a fish. Mitch obeyed. Ryan stuck the fish on the end of his spear and tried to tempt the eel out of the cabinet. There was a blurred, snapping movement, incredibly sudden, and when the water calmed again Ryan saw the eel had torn off all of the fish but its head, shredded bits of which remained on the spear point. Ryan realized he'd held the fish too close. He baited the spear again and dangled the fish a few feet away from the eel. Then, as it remained anchored inside the cabinet, head extended, watching, Ryan inched the fish closer toward the moray.

The eel refused to be drawn out. It waited until the fish was a foot away. Again there was a blur of green, a snapping motion, and all but the head of the fish was gone.

Ryan cursed. He had no choice now but to kill the eel. And right away, while they still had plenty of air. Motioning his intentions to Clare and Mitch, he stretched the heavy-duty surgical rubber cable attached to the butt end of the spear around his hand, slingshot fashion, aimed for the nearest glistening black eye and thrust the spear home.

His aim was true. The point went into the eye, on through the eel's head, and out the other side. At once the breakaway point popped loose, dragging with it the length of chain that was fastened to the spear head, so that now the eel couldn't work itself up the shaft as it could have on a conventional spear gun.

But it could still fight. The instant after it was impaled the eel released its anchor inside the cabinet and came thrashing out, all thigh-thick six feet of it, going into frantic spasms that Ryan couldn't control.

Mitch, seeing Ryan was in trouble, kicked his way into the cabin and tried to grab hold of the point end of the chain. But the moray was writhing around too fast. Mitch came away empty-handed. In its frenzy the eel twisted itself into raveled knots. Its retreating head dragged the spear shaft Ryan was holding toward its gnashing teeth. He let go too late. Its back-angled, needle-like teeth sank into his wrist. Ryan grimaced as the teeth bit through his rubber sleeve into his flesh. Dizziness almost overtook him.

He shook his head clear. Then, hampered by his tank, he fumbled for his knife. But Mitch had his blade already drawn and slashed at the moray's head. Blue-tinted blood billowed from the gaping wound. The eel's frenzied thrashing increased. The weight of its long spinning body caused its teeth to rip away Ryan's flesh and rubber sleeve.

Ryan bit down on his mouthpiece, trying to ignore the pain as he continued to hold on to the spear and limit the eel's head movements. Mitch grabbed the point end of the chain, and together they dragged the struggling moray down to the mud-covered deck. There Mitch was able to saw the eel's head off, allowing the still-writhing body to flail lifelessly about in the mud-churned water.

Ryan nodded his thanks. Mitch saw Ryan's badly gashed wrist and motioned for him to head for the surface. Ryan nodded. Pulling his tank with his uninjured hand, he kicked out of the cabin. He swam past Clare toward the forward torpedo loading hatch. Clare indicated to Mitch that she'd help Ryan and swam after him. Mitch started to follow. Then he remembered why they were there. Turning to the cabinet, he removed a flat metal box the size of a briefcase and then swam after Clare.

Once outside the U-boat, Ryan clamped his free hand about his torn wrist to stop the bleeding. The pain was intense. He squeezed tighter. Blood would attract sharks and they might not make it to the boat. Beside him Clare slipped into her backpack, then helped support Ryan's tank as they both kicked upward.

They ascended slowly. Mitch followed several feet below them, watching for sharks.

Only one shark appeared: a slender, steel-blue fifteen-footer that swam about them in a wide circle. Each circle decreased in diameter. As they neared the surface, it came in for a closer look. Mitch kicked upward, drew level with Ryan and Clare and resolutely faced the shark. It studied him with a cold, black, disinterested eye. Then it broke off and with vigorous flicks of its caudal fin nosed down and disappeared into the depths.

Once aboard the *Atlantico* Clare and Mitch helped Ryan off with the hood and jacket of his wet suit. Then, while Mitch started the boat and headed home, Clare opened the first-aid kit and attended to Ryan's wrist. The flesh was torn away from the bone and she had trouble stemming the bleeding.

'When we get ashore,' she told him, 'we must have a doctor look at that.'

Ryan grunted through his teeth. Pain was making him nauseous. Rising, he went to a cupboard and took out a fruit jar filled with moonshine. Unscrewing the lid one-handed, he downed several swallows. He handed the jar to Mitch, and said quietly, 'You handled yourself good down there.'

Mitch grinned. 'Look who taught me.'

'Teaching's one thing, doing's another. Difference has killed a lot of people.'

'Maybe. But not when you're a team, like we are.'

'Jesus,' Clare said. 'What is this, the Ryan-Mitchell mutual admiration society?'

'I'll drink to that,' said Mitch. He took a slug and returned the jar to Ryan.

'You guys hogging that,' Clare said, 'or passing it around?'

'Help yourself.' Ryan handed the jar to Clare.

'Take it easy, ma'am,' Mitch warned her. 'That stuff ain't milk, you know.'

Clare ignored him. She tipped the fruit jar to her lips and took a good swallow. The clear moonshine went down like acid and for one awful moment she thought she'd burned a hole in her throat.

'Thanks,' her mouth said. But no sound came out. Then, tears in her eyes, she returned the jar to Ryan and hurried out on deck.

Mitch gave Ryan a guilty look. 'Well, she can't say I didn't warn her.'

'That you did, my man. That you did.' Ryan chuckled softly to himself. 'Don't worry, pal. If the lady ever gets her voice back, I'm sure she'll be the first to say that she doesn't blame you one little bit.'

8

Later, as they entered Beaufort Inlet and moved along the sound, Ryan took the wheel while Clare and Mitch sat at the table and carefully pried open the metal box Mitch had taken from the U-boat. Inside was a sealed oilskin pouch that was thickly coated with diesel oil. They opened the pouch and found two code books, some documents, transcripts of Falcon's messages, a handwritten memo, and a photograph of a young man. He had blond hair, penetrating blue eyes and an engaging boyish smile.

'Wonder who he is?' Mitch said.

'Captain, probably. Or maybe his son.' She showed the picture to Ryan. 'What do you think?'

Ryan studied the face and shrugged. 'His son, most likely. Why would the captain want a picture of himself?'

Clare nodded in agreement. 'I know a little German. Maybe it says who he is in one of these documents.' She scanned each page, then shook her head. 'Nothing in here.' She turned to the handwritten memo, suddenly exclaiming: 'Hey — wait a minute. I think . . . ' She read on. Ryan and Mitch waited impatiently for her to finish. When she had, she said, 'My God, I don't believe it.'

'What?' Mitch said. 'What don't y'all believe?'

'Well, unless I'm mistaken — and I very easily could be — this is a picture of that spy, Falcon.'

'Spy?' Mitch frowned. 'What spy?'

Briefly, Ryan related what Chief Petty Officer Maynard had told them about the spy, Falcon. Mitch was enthralled. But before he could swamp them with questions, Ryan cut him off and asked Clare why she thought the picture was of Falcon.

'Well,' she said, pointing at the memo, 'for one thing it says 'Falcon' right there. And for another, right after it, it says *'Spion,'* which I'm pretty sure means spy. Of course, my German's kind of rusty, so I could be wrong. But — '

'I know someone who speaks fluent German,' Ryan said. 'She'd know what all this said in a minute.'

'Terrific,' Clare said. 'Do you think you could arrange it so we could see her tomorrow? I'm anxious to know if this really is the spy.'

'I'll try,' Ryan said. 'Soon as we get ashore, I'll call her. Find out if it's convenient.'

They were in luck. After they had docked and taken everything into the shop, Ryan called Mrs. Louise Klammer. The elderly former librarian was pleased to hear from Ryan and agreed to translate the German. Ryan thanked her, said he'd be at her house at ten in the morning, and hoped that she wouldn't mind if he brought along a friend.

'Of course not,' Mrs. Klammer said. 'Now that I'm retired, I look forward to company.'

Hanging up, Ryan told Clare the news. She was delighted. But then she insisted on driving Ryan to the emergency hospital to have his arm treated. 'Why don't you come with us?' she added to Mitch. 'Afterward, we can all have dinner together.'

'Sorry, I can't. I already promised I'd eat supper over at Wanda's. But thanks for askin'.' He hurried out.

'C'mon,' Clare told Ryan, who was tinkering with a dismantled engine. 'Quit stalling and lock up so we can get to the hospital.'

He did as she asked and followed her out to the Porsche.

The doctor on duty at the emergency hospital was young and efficient. He gave Ryan a tetanus shot, pills for the pain, and a prescription for salve to be applied with each change of dressing. He also said Ryan was damned lucky the bite wasn't worse. Ryan disagreed. Lucky people, he said, didn't get bitten at all.

They bought a respectable Burgundy and a large pizza after leaving the hospital, then drove to Clare's motel and ate dinner while watching the news on television. Following the news was an hour-long special program featuring an 'in-depth' look at the two presidential nominees. It was mostly key moments in their careers, their most-quoted remarks, and interviews with friends and adversaries.

Ryan wasn't overly impressed with either candidate. But then, as he admitted, he wasn't impressed by any of the other politicians in Washington, either. They all seemed too busy looking out for themselves to worry about their constituents or the American people as a whole.

Clare agreed that there certainly were politicians who fitted that description, but added that there were also some pretty dynamic men on The Hill, men who had strong beliefs and who were willing to fight for them, tooth and nail. 'Oh, sure,' she continued, 'sometimes they have to give a little to get a little, but that still doesn't mean they don't believe in what they're doing or aren't still determined to get their bills passed.'

Ryan said only, 'I guess you're entitled to your opinion,' and went on eating his pizza.

Clare felt a little wounded, but decided not to press the subject.

On television a commercial had just ended and the narrator was explaining that the network had dug a little deeper into the nominees' backgrounds. As a result they had come up with a number of family-album snapshots that showed Cassidy and Fontaine in some amusingly revealing poses.

There was baby Jimbo Cassidy on a rug in diapers; gawky, ten-year-old Hank Fontaine in a grubby Little League uniform; youthful, Norman Rockwell-faced Cassidy in military dress; teen-aged Fontaine winning a high school debate scroll; teen-aged Cassidy on the steps of the American embassy in Berlin prior to World War II; Fontaine in an Air Force uniform; and, lastly, a head shot of Cassidy that was taken, the narrator said, a few days before he entered the U.S. Coast Guard.

Ryan wasn't listening. 'Sweet Jesus,' he said softly. He grabbed up the head shot of the spy, Falcon, that lay on the table among their U-boat findings and compared it to the twenty-two-year-old Cassidy now smiling at them on television. 'Will you look at that?'

The likeness was uncanny.

'My God,' Clare exclaimed. 'They could be identical twins!'

Ryan laughed quietly to himself.

'What?' Clare said.

'I was just thinking . . . wondering what would happen if Cassidy and Falcon turned out to be one and the same guy.'

Clare's mouth fell open. 'Good God!' she said, shaken. 'Don't say things like that — even in jest.'

'Yeah,' Ryan said. He grinned as he thought about the monumental repercussions it would cause. 'It would kind of put a crimp in our boy's ambitions, wouldn't it?'

For a moment they stared at each other in stunned silence. Then, gradually, both started laughing as they realized the utter absurdity of such an idea.

9

The next morning Ryan and Clare took the written material they'd found aboard the U-boat to Louise Klammer's house on Elm Street. The old green clapboard house was rundown and badly needed painting, but inside it had a personality as warm and friendly as Mrs. Klammer. It also smelled of fresh coffee and hot oatmeal cookies, which she insisted they eat in the tiny sunlit parlor while she translated the material.

Mrs. Klammer was a small, energetic woman in her early seventies with a halo of white hair and cataract-clouded blue eyes. But she could still see well enough with her Coke-bottle glasses to read, and before they'd finished their second cup of coffee, she'd translated everything but the code books.

She started with the hand-written memo. It was from German Intelligence, she explained, and referred to a certain photograph that evidently had been attached to it at one time — a photo to be used by a *Kapitan* Ernst Richter for identification purposes in the event he had to meet with someone named Falcon. 'I would assume that's a code name,' she said. 'My late husband was in Army Intelligence during World War Two, so I'm not unfamiliar with certain terminologies.'

'Is that all it says?' Clare said, disappointed. 'Doesn't it mention anything about who Falcon was?'

'No, my dear. I'm afraid not. But, then, since I suspect this memo and these other documents were confidential at the time, I doubt if they would reveal such classified information.'

'No, of course not,' Ryan said, adding: 'What about the other documents? They contain anything worth knowing?'

'Well, naturally, I haven't had time to examine them in detail, but I can tell you that this book is the captain's log — it's filled with dates, bearings, and daily routine occurrences during the U-boat's voyage across the Atlantic from its pen in

St.-Nazaire in May, 1942. And these two' — she indicated the small leather-bound notebooks — 'are code books that I can't decipher. As for the rest, they're official reports concerning the U-boat's mission.'

'What was that mission?' asked Clare. 'Does it say?'

'To intercept one of our convoys,' said Mrs. Klammer. 'The captain received the date and route of the convoy from Falcon in an unfinished transmission. But apparently something went wrong, because there's no mention in the log of any attack or sinkings.'

'Maybe the U-boat was sunk?' Ryan said. Earlier he and Clare had decided not to tell Mrs. Klammer what they were involved in. They had no idea where the trail might lead them, and Ryan saw no reason perhaps to cause problems for a kindly old librarian whom he'd befriended when she had helped him find books on marine salvage. 'You know, before it intercepted the convoy?'

'That would certainly make sense,' Mrs. Klammer agreed. She rubbed her milky-blue eyes, weary now from the strain. 'Well, my dears, I'm afraid that's about all I can tell you. As I say, I didn't have time to examine everything as thoroughly as I would've liked, but — '

'Nonsense,' Clare said gently. 'You've been a terrific help, Mrs. Klammer. I don't know how to thank you enough.'

'Oh, I was only too glad to help. All these years, keeping my German up for goodness knows what reason — and now, suddenly, it comes in handy. Most remarkable, wouldn't y'all say?'

'Most remarkable,' Clare agreed. 'And very fortunate for us.'

'For me, too. You've no idea the thrill I got from being able to read all this.'

They left shortly after that. As they walked along the sidewalk under the elms to the Porsche, Clare suddenly announced that she wanted to continue trying to dig up information concerning the spy.

'Instead of diving, you mean?' Ryan said.

'Yes. With that wrist of yours, you shouldn't be in the water anyway — '

'Never mind my wrist. I can still — '

'Naturally,' she continued as if he

hadn't spoken, 'I'll still pay you — as if you were diving, I mean. And if we don't uncover anything important after a few days, then I'll call Karl and tell him it's a waste of time and we'll start diving on the sub again. Deal?'

'If that's what you want, sure.'

'It is.'

'Okay if I ask you something first?'

'Go ahead.'

'Why the big sudden interest in this spy?'

'I don't know.' Clare thought a moment, then shrugged. 'Guess I find it intriguing that he was never caught.'

'That's all?'

'What d'you mean?'

'You sure there's nothing more to it than that?'

'Such as?'

'I don't know. You tell me.'

She paused and looked up at him, her green eyes trying to penetrate his hard yellow-gray gaze. Then, abruptly, she laughed. 'If you're suggesting,' she said slowly, 'that I'm trying to make some kind of connection between Cassidy and

Falcon just because they look alike — well, forget it.' Again, she laughed. 'I may be eager to get ahead, but not that eager.'

When Ryan didn't laugh, didn't even smile, she added, 'You don't think there is, do you? Any connection, I mean.'

'Nope. None at all.'

'Good. Then our next step is to decide where to start looking for more info on Falcon. Where do you think we should go first — Coast Guard or newspapers?'

'Newspapers.'

'Okay,' Clare said. 'Newspapers it is. Now, since this is your town, you choose which one we check out first.'

'That's easy,' Ryan said. '*The Carteret Observer*. It's the only paper Morehead City has.'

The Carteret Observer was a small publication located downtown on Arendell. After Clare had shown her credentials, the editor, Wells Beaman, agreed to let them examine the back issues during the years of 1941 through 1944.

The issues were on microfilm. Ryan and Clare spent the next two hours in a back room seated before an old, manually operated viewer. The news was mostly local, grindingly dull, and at times the print so small and blurred it was barely legible. Nor was there any mention of Falcon. Not until 1942. Then on a front page dated Monday, May 11, there was a high school yearbook photograph of Mary Jo Buffram (nee Sutter) and a brief account covering her grisly death on Bogue Banks.

The name meant nothing to Ryan or Clare. And since there was no mention of Falcon, after a brief glance at the article Ryan continued to crank the handle. He pulled a week's issues across the lighted viewing screen. And then, suddenly, unexpectedly, there was another photograph of Mary Jo, accompanied by a detailed article under a headline reading: MARY JO BUFFRAM — MURDERED BY SPY?

Ryan and Clare looked at each other, and read the accompanying article. It described how on the previous night police had found a transmitter buried in the sand a short distance from the grave in which, last Sunday, Mary Jo Buffram's strangled body was discovered. 'Police claim that the close proximity of the transmitter to the corpse suggests that Mrs. Buffram might have stumbled onto whoever was using the transmitter, alarming the person or persons sufficiently to kill her.'

At first it had been suspected that Mrs. Buffram had been killed by her husband, Marine Sergeant Alvin J. Buffram, who was AWOL from his base at the time of the murder and admittedly looking for his wife. But later it was proved that Sergeant Buffram was in custody at his base at the time the medical examiner had estimated Mrs. Buffram was killed, and subsequently he had been cleared of the murder charge.

Why Mary Jo was on the beach near Salter Path at night, alone, remained a mystery. Especially since her address at the present time was believed to be in Swansboro, a distance of more than ten miles from where her body was found. Local authorities were still investigating her death and the possibility that her murderer was a spy rumored to be operating in the vicinity of Bogue Banks.

The story went on to say that Mary Jo, a former volunteer worker at the USO canteen in Wilmington, North Carolina, was employed by T. P. Murchinson's, a drugstore in Swansboro. Mr. Murchinson described Mary Jo as a 'very sweet and friendly girl who loved to have fun and go dancing' and who 'didn't have an enemy in the world.'

'She had one,' Ryan said grimly. 'A spy named Falcon.'

They continued viewing the microfilm until they reached the final issue of *The Observer* for the year 1944. But there was no further mention of Mary Jo Buffram. Or Falcon.

'Well?' Clare asked Ryan as they returned the microfilm to the filing cabinet. 'What do you think of our friend Falcon now?'

'He's getting more interesting by the minute.'

'Isn't he, though.' She added: 'D'you think the C.G. would have a file on him?'

Before Ryan could answer, the editor entered. 'Well, folks, did y'all find what you were looking for?'

'Maybe,' Clare said. 'First, though, I wonder if we could ask you a couple of questions?'

'About what?'

'A girl who was murdered around here,' Ryan said. 'It was back in 'forty-two, so you may not remember. But — '

'Are y'all referring to Mary Jo Buffram?' Wells Beaman asked.

'Yes.'

'It's really no great trick,' Beaman said. He was a small, dryly humorous old man with unruly white hair. 'Remembering her name that easily, I mean.'

'Why? Because of her connection with the spy?'

'No. Though between the mystery of Falcon never being caught, and the pleasant fact that murder is not a common problem around here, poor Mary Jo did become unwittingly famous — in a small way, of course. Everything is small here compared to normal big-city ways. No,' Beaman added, pushing his glasses up onto his wrinkled forehead, 'the reason I knew her name so readily, folks, is because someone else was in here about six months

116

ago inquiring about Mary Jo.'

Ryan shot Clare a questioning look. Then, to Beaman: 'Can you tell us who that was?'

'Well, I don't remember his name. But he was a big man, 'bout forty, I guess, with lots of thick wavy gray hair and a noticeable limp.'

'Did he happen to say why he wanted the information?'

'No-o . . . I don't think so.'

'How about who he worked for?' Ryan said.

Beaman smiled under his droopy white mustache. 'It was your opposition, Miss Winslow — Senator Cassidy.'

Ryan and Clare exchanged surprised glances.

'Are you sure about that?' Clare said.

'Oh, absolutely.'

'And he asked about Mary Jo and Falcon?'

'Yes. I'm not sure if he said why or not.' Beaman smiled apologetically. 'My memory's not what it used to be, I'm afraid. But I do remember he wanted to know if I knew of anything unusual about her death.

You know, stuff that hadn't been printed in the newspapers.'

'Do you?'

'Not a thing, unfortunately. But, as I told him, the folks to talk to about Mary Jo are the Murchinsons in Swansboro. They were her friends, and if anybody would know all the facts, it'd be them.'

'Thanks,' Ryan said. 'You've been a big help.' He led Clare out.

Wells Beaman moved to the window and watched as Ryan and Clare walked to the nearby Porsche. Then, satisfied that they weren't returning, he went to the telephone and dialed a Washington, D.C. number. After two rings a receptionist answered: 'Atlas Janitorial Service. May I help you?'

'This is Wells Beaman, Shirley — Mr. Callum, please.'

'One moment, please, Mr. Beaman.'

Beaman heard the call transferred. Then a man's voice, low and resonant, answered gruffly: ''lo, Wells.'

'Afternoon, Dean. Been a while.'

'Six months, about. What all can I do for you?'

'I'm hoping I can do something for you, old friend.' Beaman then explained about Ryan and Clare's interest in Mary Jo Buffram and the spy who supposedly killed her.

In his small, cluttered office on H Street in the capital, Dean Callum listened intently. Well over six feet, with thinning brown hair and dark sunken eyes, he had the deep passionate voice of a preacher. He always wore black. And though he wasn't a reverend, he constantly quoted the Scriptures. An old Bible lay on his desk, and a print of Jesus Christ hung on the wall before him. He neither smoked nor drank, and had not touched a woman since his wife died many years ago.

'What'd these people look like?' he asked when Beaman had finished. Then, after the editor had described Ryan and Clare: 'Did they say why they wanted to know about Mary Jo?'

'No. But Miss Winslow works for Governor Fontaine, so I presume it must have somethin' to do with politics.'

'What about the man?'

'He owns a marine salvage business here in Morehead. I don't know what his connection could be, but — well, I just thought y'all ought to know they were here, is all.'

'Thank you, my friend. May the Lord always watch over you.' Dean Callum hung up and pressed both hands, palms down on the Bible. They were huge, big-knuckled hands. On the back of the left one was tattooed USMC and on the back of the other, MJB.

He spoke a silent prayer. Then he raised his brown, sunken eyes to the plaque hanging below the print of Christ. It read: 'Vengeance is mine, sayeth the Lord.'

Dean Callum stared fixedly at the plaque. His whole body seemed to shudder with barely controlled rage. Then with an almost gentle smile, he opened his telephone book and began looking for the number of Murchinson's drugstore in Swansboro.

10

During the drive to Swansboro Ryan and Clare tried to figure out who the gray-haired man with the limp might be. He obviously worked for Senator Cassidy, but in what capacity Clare didn't know. She'd never seen anyone resembling him in Cassidy's presence, or with the senator's staff.

What was even more puzzling was that neither she nor Ryan could find a satisfactory reason as to why Cassidy would be interested in Mary Jo Buffram or Falcon. Clare said she would call her boss later and see if he knew why, and if Karl couldn't help, then she'd contact some of her reporter friends and see if they had any ideas. 'Meanwhile,' she added, 'let's hear what the Murchinsons have to say. Who knows? Maybe they'll give us all the answers we need.'

Ryan sighed, frustrated. 'I keep thinking we're missing something that's staring us right in the goddamn face. But just what it is — well, beats the hell out of me.'

They drove the twenty-odd miles west along the coast to Swansboro. Ryan had been there before, many times, and within a few minutes of entering the small town on the cape, he pulled up in front of T. P. Murchinson's.

The old drugstore was now a crass, commercially successful, neon-chrome-glass coffee shop and pharmacy that the older customers claimed had hastened the death of the owner, ol' T. P., as he was affectionately called. His only heir, a son named T. S., had never found his father's shoes comfortable. Now, at sixty-two, he still worked every day filling prescriptions.

He was behind the drug counter now as Ryan and Clare entered the pharmacy. Ryan noticed that the druggist looked at them then quickly looked away, and wondered why.

'Yes?' T. S. said as they confronted him. 'May I help you?'

'A Mr. Beaman, editor of *The Carteret Observer,* suggested we come and talk to you,' Clare said.

'What about?'

Ryan remembered the look the druggist had given them and decided to try a bluff. 'Didn't Wells tell you when he called? He promised he would.'

The bluff worked. T. S. hesitated, caught off-guard, then said: 'Yes . . . uh . . . he . . . uh . . . I just wasn't sure if you were the people he was talking about.'

'We're them,' Ryan said cheerfully.

Clare hid a smile. She then introduced herself and Ryan, and showed the druggist her credentials.

T. S. wasn't impressed. 'Why would someone as important as Governor Fontaine be interested in Mary Jo Buffram?'

'He's not,' Clare said. 'At least, not directly. But he is interested in her connection with that spy — Falcon — who supposedly killed her.' She went on to explain about the sunken U-boat and Governor Fontaine's desire to raise it and to turn it into a war memorial located in Wilmington. 'Naturally,' she added, 'the fact that Falcon was never caught adds great intrigue to the project, so if there's anything you know about Mary Jo that might help us learn more about the spy — '

'Mary Jo was not killed by any spy,' T. S. broke in harshly.

'She wasn't?'

'Of course not. That was all part of a cover-up to hide the real killer's identity.'

Ryan frowned, intrigued. 'You saying you know who that killer was?'

'I am,' T. S. said pompously. 'And so do many others — though time and bribes have undoubtedly made them forget.'

'But not you?'

'No.'

'Were you ever bribed?'

'Bribes were offered' — T. S. sounded contemptuous — 'but I never accepted a cent from them.'

'Them?'

'People — influential politicians with big bucks.'

'A politician murdered Mary Jo?' Clare said, incredulous.

'One of the biggest.'

'Who?' Ryan asked.

'I can't answer that.'

'Why not? You afraid?'

T. S. thought a moment before saying: 'I wasn't. Not for a long time. Then, about six months ago, a man came to see me.'

'A gray-haired man with a limp?' Ryan guessed.

'Y-Yes.' T. S. looked surprised. 'How did you — ?'

'Mr. Beaman was visited by the same man,' Clare put in. 'He couldn't remember his name, though. Can you?'

'He never gave it. He just said he worked for Senator Cassidy, and asked me a lot of questions concerning Mary Jo Buffram and Falcon.'

'What kind of questions?'

'I . . . I'm afraid I can't say.'

'Why not?' Ryan asked.

'Look,' T. S. said irritably, 'I'm very busy right now, so if you'll excuse me — '

Clare stopped him. 'Please — wait, Mr. Murchinson. We're not trying to pry into your private life, or cause you any unnecessary problems, but, please, can't you just tell us all you know about this spy and why you don't think he killed Mary Jo?'

T. S. hesitated, uncertain. Finally, he

said, 'I'm sorry. There's nothing to tell. Good day.' He turned and hurried into his office in back.

Clare looked at Ryan. 'What now, Coach?'

'Lunch,' said Ryan. His mind was churning. 'I've got this grumbling in my gut, and I want to make sure that it ain't because I'm hungry.'

They had hamburgers and french fries in the adjoining coffee shop. Ryan barely spoke during the meal and Clare was smart enough not to press him into conversation.

As he ate, Ryan tried to remember everything that they had seen or read or heard concerning Cassidy and Falcon since he and Clare had first noticed the likeness between the senator and the spy. He visualized every little detail, over and over, storing some things, tossing others aside, and it wasn't until they were standing at the register paying their check that it suddenly hit him.

'C'mon,' he said, taking Clare by the arm. 'Let's get out of here.'

'W-Where're we going?' she protested

as he led her outside, across the street toward a big brick building on the next corner.

'Library.'

'Library? What for?'

' 'cause it's time to get rid of my bellyache.' He'd say no more despite her questions, and finally she quit and let him lead her along in silence.

Inside the library Ryan checked the reference card file and found there were three biographies on the Cassidy family. But only one — *The Cassidy Clan* — was on the shelf.

'Mind if I ask what we're looking for?' Clare said as they took the book to one of the reading tables.

'Remember those pictures we saw of Fontaine and Cassidy on TV,' Ryan said, 'when they were growing up?'

'Yes.'

'Well, I suddenly remembered what it was that's been nagging at me.'

'Go on.'

'One of the pictures showed young Cassidy standing outside the American embassy in Berlin. The announcer said he'd gone to school there, while his father was in the State Department.'

'I remember that. But . . . so what? I mean, what're you getting at?'

'I'm not sure, yet,' Ryan said. 'Right now, all I'm tryin' to do is pacify a bellyache. But if I remember correctly, I read somewhere that Cassidy's father was a Nazi sympathizer — '

'That's right,' Clare exclaimed. 'He was.'

Ryan tapped the book before them. 'Well, it should all be in here. That — and everything else about the Cassidys' wartime activities. And if we're lucky — well, maybe their political philosophies will shed enough light on Shining Jim to explain why he's interested in the murder of a young girl by a Nazi spy over forty years ago.'

For several moments Clare didn't say anything. Then, as the enormity of what Ryan was implying struck her, she said in a hushed, shocked voice, 'This is crazy, Ryan . . . you know that, don't you? Absolutely, utterly crazy . . . '

His only response was to open the book and to start reading. Her mind whirling,

Clare moved her chair closer and read along with him.

The book had been written in 1954, when Senator James L. Cassidy was thirty-four, and the center section consisted of photographs of the entire Cassidy family.

Clare took the picture of Falcon from her purse and compared it to two photographs of James, one aged nineteen, the other twenty-eight, and again the likeness was uncanny. Not only that, but Falcon's basic features resembled those of all the male Cassidys.

'Incredible,' Clare exclaimed softly. 'Just incredible.'

'So's this,' Ryan said. He read aloud: ' "In July of 1939, Joseph Cassidy, not yet a senator, was recalled home to the United States after issuing some very serious accusations against the British and French governments. These accusations charged them with attempts to undermine the Third Reich and to blame Adolph Hitler for 'reckless warmongering.' Cassidy, a statesman with business interests in Germany, further strained diplomatic relations between the United States and Great Britain and

France by openly demanding that the Third Reich be allowed to continue its 'nonaggressive build-up of weapons' which was in direct violation of the Treaty of Versailles. Later, in Washington, D.C., Joseph again inflamed diplomatic relations by trying to persuade President Franklin D. Roosevelt to sever all friendly ties between America and her future World War II allies, and to join forces with the Third Reich in an effort to make Nazi Germany the master of all Europe.'

'Well, well,' Clare said as Ryan paused, 'now we know for sure, don't we?'

Ryan nodded. 'It still doesn't prove there's any connection between Cassidy and Falcon, though. Just that his father was pro-Nazi.'

'True. But you've got to admit, Ryan, the boy certainly grew up in the right environment.'

'For what? To have spy connections . . . or to be a spy himself?'

'To have spy connections, of course. Nobody,' she added, 'not even his worst enemy, would be crazy enough to accuse James L. Cassidy of ever being a Nazi spy.'

But the seed, however tiny, had been planted. And as they read on, they looked for any remote social or political activity that might possibly encourage that seed to flourish. But other than a brief chapter concerning Joseph Cassidy's unpopularity with the press and his gradual demise on the political scene once the war ended, there was no further evidence to suggest that James L. or any of the other Cassidys were connected with spies or Nazi Germany in any way.

There was one short paragraph on James L. Cassidy that they found interesting, though. It followed an account of his brief and uneventful stint in the U.S. Coast Guard and, in essence, said that due to the many well-documented reports verifying his father's pro-German leanings, certain government officials and high-ranking Pentagon brass were against James's transfer into Naval Intelligence, where, they pointed out, he would have immediate access to highly classified material. Many others in the capital agreed with them, citing it as being an unnecessary risk. But others, in greater numbers, rallied around the Cassidys, claiming that young James's life and dedication to his country were above reproach; and in the end the legendary Cassidy influence prevailed and James entered Naval Intelligence and eventually became its youngest and most brilliant cryptanalyst.

'Well, we know one thing for sure,' Clare said as they closed the book on the Cassidy clan. 'James Cassidy was in the perfect position to pass secrets on to the enemy.'

'So were all the others working in ciphers,' Ryan reminded.

'Agreed. But I doubt if too many of them also grew up in Nazi Germany or had a father who was pro-Hitler.'

Ryan looked long and hard at her. 'Then . . . you *do* believe it's possible?'

'What?'

'That Cassidy an' Falcon might be connected?'

'No, of course not — ' She broke off, suddenly realizing that, in effect, that was what she'd just said. Then she said, in a hushed voice, 'Do you?'

'The thought has been chewing on me.'

'Since when?'

'Since our druggist friend across the street clammed up on us.'

Clare nodded. 'That bothered me, too. It's just that — well, you know, if we were talking about anyone else but Jim Cassidy . . . a United States senator . . . the man who may be our next president . . . '

'Yeah, I know,' Ryan said. Then: 'Don't worry. I find it just as hard to believe as you do.' He paused, thought a moment and then took her arm. 'C'mon . . . '

'Where're we going now?'

'Take another shot at Murchinson. See if somehow we can loosen up his tongue.' They hurried out of the library.

11

T. S. Murchinson at first refused to see
them. He was in his office and instructed
his assistant to tell Ryan and Clare that
he was too busy to talk.

'Fine. Then you tell him this,' Ryan
said grimly. 'Either he talks to us — now
— or Governor Fontaine will have him
subpoenaed an' then he'll have to talk to
a judge. An' a judge, remind him, might
not keep things quite as confidential as us.'

The bluff worked. Shortly, the assistant
pharmacist returned and said that Mr.
Murchinson would see them in his office.

'Thanks,' Ryan said. 'I had a feeling he
might.'

The small, windowless office was an
extension of T. S.'s personality: austere and
waspishly neat. 'I don't know what you
hope to gain by this,' T. S. said as Ryan
and Clare sat across the desk from him.
'I've already told you everything I know.'

'Not according to Wells Beaman,' Ryan

said. 'He told us you an' Mary Jo Buffram were real close.'

T. S. licked his thin white lips. 'We were good friends, if that's what you mean.'

'How good?'

'Were you engaged, for instance?' Clare put in.

'No.'

'You would you have liked to have been, though,' Ryan said, probing.

'What I would've liked or not liked,' T. S. snapped, 'is none of your business.'

'A judge might think it was — *if* he thought you killed her.'

'Killed — 'T. S. almost choked. 'That's absurd. Why would I want to kill Mary Jo?'

'Jealousy, maybe?'

'People *do* kill for jealousy, you know,' Clare said.

'An' she *did* love a good time,' Ryan added. 'Your father told that to the newspapers.'

T. S. licked his lips again, emotionally distraught. 'I . . . I loved Mary Jo,' he said brokenly, 'and . . . and I could never have done anything to hurt her. You've *got* to believe that.'

Ryan sensed the man was telling the truth. 'I believe it.'

'Me, too,' Clare said. 'Besides, you said you knew who the real killer was.'

'A famous politician,' reminded Ryan.

T. S. looked trapped. He avoided their gazes and nervously shuffled the invoices on his desk.

'Mr. Murchinson, let me ask you something,' Clare said. 'Why do you honestly think Senator Cassidy's man came to see you about Mary Jo and Falcon?'

'To find out how much I knew, of course. Why else would a senator be interested in a forty-year-old murder?'

'Wait a minute,' Ryan said. 'Did I miss a play there, or are you saying that Senator Cassidy is the 'famous politician' who murdered Mary Jo?'

'I'm not saying anything,' T. S. said. His thin lips went white. 'And I'll sue you if you say I did.'

There was a strained silence. T. S. kept his eyes sullenly lowered, and meticulously straightened everything on his desk. Clare, sensing they'd antagonized him, said gently, 'Don't worry, Mr. Murchinson. You have no fear of that. After all, we are all on the same side.'

If T. S. believed her, he showed no sign of it. He squared up the onyx pen holder. Lined up the digital clock. Began unhooking a chain of paper clips. Placed each one in a magnetized container.

'Let me put it this way,' Ryan said. 'Supposing Miss Winslow an' I suspected somethin' about Senator Cassidy that would prevent him from becoming president. An' supposing we needed your help to prove what we suspect?' He paused to let the words sink in. 'Would you be willing to talk about Mary Jo's murder then?'

T. S. studied them a moment and Frowned. Then, as if suddenly making a decision, he said bitterly, 'I'd do anything to ruin that man. Everybody thinks he's so pure and wonderful, but he isn't. He's evil. A modern-day Jekyll and Hyde.' His voice trembled with emotion. 'Mary Jo was the only girl I ever cared about . . . loved . . . and Cassidy destroyed her . . . murdered her. I *know* he did!'

'Can you prove it?' Ryan said.

'No. And even if I could, it wouldn't

matter. Nothing would change. Nobody'd listen. No one cares about the truth when it concerns a Cassidy. The family's too rich, too powerful to be affected by something as mundane as the truth.'

'Don't include Governor Fontaine when you say that,' Clare said. 'He's not afraid to challenge Cassidy — on any matter.'

T. S. said nothing. He licked his lips.

'Why don't you just tell us all you know?' Ryan urged. 'Let us decide how 'mundane' it is.'

'Very well. But, believe me, it's just a waste of time.' He paused, trying to collect all the pieces before starting, and then explained that Mary Jo first met Cassidy at the Wilmington USO canteen while he was an ensign in the Coast Guard. He was waiting to be transferred to Naval Intelligence, and he saw Mary Jo as often as he could leave the base. They were wild about each other. And after a few weeks they decided to get married. But his family wouldn't hear of it, and made such a fuss that Cassidy stopped seeing Mary Jo. She was crushed. She wrote to him, tried to see him at the base — even called his family and begged them not to interfere. But it was hopeless. Cassidy refused to have anything to do with her, and pretty soon his father sent a lawyer to buy Mary Jo off. But she was too nice a girl to be bribed. Instead, she kicked him out and moved away — to Swansboro.

'That was when I met her,' T. S. said sadly. 'She came into the drugstore one day looking for work, and my daddy hired her to help me at the fountain.' He smiled, remembering. 'She was so pretty. So warm and nice. We became friends right away. Close friends. And from then on she told me everything. You know, about herself . . . how her parents had died when she was young and she'd grown up in foster homes. Then she met Jimbo — that's what she called Cassidy, even after they split up — and when she was with him, she felt like a real woman for the first time . . . '

'Did she ever say why his parents didn't want him to marry her?' Clare asked.

'They thought she was after his money.'

T. S. made an angry face. 'That wasn't true, of course. Mary Jo didn't care about money. She didn't care about anything — except Cassidy. All she wanted was to be with him, to love him, and to have him love her.'

'Too bad Cassidy didn't have more guts,' Ryan said. 'Maybe if he had, he would've told his parents to shove it and married Mary Jo anyway.'

T. S. nodded his narrow, balding head. 'That's what hurt Mary Jo most of all. The fact that Cassidy didn't love her enough to stand up to his family. Of course, it didn't surprise me. I never thought that jerk loved her from the start.'

'Mean, he was just stringing her along, you think?'

'Exactly. I even told her that once.'

'What'd she say?'

'Just laughed. Said I was only saying that because I was jealous, and wanted her for myself. Which was true, I guess . . . except . . . ' T. S. sighed, then continued: ' . . . except that — well, what she didn't understand was, I loved her so much, it didn't matter that I couldn't have her. I just wanted her to be happy. With someone.'

He sounded so sincere, so miserable, Ryan felt a beat of sympathy for the aging druggist.

Clare, meanwhile, said, 'How'd she get involved with Alvin Buffram?'

'She met him at a dance over to Jacksonville. He was stationed right there at Camp Lejeune. They both loved to dance, and, well, she being so lonely after losing Cassidy, it wasn't long before they got real intimate and Alvin asked her to marry him.' T. S. sighed again, anguished. 'I tried to tell her that she was rushing things, but she wouldn't listen. She knew I loved her, and kept thinking I was just trying to keep her for myself.'

'But if she was married,' Ryan said as it hit him, 'and Cassidy wasn't around, what makes you think the senator killed her?'

'Because she started seeing him again.'

'When?'

'About a month before she was murdered. She wouldn't admit it was him, of course, but I knew. Knew it just as surely as if I'd seen them together myself.'

'Why?' Clare asked.

'Because of the way she acted. She started arguing with her husband, telling him that he had no right to expect her to stay home nights while he was on the base, and . . . and then, when I asked her if she was seeing another man, she got terribly angry and said she'd never speak to me again if I ever mentioned anything like that again.'

'Do you think she really was seeing another man?' Clare asked.

'Of course. I just told you — Cassidy.'

'But if you never saw them together,' began Ryan, 'how — '

'For two reasons,' T. S. said. 'First, Mary Jo wasn't the cheating kind. Other than Cassidy, who had some strange hold over her, she wouldn't even look at another man. Not while she was married. On that, I'd stake my life.'

'What's the other reason?'

'This . . . ' T. S. took a gilt-framed photograph from the desk drawer and handed it to Ryan.

Ryan looked at the five-by-eight head shot of James L. Cassidy and felt his heart skip. Except that it was larger, it was identical to the picture of Falcon that they'd found aboard the U-boat. Scribbled in the lower right-hand corner was: 'To Mary Jo. All my love, Jimbo.'

Ryan handed the picture to Clare and kept his voice casual as he said, 'Interesting photo, huh?'

Clare managed to conceal her surprise. 'Y-yes,' she said quietly. 'Very.' She returned the picture to T. S. 'May I ask where you got this from?'

'The old soda fountain out there.' T. S. indicated beyond the door. 'Mary Jo kept it on the shelf behind the milkshake blender. Afterward, when she — she was dead, I kept it for myself. Don't know why, exactly. Probably just to remind myself of what a lousy swine Cassidy was . . . and how much I hated him.'

After a pause Ryan asked: 'Any idea where the picture was taken?'

'In Berlin, Mary Jo said. Just before we declared war on Germany. Joseph Cassidy was pro-Nazi, you know, and had his son in some kind of special training school there.'

'Could there've been more than one picture like this?'

'Yes. How did you know?'

'I didn't,' Ryan said. 'Just guessing.'

T. S. studied the picture a moment before saying: 'Mary Jo liked it so much, she begged Cassidy to get her another — a smaller one for her wallet. He did. And she carried it everywhere with her — even after she was married. That's the other reason why I know Cassidy killed her,' T. S. added bitterly.

'How do you mean?'

'Well, Cassidy's lawyer tried to buy both those pictures back from Mary Jo. But she refused. Said they were all she had left as a memory.'

'Go on,' Ryan said.

'The small picture wasn't in her wallet when the police found her body!'

After they left the drugstore, Ryan and Clare walked around town to think things over. Neither said much. Each was too deep in thought. But as they slowly retraced their steps and found themselves approaching the sleek white Porsche, Clare finally said, 'Well? What do you think of Shining Jim now?'

Ryan shrugged. 'I guess he's been in smoother waters.'

'That may be the understatement of the year. The decade, even.' She took the picture of Falcon from her purse, looked at it, and Said, more for herself than Ryan: 'You know what I've got to do next, don't you? I have to tell Karl.'

'Everything?'

'Everything.'

'Should be some conversation.'

'Yeah, really.' Clare frowned, her eyes green as the sea. 'I know exactly what he's going to say, too.'

'Before or after he calls for the guys in white coats?'

'Hopefully, before . . . ' She sighed. Shook her long yellow hair back from her face. 'I can't say that I'd blame him, either. Despite everything we've read and heard, I still don't actually believe it myself. Senator James L. Cassidy, America's Sir Galahad in shining armor, a former Nazi spy? I mean, good God, there just *has* to be another explanation!'

12

It was after six when they got back to Atlantic Salvage. Mitch had already left for the day, and his note pinned on the office door told Ryan that there'd been no calls. Clare used her credit-card number and called Governor Fontaine's campaign headquarters in Washington, D.C. The switchboard operator said that Mr. Slater was in Atlanta with the governor at a political fund-raising dinner. She gave Clare the name of the hotel and Slater's suite number. Clare called the Atlanta Hilton, asked for Mr. Slater, and was told that he had not yet returned from a meeting.

'I'll call him after we've had dinner,' Clare told Ryan. 'That'll give me plenty of time to figure out exactly how I'm going to explain everything.' She started out of the shop, calling, 'Pick you up around seven. Bye!' And a few moments later Ryan heard her drive off.

Alone, he drank a cold beer and locked up, then Started working on a crossword puzzle. He couldn't concentrate, and ended up taking a shower. He stood under the steaming water for a long time, his mind churning. What the hell was he doing getting involved in something as explosive as suggesting that Senator Cassidy was once a Nazi spy? Jesus, never mind the fact that it was a totally insane notion to start with — that was bad enough. But actually to think that he could make that kind of incriminating accusation, and still hope to maintain a low profile — keep his real identity a secret and stay out of prison — well, that was nothing short of sheer, fucking lunacy! Hell, within minutes of Cassidy's first phone call to the FBI, Ryan knew he'd have every goddamn agent available on the case.

Then, where did he hide?

Yet, on the other hand, Ryan thought, intrigued, what if Cassidy really was Falcon? He *couldn't* be. That kind of CIA oversight concerning a prominent politician in Cassidy's exalted position was impossible.

Wasn't it?

It *had* to be. But what if, by some freaky, colossal CIA fuck-up, it wasn't impossible and Shining Jim really and truly was Falcon? *I mean, what then, Kyle Lane? Do you sit back and ignore the fact that the next president of the United States was once a Nazi spy? Or do you go out and put your stupid ass in the proverbial sling and try to expose him?*

I don't know, Ryan thought as he felt the water scalding over him. *Sonofabitch, I honestly don't know.*

But, deep down, he did.

Knew it as well as he knew the feel of his own flesh.

And the knowledge of what he'd do, despite what would happen to himself, suddenly sent a chill through him.

That evening Ryan and Clare drove to Salter Path and ate dinner at Squatters Seafood Restaurant, an old, rustic, ocean-front shack built out over the water. They sat at a window table overlooking the boats tied up outside. They dined on oysters and red snapper, and drank a friendly dry white wine that was so chilled, it made the back of their throats ache.

The moon came up while they were eating. Afterward, they took off their shoes and walked along the water's edge. The surf ran cool about their bare feet. Presently, they sat on a piece of driftwood and watched the moon-whitened waves breaking on the beach.

'There's something I been meaning to ask you,' Ryan said.

'What's that?'

'The U-boat — how'd your boss know where it was sunk?'

'An officer friend of his told him. He works at the Navy Yards in D.C. Apparently he discovered some old records that told where the sub went down. Karl talked the war memorial idea over with the governor and then told me to come down here and hire a diver to find the U-boat. The rest, as they say at GIGO headquarters, is history.'

'GIGO?'

'Meaningless political statistics. 'Garbage in, garbage out.' GIGO.'

'Jesus,' Ryan said. 'Sounds like the story of my life.'

Clare laughed, a sound not unlike the

sea. 'C'mon,' she said, rising. 'If I'm going to call Karl, we'd better get going.' Shoes in hand, they walked back to the car.

Neither of them realized they'd been sitting less than ten feet from the spot where, forty years ago, Falcon had murdered Mary Jo Buffram.

Later, back in her room at the Atlantis Lodge, Clare called Karl Slater at the Atlanta Hilton.

'Before I tell you anything,' she said cautiously, 'I want you to understand something: I'm well aware of how incredibly crazy it sounds, and I won't blame you one bit if you don't believe a single word of it. Okay?'

'Very well,' Slater said. He already sounded dubious. 'Go ahead.'

As briefly as she could, Clare explained all the similarities that she and Ryan had discovered between Senator Cassidy and Falcon. It took a while. When she was finished, Slater remained silent so long, she asked, 'Karl? Karl, you still there?'

More silence. Then, 'You're right,' Slater said. 'It is crazy and I don't believe one word of it. Not only that,' he continued, 'but you've got far better things to do — such as finding more souvenirs, working out how to get the U-boat raised and — '

'I know, I know,' Clare said. 'But, Karl, you should see those photos. Cassidy looks identical to — '

'Please, Clare, I've got a million things to do.' Slater sounded impatient and irritated. 'So, unless you have something constructive to tell me . . . '

'No, Karl. I haven't right now.'

'Fine. Good night, then. Oh, and Clare — '

'Yes, Karl?'

'If you want to remain in the running for press secretary, do yourself a favor and don't mention any of this to the governor. He just might not understand your misdirected enthusiasm.' He hung up.

Glumly, Clare did the same. Ryan read her expression.

'Didn't go for it, huh?'

'Not one word.'

'Yeah, well, what'd you expect?'

'This kind of reaction, I guess.' She sighed, depressed. 'How can I blame him, when I don't really believe it myself?'

'Then . . . it's back to diving?'

'I guess. For now, anyway.'

But at three thirty-one in the morning she felt differently. Turning on the bedside light, she called Ryan and told him that she'd changed her mind.

' 'bout what?' he asked sleepily.

'The U-boat.'

'What about it?'

'We're not going to dive on it. 'Least, not right now. We're going to keep on digging. Find out if Cassidy's really Falcon or not.'

Despite his sleepiness, Ryan felt pleased. 'What about Slater?'

'I'm not going to tell him. I know I'm taking a risk that could blow my career clear over Capitol Hill, but I've been lying here all night, thinking, and I just can't convince myself that everything we've come across is nothing more than coincidence.'

'I hate to say it,' he said, 'but neither can I. So, what's our next move?'

'I was hoping you'd tell me.'

'Well,' he said, 'a man I once knew

always used to say: 'If you want to know the bear, embrace him in his cave.''

'Meaning?'

'We confront Cassidy with the facts — see how he reacts.'

'You really think that'll work?' She sounded dubious.

'It has on other occasions.'

'All right. We'll try it. Now all we've got to do is find a way to reach Cassidy.'

'Shouldn't be too hard. On the late news it said he's campaigning throughout the South right now, and is due to speak sometime this week down in Wilmington.'

'Terrific. That solves *where* the 'bear' is — now all we need is a way to get into his 'cave.' Avery!' she suddenly exclaimed. 'Of course!'

'Of course, what?'

'It just hit me. There's this senator — Avery Brickland — who's made it known through the Washington grapevine that he's interested in getting to know me better. He's as close to Cassidy as anyone on The Hill. And a phone call in the morning — two phone calls, to be exact: one from me to Avery, the other from him to Cassidy — will hopefully get us what we need.'

'Great. Do it,' Ryan said. 'Anything else?'

'Uh-uh.'

'Then I'll go back to sleep.'

'Yes, I'd better do the same.' She yawned. 'I've a feeling tomorrow's going to be a full day.'

'Today,' he corrected, noticing the time.

'What?'

'Nothing,' he said, chuckling. 'Just go to sleep.'

13

In the morning, after an early breakfast, Clare called Avery Brickland at his Senate office in Washington. The secretary recognized Clare's name. She was pleasant enough, but there was a touch of curiosity in her voice, as she obviously wondered what the 'enemy' wanted with Senator Brickland.

When Avery came on the line, he sounded warm and charming but equally curious. 'Well, well, Ms. Winslow, this is a pleasant surprise.'

'Hello, Senator.'

'And what can I do for the opposition this morning?'

Clare came right to the point. 'I need a favor, Senator.'

'You personally, or your party?'

'Me.'

'I see.' Avery frowned, intrigued but cautious. A small, slender blond man in his mid-thirties, he'd wanted to get close to Clare for several months now but whenever they'd met at various parties she had always brushed him off. As Senator Cassidy's fair-haired boy it was something he wasn't used to, and it made him all the more interested in her. Now, out of the blue, she wanted a favor from him. Wondering what it was, he decided to use it as a chance to get close to her. 'Well, perhaps we could discuss that favor over lunch today?'

'I'd like that, Senator — but I'm afraid I'm in North Carolina and won't be back in the capital until next week.'

'Oh,' Avery said, disappointed. 'Then we'll have to wait until next week, Ms. Winslow, won't we?'

'Clare.'

'Clare.'

'Next week will be too late, Senator.'

'For lunch or the favor?'

Clare smiled to herself. Avery was shrewder than he seemed, she realized. She'd have to be careful when they met; make sure that she didn't get herself boxed in. 'The favor, Senator.'

'Please, call me Avery.'

'Thank you.'

'And just what is that favor, Clare?'

Briefly, Clare explained that a freelance writer friend — Mr. Ryan — wanted to do an in-depth profile on Senator Cassidy. He knew the senator would be in Wilmington this week and had tried to set up an interview date. But because of the presidential candidate's hectic campaign schedule, he couldn't get to see him.

'And you thought a phone call from me might help, correct?'

'Well, you are a close friend of the senator's.'

'That I am. And you, Clare, are not telling me the whole truth.'

'What do you mean?'

'Please, let's not play games. What do you gain out of this meeting?'

'An equally favorable profile on Governor Fontaine. That's assuming, of course, I can first produce the interview with Senator Cassidy.'

'Sounds fair,' Avery said. He enjoyed any kind of political intrigue. 'Now, if I only knew what *my* gain for getting you that interview is . . . '

'I was hoping we could discuss that, Avery, when we had lunch.'

'Why not?' he said charmingly. 'Far less important decisions have been settled over a chilled bottle of champagne.' He then promised to contact Senator Cassidy that day and to call Clare back the moment he had an answer. She thanked him, said she was looking forward to lunch next week, and hung up.

As she did, she found herself surprised by her ability to lie so glibly. Momentarily, she wondered if she was becoming the same kind of political animal that Washington was full of and that she so despised. She hoped not. Then, deciding that the bottom line — Cassidy's guilt or innocence — overshadowed all else, she quieted her conscience by promising to feel guilty later. She left the motel and drove over to Atlantic Salvage.

Ryan had been working out at the local karate dojo, and pulled his pickup right in behind the Porsche just as Clare parked outside the shop. 'Everything's all set,' she told him as they walked inside. 'Avery's going to call me back as soon as he's talked to Cassidy.'

'Fine,' said Ryan. 'Then all we got to do is drive down to Wilmington and find out how right or wrong we are.'

Clare laughed, more from nerves than amusement. 'Let's hope it's just that easy — ' She broke off as Mitch joined them by the office. He'd been repairing a customer's outboard motor and was covered with oil and grease.

'You got a phone call,' he told Ryan. 'Some guy. Wouldn't talk to me, though. Said he'd call back later — when you 'n Clare was both here.'

'Must've been Karl,' Clare said. 'He's the only person I know who has this number.'

'Maybe he's had a change of heart?' Ryan said. 'Decided that, true or not, a little bad publicity about Cassidy might help boost the Fontaine image.'

'With anyone but Karl, I'd have to agree with you. But he's different. Karl might look you in the eye and shoot you, but mess around with smear tactics — that's not his style.'

The office telephone rang. Ryan entered

to answer it and listened briefly, then said harshly, 'Who is this?'

'That doesn't matter,' a cultured man's voice said. 'All you and Ms. Winslow have to concern yourselves with, is . . . losing interest in a certain senator's past.'

'An' if we don't?'

'Then you're placing yourselves in a highly dangerous position. One, I might add, that can only result in a most unhappy conclusion.'

'Listen, you — ' began Ryan. The line went dead. He left the office and rejoined Clare and Mitch.

'Who was that?' Clare asked, reading the anger on his face.

'Some jerk warning us not to poke around in Cassidy's past.'

'Are you serious?'

Ryan nodded. 'So was he.' Then, to Mitch: 'That guy who called earlier — what'd he sound like?'

'A big-city Yankee.'

'How old?'

'Forty, easy. An' real polite. You know, like a waiter in a fancy restaurant.'

'Same guy,' Ryan said. He thought a

moment. Still angry, but calmer. 'What exactly did you tell Senator Brickland?' he asked Clare.

Briefly, she explained. As Ryan listened, he thought of all the people they'd spoken to in the last few days and tried to decide which if any of them could've made the threatening call. He hadn't recognized the man's voice, so obviously he was working for whoever was behind the call. But who'd hired him? Ryan listed the names in his head and realized that only four people even knew that he and Clare were digging into Cassidy's past: Fontaine, Slater, Wells Beaman, and T. S. Murchinson. And since Fontaine and Slater would profit by winning the election and Murchinson genuinely seemed to hate the senator, that left Beaman as the only possible suspect.

But how could the editor of a tiny local newspaper be connected to a senator of Cassidy's magnitude? And, more importantly, why would he warn Cassidy just because two strangers asked him a few questions about an unknown spy and a girl murdered forty years ago? Unless — unless Cassidy really was Falcon and

Beaman somehow knew that?

No way, Ryan thought emphatically. A man as powerful as Cassidy, and with as much to lose, would never risk leaving a loose end like Beaman alive to ruin him. He'd kill him. Or have him killed. Therefore, the very fact that Beaman was still alive proved that he knew nothing that could endanger Cassidy. But if that was true, thought Ryan, then why did Beaman call the senator? And if he didn't, who did? Someone must have. Otherwise, Cassidy wouldn't have known anyone was prying into his past. And he had to know that or he wouldn't have hired someone to make the threatening call.

It was all very confusing. And frustrating. Because other than Cassidy himself, who else would know enough or care enough about the senator, or his incriminating past, to make that kind of call on their own initiative?

Then it hit him. 'Sweet Jesus!' he said suddenly. 'It's Senator Avery!'

'Avery?' Clare said, confused.

'Of course. It has to be. Don't you see?' Ryan added. 'He's the only one who cares.'

'Cares? Cares about what?' Clare looked even more confused. 'Ryan, I don't know what you're talking about. You asked me to repeat what I told Avery, and — '

'No,' Ryan said. 'I don't mean about that. I mean, Senator Avery's the guy behind the threatening call. He *has* to be.'

'Why? I mean, that's impossible. Avery doesn't even know what we're doing down here. I was very careful not to say anything that would give him even the slightest hint.'

'You didn't have to,' Ryan said. 'He already knew.'

'How?'

'Wells Beaman.'

'But — why would the editor of a little local newspaper call Senator Brickland just because we asked a few questions about Falcon and Mary Jo? I mean, what's the connection?'

'I asked myself almost the same question,' Ryan said. He smiled, wolfishly. 'How about a gray-haired man who limps?'

'Good grief, that's right. Beaman did say — ' She broke off, frowning. Then:

'Hey, no, that doesn't work. Beaman said Gray Hair worked for Cassidy, not Avery.'

'I know he did.'

'Then . . . ?'

'Who's Cassidy's pet clone? Avery, right?'

'Yes.'

'Okay, then. Don't pet clones always try to serve their masters as well as they can — especially when it serves their own best interests as well? Which, in this case, means scaring off anyone trying to stop your buddy from becoming head honcho at the White House.' He paused, waiting for her to agree. When she didn't, he said: 'Well? Makes sense, doesn't it?'

'I guess.' Clare sounded doubtful. 'I don't know. I don't particularly like Avery, but whether he's capable of knowingly letting an ex-Nazi spy become president just to further his own political ambitions — well, like I say, I don't know.'

'What if he *doesn't* know — that Cassidy's a spy, I mean? Just thinks he's helping him cover up an old love affair that ended tragically?'

164

'Mary Jo, you mean?'

'The same. Just a patriotic young girl he met at the USO, right? A pretty thing whose murderer was never found? No big deal, you say? Well, maybe not for the average guy. But for a Cassidy — a senator about to become president — well, that kind of story in the wrong hands could heat up the front pages of every newspaper in the country, an' maybe tarnish even Sir Galahad's shiny white image.'

'I see what you mean . . .' Clare thought a moment before adding: 'It certainly is possible, all right. Very possible.'

'In an election year,' Ryan said, 'even probable.'

'You guys ain't gonna quit, though, are you?' said Mitch. He'd gone off to wash up while they'd been talking and now stood nearby, drying his clean hands on a grimy towel. 'Just 'cause this dumb jerkwater threatened you, I mean?'

'That's not up to me,' Ryan said. He looked at Clare. 'That's strictly a management decision.'

'No, of course we're not going to quit,'

she said firmly. 'All that threat proves is, we must be closer to the truth than we realize.'

'Truth, or trouble,' Ryan said, admiring her guts.

14

After lunch Ryan and Clare made a list of all the evidence they'd gathered that indicated Cassidy and Falcon were one and the same person. Then they took the list and all the written material — including Falcon's photograph — from the U-boat to the local printers and had Xerox copies made of everything. They made two copies and kept one set each. Then they drove back to Atlantic Salvage and locked the originals in Ryan's floor safe. It was now late afternoon. Clare called her motel. But there were no messages. Not wanting to miss Avery's call concerning their meeting with Senator Cassidy, Clare suggested they both wait at her motel. 'While we're waiting,' she added, 'we can go over all the facts and everything a final time — make sure we haven't overlooked anything.'

Clare's motel room had a small patio overlooking the ocean. She and Ryan sat outside in the fading sun, and drank tall icy wine-coolers as they pored over all the facts, documents, and assumptions they had compiled about Cassidy and Falcon.

It was early evening before they realized it. Clare turned the news on. The television showed news clips of both presidential nominees addressing voters throughout the South. The basic dialogue was the same, but delivered from different viewpoints. Cassidy was eloquent, charming, charismatic. Fontaine brilliant but hesitant. Tense but sincere.

'It's a tribute to his political savvy,' Ryan said as they watched Fontaine presenting his agricultural issues to a bunch of semi-literate 'good ol' boys,' 'that he's even in this race at all.'

Clare agreed. 'It's too bad, too. Because all of Cassidy's charm and charisma won't turn the economy around or blunt the Soviet edge. Only Fontaine's political genius can do that.' She paused as the telephone rang.

It was Avery. He'd had a few drinks, and explained that he'd broken away from a fund-raising dinner to call and tell her that Senator Cassidy would talk to her Mr. Ryan after his campaign speech in Wilmington. Clare asked him when the senator would be in Wilmington. Day after tomorrow — if all went according to schedule.

'Wonderful,' Clare said. 'You've been a great help.'

Avery laughed and said 'I hope you remember how wonderful I've been when we have lunch next week.'

'I'll certainly try,' she said. 'Good-bye, Senator.'

She hung up before he could protest. Then she looked at Ryan, whose yellow-gray hunter's eyes were staring out to sea.

'It's all set,' she told him. 'We meet with Senator Cassidy sometime on Thursday.'

'Good. Did he say anything that might possibly connect him to the guy on the phone?'

'Uh-uh.'

'You sure?'

'Positive. As a matter of fact,' she said, 'from the way he's acted — helping us and everything — I find it hard to believe that he's involved at all.'

'He may not be. But if he isn't, that makes Beaman our only suspect. And somehow, he doesn't seem the type to hire guys to make threatening phone calls.'

'I agree. Well' — she shrugged — 'it was just a thought.'

'Here's another. All this brain work's made me hungry. How about we go eat something?'

'I never thought you'd ask,' she said, laughing. 'My stomach thinks my throat's been cut.'

Outside, they got into the Porsche, buckled up and Clare fired the engine. She started to back up — then suddenly braked as something crunched under a rear tire.

'What the hell was that?' she exclaimed.

They got out to take a look. Broken pieces of black plastic lay under the left rear tire. Among the jagged fragments was a note. The words were made up of letters cut out of magazines. Ryan read aloud: 'Next time a bomb. Think. Is it worth it?'

'Oh, my God,' Clare said, shaken.

'Take it easy, now.'

'Take it easy yourself.' She looked at her hand. 'Christ, I'm shaking like a leaf.'

'Don't feel alone,' he said gently. 'I'm shaking some bolts loose myself.'

'I'm not usually this big of a baby ... but ... well, nobody's ever threatened to kill me before, and — and it's really scary.'

Ryan angrily kicked the broken bits of plastic away from behind the tire. 'Crazy bastard ... I'd better check out the rest of the car to make sure he hasn't played any more games.'

When he was satisfied the car was safe, they drove to a restaurant overlooking the Atlantic Beach marina. Neither said much. The meal was excellent, but Clare barely ate. Instead she sat, absently toying with the ice cubes in her glass, and stared thoughtfully out the window at the boats in their slips and the dark empty ocean.

Across the table Ryan watched her. He sensed she was still scared. That was good. It was smart to be scared. He was a little scared himself. He knew the kind of people they were up against, how much power and influence they wielded, and

171

wondered if he deliberately pulled out now whether she'd also quit. He doubted it. Scared as she was, the fighter in her wouldn't let her back off. He admired her for that. He didn't understand all her moods yet, especially her unpredictability. But that was part of her appeal. Just as appealing was her ability to appear both capable and vulnerable at the same time. It made Ryan want to reach out and touch her. Kiss her. Make love to her. But he'd controlled his emotions so thoroughly and for so long now, any display of affection made him feel awkward and uncomfortable.

He wondered if Cassidy or Avery were really behind the threats. And how, if they weren't bluffing, he could protect Clare from an unknown, invisible enemy. It was a sort of 'hair-trigger existence,' and as Ryan studied the silent, tight-lipped, sea-eyed girl before him, he realized that if they were going to continue prying into Cassidy's past, he would have to be on guard at all times.

First, though, he had to be sure that Clare still wanted to keep digging. And later, when they'd left the restaurant and were standing at the railing overlooking the marina, he reminded her that it wasn't too late to back off from Cassidy. 'After all,' he said, 'we don't have any real concrete proof that the senator is Falcon. What's more, if the threats aren't a bluff, we could be dead before we find any.'

'True,' she said. 'And if I tell Karl about the threats, he'll probably fire me for not continuing with the dive, as ordered.'

'Well, there you are then. Makes sense that we forget about Cassidy and go back to diving. Right?'

'I guess.' She looked hard at him. 'Is that how you'd handle it?'

'You bet,' he lied. 'No sense in beating your head against a stone wall. It doesn't make much sense.'

'No,' she said. 'You're quite right. It doesn't. No sense at all.' She asked him to take her home then. He did. He was pleased with himself. At least now she'd be safe.

But outside the motel, as he was about to walk to his pickup, she stopped him and said: 'Thanks for trying to protect me back there, Ryan. It was sweet of you. And I really appreciate it.'

He didn't know quite what to say.

Clare smiled and reached up on her tiptoes and kissed him lightly. 'Goodnight,' she said. 'See you in the morning — as usual.' She hurried inside.

He knew then what he'd known all along: that she'd never had any intentions of quitting . . . and he loved her for it.

15

Thursday morning Ryan left Mitch in charge at Atlantic Salvage and drove Clare the seventy-five miles to Wilmington.

It was a pleasant, sunny drive through wooded areas and along the coast, past quiet little hamlets with rural names like Hubert, Piney Green, Verona, and Holly Ridge, and Ryan and Clare felt more relaxed when they arrived at the old Confederate town.

Ryan had kept his eye on the rear-view mirror throughout the trip. But no one followed them. Relieved, he hoped that the threats had been a bluff.

Senator Cassidy's PR workers had done a thorough job in Wilmington. The quiet, tree-lined streets and historical buildings were draped with red, white, and blue signs and banners proclaiming the presidential nominee's arrival and speech date.

'I'm surprised they don't call it the 'second coming,'' Ryan grumbled.

'Be patient.' Clare laughed. 'That comes *after* the election.'

Markers pointed the way to the place where Senator Cassidy would deliver his speech at noon. Ryan and Clare followed them along Market Street Road to Chandler's Wharf, turned left on Waterfront, crossed the big iron bridge, and drove alongside the Cape Fear River to the Battleship Memorial Ground.

'This'd be a great place to install the U-boat.' Clare pointed. 'That way, people could see both memorials at once.'

They joined the heavy traffic that moved slowly toward the parking area. It was only eleven thirty but already a large, excited crowd had gathered in front of the restored World War II battleship, USS *North Carolina*. They were nearly all fervent Cassidy supporters. Most wore either 'Vote for Shining Jim' campaign buttons or waved tiny American flags that volunteer workers handed out in the parking area. A makeshift podium festooned with patriotic streamers, Cassidy banners, and American and Confederate flags had been erected by the ramp

176

leading up to the massive battleship. As Ryan and Clare squeezed through the crowd to the podium, they noticed several Cassidy 'mob-quieters' persuading a group of Young American Nazis not to wave their signs during the senator's speech. Ryan and Clare exchanged ironic looks.

Exactly at noon James L. Cassidy strode down the ramp from the battleship with the same smiling, waving determination of MacArthur 'returning' to the Philippines. He was accompanied by his youthful staff and several Secret Service agents, and he mounted the podium to a genuine, ear-shattering cheer.

'Ladies and gentlemen,' he said when the applause had finally quieted. 'Friends, and above all, fellow Americans. The fact that you've greeted me in this tremendously gratifying manner only reinforces my opinion that there are no prejudices here (more applause) . . . no subtle hatreds that my opponent has so often pointed out exist between Southerners and Yankees like myself (loud laughter) . . . only Americans, who desire, as all true Americans do, a country that is strong, prosperous, independent, and . . . economically sound . . . '

There was instant applause. It lasted so long that the tall, tanned, handsome senator grew tired of motioning for silence and continued speaking as the crowd gradually quieted.

The speech was relatively short. Cassidy dealt with inflation, rising crime, ecological dangers, the nation's increasing dependency on foreign oil, the God-given constitutional right of every American to be free and to be able to speak freely, and the fact that it was time America stopped playing weak sister to the Communists and terrorist-type governments scattered throughout the world!

During the speech there were occasional bursts of cheering. And when Cassidy finally stopped talking, the huge crowd erupted in applause.

'Dynamite speech,' Clare said grudgingly.

'Yeah,' said Ryan. ''specially for a Nazi spy.'

That said it all for both of them. And as they left with the departing crowd, neither was anxious to go to the Wilmington Hilton Inn and accuse Senator Cassidy of being a traitor.

As they drove back across the river toward the hotel, the enormity of what they were about to do became increasingly oppressive. Reading Clare's tense, tight-lipped expression, Ryan said gently, 'It's not too late to change your mind, you know.'

'I know,' she said. 'What would you do?'

'Me?' He shrugged, tried to make what he was about to say sound unrehearsed and casual. 'I'd hedge my bet.'

'Meaning?'

'I'd talk to Cassidy alone.'

'What? No way! I — '

'Hold on,' he said. 'Let me finish.'

'Don't bother. I already know the end of that tune. Listen,' she continued angrily, 'I'm not stupid, Ryan. Don't you think I've already realized that if Cassidy is Falcon and we confront him with it, we've set ourselves up targets?'

'Okay, then, since you've realized it, don't you also realize that it doesn't make sense to give the man *two* targets? Or at least, not both at the same time.'

'I'll buy that,' she said. 'And since I'm running this show, *I'll* be the one to confront Cassidy, while you stay outside and protect my rear.'

'No way,' Ryan said.

'All right,' Clare said. 'Then we face him together, like we originally planned.'

They had reached the hotel. It was old, elegant, and sat squarely on the water-front across the river from the battleship. Avery had told Clare that Cassidy would be returning there after his speech, and she and Ryan sat in the lobby along with the mob of reporters, photographers, and local TV newsmen.

They made Clare nervous. She was afraid someone might recognize her in the 'enemy camp,' and suggested to Ryan that they hide in the coffee shop until Cassidy was in his suite. Ryan agreed. Unnoticed by members of the media, who were watching the hotel entrance, they entered a restaurant off the lobby and sat at a window table so they could see when Cassidy arrived.

It was lunchtime and most of the tables were occupied. Waitresses and busboys rushed to do their jobs. Ryan and Clare kept their faces turned to each other, neither noticing the man reading a newspaper in the corner. He was a short but powerfully built man in his early forties. He had thick, wavy gray hair, a blunt-featured, obstinate face and pale blue eyes rimmed with pink. As he pretended to read his paper, he watched Ryan and Clare with the same cold, detached interest as a shark eyeing its next meal.

Shortly, Cassidy and his exhilarated young staff swept into the hotel. They paused in the lobby long enough for the senator to work his magic with the press, then headed up to their suite.

'Time to go,' Clare told Ryan.

He nodded, but didn't move.

'What's wrong?'

'Maybe nothing. Don't,' he said as she started to look around. Then, as she faced him he whispered: 'There's a man sitting in the corner over your left shoulder. A gray-haired man with a face that says nothing.'

'Gray-haired?'

'Right. What's more, I think he's got a sour leg.'

'How do you know? He's sitting down, I mean.'

''cause every time he shifts around, he only uses his left leg to take the weight.'

'Very observant.'

'It pays to be.' He got up, adding: 'C'mon. We got a senator to talk to.'

They paid the check and returned to the lobby, the told the desk clerk to notify Senator Cassidy that a Mr. Ryan and a Miss Winslow were here for their scheduled interview. The clerk called the senator's suite and passed the information along. He told Ryan and Clare to go on up to suite 311 and they headed for the elevator. The lobby was empty now, save for a few elderly guests. As Ryan waited with Clare for the elevator, they glanced into the restaurant and saw the gray-haired man limp to the register and pay the cashier for his check.

'You were right,' Clare said. 'Think it's the same man who talked to Beaman and Murchinson?'

Ryan shrugged. 'Cassidy's upstairs, he's down here. I'd say it's a pretty safe assumption.'

They got off the elevator on the third floor and walked along the plum-colored hall to the two large, solemn-faced Secret Service agents guarding the senator's suite.

'Winslow and Ryan,' Clare said. 'Senator Cassidy's expecting us.'

'May I see your ID?' the older agent said.

They showed him. He scrutinized their driver's licenses carefully. Satisfied, he handed them back and told the younger agent to open the door.

If it was disciplined and quiet in the hall, it was chaos in the suite. Cassidy's staff looked as if they'd been thrown about the room. Some stood. Some sat. Others lay sprawled about on whatever furniture happened to be nearest. And all talked at once. Loudly.

A bright young woman with huge owlish glasses emerged from the pile of bodies. She smiled at them. 'Hi, I'm Maggie. This way, please,' and led them through the human obstacle course to the closed bedroom door. ''fraid it'll have to be talk and run,' she said cheerfully. 'The senator's behind schedule now, and, quite frankly, he's sacrificing five minutes of valuable shut-eye to squeeze you in.'

She'd been staring at Clare as she spoke to both of them. She now added: 'Don't I know you from somewhere, Ms. Winslow?'

'I don't think so,' Clare lied.

Maggie shrugged, dismissing it. 'So many faces.' She knocked on the door.

'Come in.'

Maggie led them into the bedroom. Senator Cassidy was reading a speech on the bed. Maggie introduced Ryan and Clare to him and hurried out.

'I'm sorry if I have to rush through this,' Cassidy said when they were seated. 'But as Maggie probably told you, I'm going full speed now and still falling behind.'

'We understand,' Clare said. Giving herself no time to be scared, she handed the photograph of Falcon to Cassidy, adding: 'First, Senator — is this you?'

Cassidy looked shocked as he recognized the picture. 'Y-Yes, of course. But — where the hell did you get this?'

Clare explained, without mentioning Falcon or whom she worked for. When she was finished, Cassidy's handsome, tanned face was a mixture of shock and bewilderment.

'U-boat?' he said, finally finding his voice. 'A Nazi *U-boat!* Good God, you can't be serious?'

'Assuming we are,' Ryan put in, 'have you got any idea how the photo got there?'

'Not the vaguest. As a youngster I spent considerable time in Germany, but I never once boarded a U-boat or — or came in contact with anyone who — and anyway,' he said, interrupting himself, 'that photo was taken only a day or so before my father and I returned to the States. So there's no way it could've found its way onto a U-boat.'

'It did, however,' Clare said. 'I assure you, Senator, there were three of us present when it was found, and — '

'I wasn't suggesting you didn't find it

there, Miss Winslow — I'm merely saying that I've no idea how it *got* there.'

He sounded so sincere, Ryan and Clare exchanged glances that asked each other if they should continue or just let it go at that.

'Have you?' Senator Cassidy asked, catching their looks.

'One,' Ryan said. 'But it ain't pretty.'

'All the more reason to hear it,' Cassidy said. He looked up as there was a knock, and Maggie stuck her head in and said, 'Sorry, Senator. But you've got calls to make and a plane to catch.'

'Yes, yes, I know.' Cassidy sighed wearily, and for a moment didn't look so handsome. 'Give me five minutes more, eh, Maggie?'

'You got it.' The door closed behind her.

'All right,' Senator Cassidy told them. 'Now, why don't you tell me exactly what this is all about?'

Between them, Ryan and Clare did. The only thing not mentioned was whom Clare worked for. Cassidy was not a good listener. But Ryan kept him from interrupting and when they were finished, the senator knew exactly what he was being accused of.

He was stunned. 'My good God!' he said after a long pause. 'Surely you don't believe any of this?'

'Why not?' Ryan said. 'Some of it we know is true.'

'Oh, I'm not denying my relationship with Mary Jo, if that's what you're referring to. I meant, about my actually being a Nazi spy.'

'If we believed it a hundred percent, Senator,' Clare said, 'frankly, we wouldn't be here. We would've gone to the FBI and let them worry about it.'

'But you do believe it's possible, even plausible that a United States senator nominated for the presidency *might* have once been a spy. Correct?'

'With all the supporting evidence,' Ryan said, 'we think it's possible, yeah.'

'But that's absurd! Don't you think the government, the FBI, CIA, whatever, has already made a thorough investigation of my background?'

'Of course,' said Clare. 'That's one of

the main reasons we've kept this to ourselves — because it *does* seem strange that no one else caught this before we did.'

'On the other hand,' Ryan said, 'people do make mistakes. Even government agencies. We just want to make sure this isn't one of those times — before it's too late.'

'Before I become president, you mean?'

'Or even if you don't,' put in Clare. 'The public still has the right to know the truth about one of their most powerful senators.'

'I couldn't agree more,' Cassidy said. 'And the truth is Ms. Winslow, except for my relationship with Mary Jo which, I admit, I handled poorly, there isn't an ounce of truth in any of this. So I suggest,' he added, suddenly growing angry, 'we discontinue this whole discussion, and you two imposters get out of here before I have you charged with attempted slander!'

'Slander? Imposters?' Clare frowned, puzzled. 'What're you talking about, Senator?'

'Simply this — you tricked my friend, Senator Brickland, into believing Mr. Ryan, here, wanted to interview me. Whereas in truth, this was nothing more than a despicable attempt by you, Ms. Winslow, to disrupt my schedule and to try to frighten me into quitting my campaign — '

'That's not true, Senator. I — '

'I'll be the judge of what's true,' Cassidy raged. He tugged his hands through his thick, graying blond hair. 'After all, I'm perfectly aware of the fact that you're employed by my opposition, Ms. Winslow . . . just as we're all equally aware of the ugly use of smear tactics — '

'That's unfair,' Clare broke in. 'First of all, neither Governor Fontaine nor my boss, Karl Slater, have any idea that we're here, talking to you; and secondly, if we were trying to smear you, as you suggest, we wouldn't even be here. We would've gone straight to the press!'

'How do I know you haven't?' demanded Cassidy.

'C'mon, Clare,' Ryan said, rising. 'We're wasting our time here.'

'Wait!' Senator Cassidy rose as they

reached the door. 'What do you intend to do now?'

'Go to the FBI,' Ryan said. 'Let them worry about 'smear tactics.''

'Please . . . both of you . . . sit down.'

Ryan and Clare glanced at each other, hesitated, then sat and watched Senator Cassidy pace back and forth for a moment.

Shortly, he said, 'You must believe that what I'm going to say is as near to the exact truth as forty years will allow . . . '

They waited Silently.

'I gave that photo to Mary Jo because she kept begging me for it. She wanted it for her wallet, she said, and since I had extras, I let her have one. Later, when my family insisted that I not see Mary Jo anymore, my lawyer tried to buy that and another picture back. She refused. And that's the last I ever saw of them.' He paused, tugging at his hair, then said worriedly, 'If, as you say, she had the photo in her purse when she was killed — surely, isn't it possible that this spy who was supposed to have murdered her took it aboard the U-boat with him before it was sunk? I mean, isn't it?'

'Sure. Anything's possible.'

'Wouldn't that also explain why the spy was never found, because he went down with the U-boat?'

'It could,' Ryan said. 'Though you've got to ask yourself why Falcon then gave the picture to the captain to lock in a security box. I mean, hell, why take the goddamn picture in the first place, and in the second, why not just throw it away?'

'I don't know,' Cassidy said. 'I wish I had a logical answer for you, Ryan, but I don't. To be truthful, I can't even think of a logical answer — though it would obviously be in my best interests to do so.' Again he paused, but this time only for an instant. Then, explosively: 'Jesus Holy Christ! Am I really sitting here trying to defend myself against such an insane, preposterous accusation?'

Then, to Ryan: 'I don't know whether this is important, or not. Especially to you. But I want you to know it, anyway. Both of you. I loved my father. Idolized him, in fact. But I never felt as he did about either Hitler or Nazism. And I've

191

never put myself or my personal goals above this country. As for treason, the very thought of it is repugnant to me. I am not a perfect man by any means. Nor do I claim to be. But I do love America, and I could never even consider doing anything that might harm it. And should the good Lord decide to smile on me and make me president, I will do my damnedest to make this country a better place to live in, and a country the whole world can respect and admire.'

He paused, tugged his fingers through his hair, and smiled the great Cassidy smile at them. 'Now, if any of what I've said rings true, I would hope that you'll consider the disastrous consequences of what your false accusations could bring — namely, the injustice of perhaps destroying an innocent man . . . a man the country may want as their next leader — and drop this absurd matter entirely.'

Ryan and Clare sat looking at each other, and at the senator, without saying a word. Both were impressed by Cassidy's apparent sincerity and, despite all the condemning evidence, were beginning to believe he was innocent.

'Well?' Senator Cassidy said shortly. 'Will you drop it?'

'I don't know,' Ryan said. He looked at Clare, trying to read her thoughts. 'First, Clare and I have to talk this over — alone.'

'That's right,' she agreed. 'As you say, Senator, the consequences, should we be wrong, could be disastrous.'

'They won't be too terrific if we're right, either,' Ryan reminded her grimly.

'True,' the senator said. 'But believe me, *please* believe me, you're not right. And — '

There was a knock, and Maggie re-entered. She held up her wrist to him, indicating her watch. 'Senator,' she pleaded. 'We really can't wait any longer.'

'Be right there, Maggie.' Cassidy turned to Ryan and Clare. 'I really do have to go.'

'Of course, Senator.'

He insisted on shaking hands with them. He brightened as he did, looking more like his virile, handsome self as he said, 'As loyal Americans, I'm sure you'll both do the right thing.'

'We'll sure try to,' Clare promised. 'Good-bye, Senator.'

'Good-bye,' he said. He watched as they made their way out. Then he went to the bedside telephone and began to dial a number.

16

After leaving Senator Cassidy, Ryan and Clare went down to the bar for a drink. They needed time to collect their thoughts and to try to figure out what to do next.

'I hate to say this,' Clare said, breaking the silence. 'But I've got this terrible feeling that Cassidy's telling the truth.'

'Me, too,' Ryan said. 'But then I keep remembering that phone call and the note under your tire. Jesus, those aren't the acts of an innocent man.'

'No, they're not. But — the way I feel now, I think there must be a logical explanation that somehow we're missing.'

'Could be. But I sure as hell don't know what it is. Other than Avery being somehow connected to Beaman and then passing the info on to Cassidy, I can't logically figure out how the senator would even know we were interested in his past.'

'I can't, either. More than that, though, I can't see Avery Brickland connected with

Beaman or hiring men to make threatening calls. It just isn't his style.'

Ryan shrugged. 'I'm fresh out of answers, then.'

'So am I. Guess the best thing to do now is to go along with what Karl wants, make a few more dives on the U-boat, see what we come up with, and then maybe decide about Cassidy. After all, it's still a few weeks before the election. And besides, we might even find something in the U-boat that proves Cassidy's guilty or innocent without any doubt. Does that make any sense?'

'A lot of sense.' He finished his drink. 'May as well head back to the ranch, then.'

'Or the huddle, as my brother the coach would say.'

'Your brother's a football coach?'

'Yes. High school in Philadelphia. Doesn't make much money, but he's the happiest man I know.' She smiled fondly as she thought about her brother. Then: 'Do you have any family?'

Before Ryan could answer, the gray-haired man with the limp entered the bar

196

and approached their table.

'Excuse me,' he said politely. 'I wonder if we might talk?'

''bout what?' Ryan said.

'A matter of some urgency.'

'To you — or us?'

'Both.'

Ryan looked at Clare, who nodded. 'Sure,' he told the man. 'Sit down.'

'Thank you.' The gray-haired man sat, rubbed his crippled leg a moment, then in the same polite, cultured voice said: 'Since time is of the essence, I shall come right to the point. A mutual friend of ours has instructed me to offer you a sum of money for a certain item you possess.'

Ryan looked at Clare, knowing she was experiencing the same sinking feeling as both realized they'd totally misjudged Senator Cassidy's character. But Ryan had to be sure.

'Exactly what 'item' are you talking about?'

'Oh, I think you know, sir.' Gray Hair smelled of expensive European cologne. His manicured fingernails had clear polish on them. His clothes were

197

immaculately tailored, yet Ryan sensed everything was a façade. The man had come from the streets, had empty eyes and was deadly. 'What I'm referring to,' Gray Hair was saying, 'is small — no larger, say, than a photograph — and reminds someone of their past.'

'Just supposing we do have such an item,' Ryan said. 'How much is our mutual friend prepared to pay for it?'

'A half million dollars — cash.'

Ryan did something with his eyes that made Clare say to Gray Hair: 'Would you leave us alone for a few minutes, please?'

'Of course, madam.' He stood up, worked the stiffness from his crippled leg, then limped toward the bar.

Ryan and Clare shook their heads, depressed and disgusted.

'Shit,' she said. 'I was just about to wipe Cassidy's slate clean. Drop the whole matter.'

'Same here.' He added: 'Half a million bucks buys a whole pile of sunshine.'

'Especially when it's tax-free.'

'Right. And don't forget, it's not going to be easy to prove Cassidy's a spy

— even with the photo and everything else we know about him.'

'Worse than that,' Clare said. 'We could get killed trying.'

'Now you're making sense,' Ryan said. 'Besides, even if Cassidy was once a Nazi spy, that doesn't mean he still is. People change, you know. And sometimes for the better.'

'Very true. And then we'd feel pretty rotten knowing that we'd been responsible for a great man like Cassidy not becoming president. Right?'

'Right. 'sides, I've been rich *and* poor. And rich is better.'

'Way better.'

'What do you think, then — we should take the money?'

'Don't you?'

'Of course.'

They paused. For a moment they looked at each other. Then at Gray Hair drinking at the bar. Then, softly, they started to laugh.

Ryan said cheerfully, 'Are you gonna tell our friend, there, to stick his offer in his ear, or am I?'

'Why don't we do it together?' Clare said, smiling. 'Let him know we *both* hate punting.'

They rose, went to the bar and refused Gray Hair's offer. He tried hard to change their minds. But they remained adamant and left. Gray Hair paid for his drink and then limped out to the lobby telephone.

With Ryan at the wheel, the two drove back to Morehead City. They felt as clean and free as the sea beside them. And although they knew they hadn't heard the last of Cassidy, they were in good spirits.

'What's our next move?' Ryan asked. 'Keep digging?'

'You bet. Like you said, it's not going to be easy to nail Cassidy. Don't forget, it's only our word against his that we found the photo in the U-boat.'

'And the word of German Intelligence,' reminded Ryan. 'They mention it in that memo to the captain.'

'Wrong. They mention 'a' photo — not necessarily that photo. At least, that's what a good defense attorney would show.'

'Clever girl. I didn't think of that. Too

bad we don't know exactly who in German Intelligence wrote that memo — he might be able to identify the photo.'

'After forty years? I doubt it. Besides, we don't have a lot of time. November eleventh will be on us before we know it.'

'Then our best bet is to go straight to the U-boat captain himself.'

'You think he'd still be alive?'

'Good chance of it. We know the crew were interned at Charleston, so he didn't die during the war. And most of those U-boat commanders were pretty young — early thirties, at most.'

'Which could only make him around seventy-something.'

'Right. And we know his name. So if we can just get hold of an action report — '

'Action report?'

'The official record the Navy keeps, detailing the action between one of their vessels an' the enemy. Your boss's friend at the Navy Yard could probably dig it up for us. Then, from the report, we might find out where *Kapitan* Richter lived, and you could fly there, show him the photo, and — '

Suddenly a rifle shot echoed in the woods alongside the highway. A bullet punched a neat, starry hole in the windshield, barely missing Ryan's head, and continued on out the open window to his left.

Ryan momentarily lost control of the steering wheel. The car veered left across the yellow divider line, swerving toward oncoming traffic in the opposite lanes. Ryan recovered quickly and swung back across the center divider and into his own lane.

'Keep down!' he shouted. 'Keep down!'

He accelerated. The Porsche roared along the highway at high speed. No more shots followed. After a few miles Ryan slowed down to the speed of the other cars traveling in their direction.

'Sweet Jesus,' he said. He was drenched in sweat. 'You okay?' he asked Clare.

She nodded, still too shaken to speak.

Without conviction, he said, 'It could've been an accident, you know. Some backwoods poacher after a deer.'

'You know damn well it wasn't an accident. So stop trying to con me,' Clare said. She fell silent, frightened beyond what she'd imagined fear was. But angry, too. Furious.

Neither spoke again until they reached her motel. Then, as Ryan parked in the space outside her door, Clare said quietly, 'Please — would you come in with me? I'm going to call Karl. Tell him exactly what happened. See if he'll believe us now.'

She reached Slater at his luxury condominium in the capital. She explained about the meeting with Cassidy, the gray-haired man's attempt to buy Falcon's photograph, and, finally, the sniper attack from the woods.

At first Slater was angry with Clare for disobeying him and not diving on the U-boat. But then, stunned by Senator Cassidy's reaction and apparent violent reprisal, the campaign manager grew concerned and promised to pass everything along to Governor Fontaine as soon as he hung up. 'And I want you to come back to Washington immediately,' he ordered. 'It's obviously not safe for you there.'

'What about Ryan?'

'Bring him with you. I want to meet him, anyway. Oh, and one other thing,' Slater added. 'From now on, until the governor and I can work out how best to protect you two, you're to call me every few hours — let me know exactly where you are and what you're doing. Understood?'

'Perfectly,' she said. Hanging up, she told Ryan what Slater had said. He knew what kind of risk he was exposing himself to by going to Washington, and yet, having already come this far, and feeling more protective about Clare than he cared to admit, he realized he had little choice but to agree.

Clare was delighted. 'I'll certainly feel safer with you along, especially if we have to fly all the way to Germany.'

Ryan frowned, surprised. 'Germany?'

'Of course. To find *Kapitan* Richter. It was your idea, remember? Before someone took that shot at us, you said the action report might tell us where he lived.'

'Yeah, yeah, I know what I said. It's just that, well, I never figured on goin' all the way to Germany.'

She sensed he had reasons for not wanting to go to Germany that he presently wasn't prepared to share with her. Rather than pressure him now, and get a 'no,' she decided to wait until later, when they were in Washington, and maybe let Karl help 'persuade' Ryan into accompanying her.

'Well, let's not worry about Germany now,' she said. 'Who knows, *Kapitan* Richter might've stayed on here after the war — might still be living in the Charleston area.'

He might also be dead, Ryan thought hopefully. *Then I won't have to use a phony passport and risk having my ass thrown in jail.*

17

The following day Ryan threw some things into a bag and told Mitch to 'mind the store' till he got back. Then he and Clare started out on their drive to the capital.

Taking the Porsche was Ryan's idea. He reasoned they would need a car once they were in Washington, and since there were no local dealers who could fix the windshield, he suggested they drive instead of fly.

The Porsche ran like a fine Swiss watch. With only one stop for lunch, the trip took roughly six hours. Ryan kept a constant eye on the mirrors. He saw nothing suspicious. And by late afternoon, when they pulled up outside Governor Fontaine's campaign headquarters, he was positive that they hadn't been followed.

'I'll wait here,' he told Clare. 'You go check if your boss is around.'

She returned shortly and said she'd just spoken on the phone to Slater, and that he wanted to see them at his condominium right away. He and Governor Fontaine were leaving for New Hampshire that night and Karl was packing right now.

At that moment, back at Fontaine's campaign headquarters, Donna Walker, a pretty young black girl, sat at her desk, dialing the Ajax Janitorial Service. For the past year she had been employed by Ajax as a part-time receptionist. But a few days ago the owner, Dean Callum, had paid her to get a job as one of Fontaine's numerous temporary telephone-answering girls. Callum told Donna to call him immediately when a woman named Clare Winslow returned to Washington, and to keep him apprised of her comings and goings.

Now, on the phone, Donna told Callum that Ms. Winslow had just left the office and was on her way to Mr. Slater's condo. Donna spoke softly so that none of her fellow workers could hear what she was saying, and added that Clare had entered alone but had driven off with a man who'd waited outside in a Porsche. Donna then gave Callum Clare's home address, which she'd copied from the files, and said that Slater lived on Massachusetts Avenue in the elite Penthrope House.

Dean Callum instructed Donna to call him again if Clare returned and hung up. He put on his long black overcoat and pulled gloves over his tattooed hands. He told the receptionist that he was leaving for the day and drove to Clare's Georgetown town house. Perhaps now, at long last, he thought as he kept one hand pressed atop the Bible in his lap, vengeance would be his . . .

The Porsche pulled up in front of the Penthrope House, an elegant condominium complex located in the plush residential section of Massachusetts Avenue. Ryan and Clare entered the lobby and identified themselves to the security guard. The guard was expecting them. He gave them Slater's condominium number, directed them up to the elevator, then notified Slater that they were coming up.

Slater's personal secretary, Ruth Livermore, met them at the door. She was Clare's age, vibrantly attractive and extremely efficient, but slightly too sugary to be trusted. She invited them in and said Slater would be out in a minute. They refused the drinks she offered and she left the room.

Ryan and Clare sat in the spacious, tastefully decorated living room, and within a few minutes Karl Slater joined them. He introduced himself to Ryan, made no attempt to apologize for demanding to see them after their long drive, and asked them what their next move was.

'Tomorrow,' Clare said, 'we're going to the Navy Yards and see if we can find an action report that'll tell us where the U-boat captain lives. We know his name is Ernst Richter, and Ryan thinks he might still be alive. If he is, and lives in Germany, we'll fly there and see if he can positively identify the picture of Senator Cassidy as being that of the spy, Falcon.'

'Let me see the picture,' Slater said.

Clare took it from her purse and showed it to him. His expression never changed. But when he returned the picture to Clare, he said: 'You're right. They could be twins. It's too bad my friend, Commander Haskell, isn't still at the Navy Yards. He would've been invaluable help.'

'Doesn't matter,' Ryan said. 'Long as the action report's been declassified we shouldn't have any trouble finding it.'

The phone rang. Ruth Livermore answered it. Placing the receiver back in its cradle, she told Slater that the governor was already on his way to the airport.

'So am I,' Slater said. Then to Clare: 'Ruth will know where I am at all times. Soon as you have any worthwhile news, call me. Understood?'

Clare nodded.

'I'm very worried about your safety, Clare. Yours too, Ryan.'

'Don't be,' Ryan said. 'We can handle things.'

'Mr. Slater — ' Ruth said anxiously.

'Coming, coming.' Slater turned to Ryan: 'One last thing. You stay with Clare. Keep an eye on her. And not a word of this to anyone until we have proof positive that Senator Cassidy is indeed Falcon. Not anyone.'

'Got our word on it,' Ryan assured him.

Later, when they were driving to Georgetown in her car, Clare asked Ryan what he thought of Slater.

'Talks too much.'

She laughed. 'Compared to you, so do statues. Seriously, though, what do you really think?'

'Seems like a good guy.'

'He is. Bit of a Puritan at times, but, well, he'll bend when he has to — like he did by asking you to stay at my place. By the way,' she added, 'I never thought to ask. Is that okay with you?'

'Depends,' he deadpanned.

'On what?'

'How loudly you snore.'

'Not loud enough to be heard through a locked door.'

'Touché.'

It was dusk when they reached Georgetown. Ryan found a parking space not too far up the street from Clare's town house. Then he collected their bags from under the hood and followed Clare into the house.

Across the street Dean Callum watched them from his car. He'd been waiting there for over an hour. Now, as Ryan and Clare climbed the neat white steps and went inside, Callum pointed them out to Rick Weems, the short, fleshy private investigator sitting beside him. Weems snapped Ryan and Clare's picture, using infrared film, and promised that he and his operatives would maintain a twenty-four-hour surveillance on both Ryan and Clare until instructed not to. He then got out and walked to his car.

Callum, meanwhile, watched the town house for a few more moments before driving off, praying all the while, clutching his ever-present Bible.

18

The next morning Ryan and Clare left the Porsche at the shop to have the windshield replaced, and drove the dealer's loaner to the U. S. Navy Yard overlooking the Anacostia River. Callum's PI tailed them in a plain white sedan, but so professionally that Ryan had no idea they were being followed.

A guard stopped them at the main gate off M Street and told Ryan that the information he needed was in Building 210. 'That's the tan job there on the left,' she said and pointed.

They thanked her and drove along the paved road until they reached the building, where they parked among the cars outside.

Inside the lobby was austere and unfurnished save for a wooden desk behind which sat a guard who directed them to the fourth floor, adding that they'd have to use the stairs as the elevator wasn't working again.

Ryan and Clare climbed the three flights of gray-painted stairs, pushed through a door and approached the information desk.

'Yes, sir?' the yeoman clerk said. 'May I help you?'

'We need to look at a 1942 action report,' Ryan said. 'It concerns a Coast Guard cutter and a U-boat. The sub was sunk off the North Carolina coast.'

The clerk scribbled down the information and told them he'd get the archivist. He disappeared into a back office and returned shortly with the archivist, a tall, slender, attractive young woman in a blouse and jeans. Her name tag read, L. Glover, and she spoke with a slight, pleasant Midwestern twang.

'I need to know more information before I can look up what you want,' she told them. 'For instance, what was the name of the cutter?'

'*Daidalos*,' Ryan said.

'And the number of the U-boat?'

'U-352.'

'How about the date of the action?'

'Sometime in May of forty-two,' Ryan

said, adding, 'I'll also need the post-mortem report and any information on the survivors, if it's available.'

'It should be,' Glover said. 'That far back, there shouldn't be any trouble with the material being classified.' She gave them a form to fill out for her records and then disappeared in back.

'I'm impressed,' Clare said.

Ryan nodded. 'Does seem to know her job, all right.'

'I mean with you. Heck, I had no idea you were so well-informed about Navy procedure and terminology.'

Ryan shrugged. 'I have friends in the Navy.'

'So do I, but — '

'A man once told me, you learn more by listening.'

'Ouch,' Clare said. She mimed zippering her mouth shut, and watched as he started filling out the form.

Miss Glover returned in ten minutes, all smiles. 'Bingo,' she said. 'Got everything you need.'

She waited while the clerk locked Clare's purse in a locker for security purposes, then she led them into the office in back, through vault doors, into a room with chairs, a reading table, and two microfilm readers lined along the rear wall. An official file folder lay on the table. Beside it sat a box containing a roll of microfilm. 'The folder contains everything that's on the microfilm,' she explained, 'so you can take your choice or look at both, whichever you prefer. Oh, and if you want copies of anything, just let me know. I can do up to fifty copies.' She went into her adjoining office and closed the door.

Alone, Ryan and Clare read the official action report that described in detail how the USCG *Daidalos* engaged and sank the German submarine U-352. The action occurred on May 9, 1942, and it was described by the commanding officer of the cutter, Captain Douglas Jeeter, and by his executive officer, Lieutenant C. R. Hampton. Along with the action report, there was a list of the survivors and the casualties of the U-boat. The crew consisted of three officers, one midshipman, eighteen petty officers, and twenty-four men, of which two officers and twelve men were dead. *Kapitan* Ernst Richter was listed among the survivors, and the accompanying interrogation report stated that he was thirty-two years old and of the naval class of 1930. He was born and raised in Flensburg, came on active duty in 1935 and served in various surface vessels until 1939 when he was given a submarine command.

'Flensburg!' Clare said, pausing in her reading. 'That's in Northern Germany, I think. Up by Denmark somewhere.'

'Let's hope he still lives there,' Ryan said.

'Let's hope he still lives, period. If he was thirty-two in '42, that'd make him seventy-two.'

They read on. Richter professed an unqualified admiration for Hitler and National Socialism. He was highly respected by his men, was a harsh disciplinarian, and wore the Iron Cross second class, for valor in action.

'Sounds like a real Nazi,' Clare said. 'Sure hope that doesn't stop him from identifying Falcon or Cassidy.'

Ryan wasn't listening. 'Look at this,' he said, turning to the last page. It was stamped confidential, but was now declassified. It was a directive from the Anti-Submarine Warfare Unit in Boston dated May 21, 1942, and it stated: 'From a study of reference A [information supplied] the following observation has been made: The fact that the enemy submarine U-352 was waiting for a convoy and that a convoy would have been in the vicinity a very short time after this encounter indicates an accurate supply of intelligence information was given to the enemy.'

'In other words,' Ryan said, '*Kapitan* Richter definitely did receive help from our friend, Falcon.'

'Yes. As Mrs. Klammer told us — in that last interrupted transmission.' She paused, rubbed her weary eyes, yawned and stretched. 'Well, at least everything ties together. Between what we've dug up, and what's written here, I'd say there isn't a lot more we can uncover — until we speak to Richter that is.'

'When're we going to do that?'

''You mean fly to Flensburg?' At his

nod, she said: 'Hopefully, right away. Of course, I'll have to clear it with Karl. But unless he or Fontaine has some unknown objection, we should be on our way by sometime tomorrow — latest. That okay with you?'

'Sure.'

'You have a valid passport?'

'Yep.'

'Terrific. I'll get this stuff back to Miss Glover, then.' Clare took the material into Miss Glover's office. She returned shortly with the archivist, who in her pleasant drawl asked Ryan if there was anything else he needed.

He thought a moment, wondering as he did how many people other than themselves had looked at the action report. Maybe one of them would lead back to Cassidy and further implicate the senator. 'As a matter of fact there is. That information card we filled out at the desk, Miss Glover, how long do you keep them?'

'You serious?' She laughed, good-naturedly. 'This department's under D.O.D. jurisdiction — we never throw *anything* away!'

'Then you'd know how many people in the last year or so have looked at these reports, right?'

'Sure. Why?'

'Well, to be honest,' lied Ryan, 'a friend of ours — a Commander Haskell — persuaded us to write a book about World War Two U-boats, and, well, we've spent a lot of effort on it already and now we're afraid someone else has got the jump on us.'

'You mean another writer?'

Ryan nodded. 'I don't want you to break any rules, but if we knew who'd looked at this action report, we'd know if we had to rush things up or were still the only game in town.'

'We'd intended on asking Commander Haskell,' Clare put in, 'but, as you know, he's no longer here — '

'Don't worry,' Miss Glover assured them. 'I've never heard of any Commander Haskell, but I'll be glad to get the information you need.'

She was only gone a few moments. When she returned, she said, 'There's been only one person who requested to see this report — a Mr. Dean Callum. I can't give you his address, of course, but I can tell you he was here on April 3rd of this year.'

'That's our competition,' Clare said, faking concern. 'For a man who limps, Mr. Callum sure gets around.'

'Mr. Callum didn't limp,' Miss Glover said.

'You sure about that?' Ryan said.

'Positive.'

'Forties, short, husky, lot of gray wavy hair?'

'Oh, no, you must have the wrong Mr. Callum,' Miss Glover said. 'This man was very large, about sixty, and had almost no hair at all. I remember him so well,' she added, 'because he had a tattoo on the back of each hand.'

They drove back to Clare's town house, again not noticing the white sedan discreetly tailing them. Once inside, Clare called Pan Am and TWA and discovered that there were no direct flights to Flensburg — only local German airlines that flew out of Hamburg or Frankfurt. Ryan, who'd been poring over a map of

Germany, suggested they rent a car. 'Flensburg's only about a hundred miles from Hamburg.'

The idea had merit. Later Clare called Slater at his hotel in New Hampshire and briefed him about the action report. Slater was tired from a day of campaigning and seemed more abrupt than usual. 'Do whatever you must do to contact Richter,' he snapped, 'then call me the minute you've spoken to him. The very minute. Understood?' He hung up before Clare could answer.

'We've got the green light,' she told Ryan. 'Now all we have to decide is whether we leave tonight or tomorrow morning.'

Then, when he didn't say anything: 'Since you're obviously leaving that up to me, let's take the morning flight. I can't sleep worth a damn on planes. And anyway, after forty years one day more or less can't make that much difference, can it?'

'I wouldn't think so.'

'Good enough.' Clare picked up the phone. 'Then I'll call and get us on the morning flight out of Dulles.'

The morning flight to Frankfurt left shortly before noon. Ryan and Clare slept late, ate a leisurely breakfast and then drove the loaner back to the Porsche dealer. Clare's windshield was fixed, but she didn't want to leave the car for several days at the airport, so they left the car at the dealer's and caught the flyaway commuter bus out to Dulles International.

They were tailed by the PI in the white sedan. He watched them board the plane to Frankfurt, then called Dean Callum and reported the news. Callum put on some old blue coveralls, left his office and drove to Claire's town house. There he let himself in with a pick-lock and began a thorough search. He was looking for anything that would tell him just how much Ryan or Clare knew about Mary Jo Buffram and Falcon.

He found all he wanted in a desk drawer: Clare's copies of the U-boat documents and Falcon's photo, and the rough translations that Mrs. Klammer had made at her house. He was puzzled by the photograph. He studied it for several seconds before turning to the documents and translations. He examined them carefully. Then, satisfied by what he'd read, he replaced everything in the drawer exactly as he'd found it and left.

Back at his office, he called the detective agency and instructed the owner to continue his twenty-four-hour surveillance of Clare's town house and to notify him immediately when she or Ryan returned from Germany. Then he held the old Bible in his huge, big-knuckled, tattooed hands and prayed fervently that he was nearing the end of his quest.

19

The giant 747 landed on time at Frankfurt. Ryan and Clare walked through a series of linking tunnels, following signs that directed them to connecting flights. The flight from Dulles had taken just under ten hours and they were stiff and weary from sitting, in spite of the stopover at Kennedy.

Ryan and Clare reached the departure area for the connecting flight to Hamburg. The young man behind the check-in counter spoke clipped, understandable English and was courteously efficient. He said their plane left in forty-six minutes, gave them boarding passes and wished them a pleasant flight. Ryan and Clare used the waiting time to walk the stiffness out of their legs.

The flight to Hamburg took less than an hour. It was still mid-afternoon when they landed, and a light rain was falling from a leaden sky. Ryan and Clare collected their baggage and followed the signs pointing to the rent-a-car counters. They rented a Fiat and were given a highway map and directions to the *Europa-Strasse* 3, which would take them directly into Flensburg.

The rain stopped a few miles north of Hamburg. Ragged bits of pale blue sky broke through the clouds. Ryan turned off the irritatingly loud windshield wipers and listened as Clare polished up her German by translating what she heard on the radio.

The autobahn passed through mostly flat, pastoral countryside. Both sides of the modern paved highway were cultivated fields, beautiful green forests, and low rolling hills dotted with sheep. All the towns had unfamiliar, hard-to-pronounce names. At Rendsburg, they drove through a tunnel under the *Nord-Ostsee-Kanal*, the wide, manmade channel, third largest in the world, which runs across the entire tip of northern Germany. It links the North and Baltic seas, allowing, by a proficient system of locks, the heavy flow of river traffic to supply the country with commercial and industrial goods.

The little blue Fiat was fast and handled well. It took them only an hour and twenty minutes to travel the one hundred and sixty-two kilometers to Flensburg.

On the outskirts the autobahn linked up with local highways and Ryan followed the signs directing them into the ancient seaport city that was known as the 'Gateway to the North.'

Clare had a brochure describing Flensburg, given to her by the Washington travel agent who had booked their flight and hotel reservations. She read aloud from it as they drove into town, pointing out the various buildings, churches, and market places as she recognized them. The large, modernistic, gray-towered building on their left was the *Rathaus*, or city hall; behind that, with its tall Gothic spire and orange-red roof poking above the treetops, was St. Nicholas church; and, as they swung left, past the cluster of old-fashioned buildings at the *Neumarkt*, and drove along the broad, heavily trafficked *Süderhofenden*, they got their first glimpse of the big, round modern bus station known as ZOB (*Zentral Omnibus Bahnhof*). Beyond, through the wintry trees, they could see the row of sleek white ferry steamers moored in the calm ice-blue waters of the fjord.

At the ZOB they stopped and asked the blue-uniformed policeman directions to their hotel. The tall blond young man spoke respectable English, to the disappointment of Clare, who was impatient to test her German.

The Hotel Flensburger Hof was located just off *Süderhofenden*, a short distance from the ZOB. Standing among the gable-roofed buildings that were several hundred years old, the hotel was a modern, cube-like structure several stories high with neon signs, a ground-floor restaurant and bar, and all the contemporary conveniences of an American Hilton.

Ryan parked among the cars out front, got the bags from the trunk, and followed Clare inside. It was now dusk and the well-heated lobby was cheerfully lit. They approached the desk, ears and noses tingling from the cold, and Clare told the clerk in German who they were.

'*Ja, ja,*' he said smiling. 'Mr. Ryan und Miss Winslow. Ve haf been expecting you.'

Their adjoining green-walled rooms were on the fourth floor. Both had the same yellow lamps, black vinyl furniture, and red Persian rugs as the lobby, along with double beds and two windows overlooking the street. The door between their adjoining rooms was open. Through it Ryan saw Clare take a robe from her bag, kick off her shoes, and head into the bathroom. Ryan heard the water running in the tub. Weary from all the traveling, Ryan stretched out on the bed with the telephone directory. There were nine Richters listed, but only three had an *E* before the surname. Ryan waited until Clare had bathed and changed. Then, as she joined him on the bed, he gave her the open directory and asked her to call the three Richters. While she did, he showered and changed clothes.

Clare's first call was answered by a young man whose first name was Erich. Clare, in stumbling German, asked to speak to Herr Ernst Richter. The young German replied that there was no Ernst

Richter at this number and hung up. Clare then tried the second number and got no answering ring. She tried again and got the same result. She then tried the third number. A child answered. Clare asked to speak to Herr Ernst Richter. The child said something in German that Clare didn't catch, giggled, then a woman got on the phone. Clare asked her if a Herr Ernst Richter, formerly Kapitan Richter, lived there. The woman said no, but added that *Kapitan* Richter was her husband's grandfather.

'My friend and I want to — uh — talk to him,' Clare said in faltering German. 'We've come from America. Do you have his telephone number?'

'*Ja*,' said the woman. She then gave Clare the same number she had previously called that hadn't rung.

'I've — uh — darn, what's that word? — tried that number,' Clare said, 'and it doesn't ring.'

The woman didn't understand all of what Clare had said. Clare could hear several children arguing loudly in the background and the woman apologized to

Clare, said she had to go, and hung up.

'I knew three was our lucky number,' Clare said as Ryan emerged from his bathroom. 'Our good friend the *Kapitan* is alive and kicking at *Telefon Nummer* 23091.' She dialed the number again and got no answering ring. 'Odd,' she said, hanging up. 'Still no ring.'

'Maybe it's disconnected?'

'Could be, I guess, but wouldn't his granddaughter-in-law have known that? Said something?'

'Maybe. Maybe she just forgot.' Ryan shrugged. 'Why don't we try again after dinner? Then, if it's still no go, we'll get the operator in on it.'

Clare agreed without much argument.

They ate in the ground-floor restaurant. The long, beam-ceilinged room faced the bar. Ryan and Clare sat at a corner table by one of the lead-paned windows and had the tavern special: kippered eel on pumpernickel bread, thick slices of sauerbraten, steamy sauerkraut, glasses of dark beer, and apple crêpes for dessert.

'No wonder German women are robust,' Clare grumbled as she and Ryan took the stairs back to their rooms.

Ryan wasn't listening. He had that same uneasy feeling in his stomach again, and though he hadn't mentioned anything to Clare, he sensed something was wrong. What, he didn't know. Probably nothing. After all, just because Richter's phone didn't ring, that didn't mean he was dead or — or even in any danger. Hell, the line could be out of order. Or maybe he hadn't paid his bill or . . .

Then why did he have a bellyache? Ryan wondered. It was the same goddamn pain in the gut that he always got when something was about to go wrong —

'Are you listening to me?' Clare said. They had paused outside the door to her room, and he realized he hadn't heard a word.

'No,' he said. 'Sorry. What'd you say?'

'I said, we'd better call Karl — let him know how we're doing.'

'Okay. But let's wait until we've spoken to Richter. That way we'll have something to talk about.'

They entered Clare's room. Clare called Richter's number but again could get no ring. She then had the operator try. The operator went off the line briefly. Then she returned and said the number was out of order and that she would report it.

'Well, at least we know it's just the phone,' Clare said. 'I didn't want to say anything, but for a while there I thought Herr Richter might be ducking us. You know, had told his granddaughter-in-law to give us the wrong number.'

Ryan had envisioned worse than that. Clare read his frown.

'What's wrong? Something bothering you?'

'I don't know,' he said, deciding not to alarm her over a gut feeling he couldn't explain. 'Probably drank too much beer, is all.'

Clare studied him, trying to see if he was telling her the truth. Then she yawned, deadly sleepy. 'If you're giving me that old 'Don't Explain' routine, Ryan, forget it. I'm too tired to be curious.'

Ryan acted as if she hadn't spoken. Entering his own room through the connecting door, he told her: 'I'll leave this unlocked — case one of us needs something during the night.'

'Good idea,' Clare said.

'G'night,' Ryan said.

20

Ryan had been awake for about an hour when the bedside phone rang. It was the desk clerk with Ryan's seven o'clock wake-up call. Ryan thanked him, climbed out of bed, went to the window and peered around the drapes.

Outside rain was threatening. Ryan studied the overcast sky. It was the color of muddy snow. Then he heard a noise behind him. He whirled around and saw it was Clare standing, night-gowned, in the doorway connecting their rooms. One green eye studied him sleepily from under a tousled wave of sun-colored hair. 'Can't be seven o'clock already,' she yawned. 'Feels like I just closed my eyes.'

'Go soak your head under the cold water,' Ryan suggested. 'It does wonders for jet lag.'

'That's what I like most about you,' she said, yawning again. 'You're always so terribly understanding.'

But she did as he suggested. When she returned shortly, fresh-looking and dressed now, she found him sitting on the edge of his bed, looking at the phone on his lap. Troubled.

'Still out of order, huh?'

He nodded.

'Think it's too early to call his granddaughter?'

'Not if she has kids.'

'You're right. Poor woman's probably been up since the crack of dawn.'

They dialed the woman's number. It rang and rang. Ryan finally hung up. He copied *Kapitan* Richter's address from the phone book and suggested they drive over to the house once they'd eaten to see if everything was all right.

They each gulped down a cup of coffee and ate a fresh-baked Danish pastry in the hotel restaurant. Then they got a street map from the desk clerk and directions to Herr Richter's house, and hurried out to the car. Rain threatened, and cold breezes off the inner fjord hit them like a damp blast. Clare shivered inside her raincoat. Ryan pulled the fleece-lined collar of his denim windbreaker up about his ears. They climbed into the Fiat. Ryan let the engine idle until it was warm, then turned north and drove along the *Süderhofenden*.

Ryan realized the fast-moving traffic was mostly comprised of workmen and office personnel. As they passed the ZOB, lines of workers were descending from the different colored buses, while loudspeakers announced the various bus departures. Clare understood parts of the announcements. She indicated one of the white and blue buses and said she thought it was taking people to the nearby Danish frontier. Ryan stored the information away — in case the uneasy gut feeling turned out to be more than too much beer at dinner.

Flensburg, although founded in 1240, is well laid out with an easy-to-follow street pattern. Despite heavy British bombing to the shipyards and submarine base, the town itself survived World War II almost undamaged. Ahead a street sign said they were now on *Norderhofenden*. The broad harbor boulevard ran alongside the banks of the *Innenforde*, and

Ryan and Clare could see up close the streamlined white ferry steamers at their moorings, and beyond, across the calm gray waters of the fjord, the big tall waterfront granaries and the oceangoing freighters and tankers tied up to the docks.

Kapitan Richter lived on Knappen, a side street just off *Duburger Strasse*. Ryan followed the desk clerk's red pencil line on the street map, driving along *Norderhofenden to Schiffbrücke* until he came to *Toosbuystrasse*. Then he turned left, away from the water, and drove between a double row of old tall buildings with lots of windows and the ever-present pointed red roofs. On their right was a large Danish bookshop; to their left was *Grosse Strasse*, one of the main shopping streets that had been blocked off so that tourists could stroll unhindered by traffic.

They turned right at *Duburger Strasse*, right again on Ritter. And then turned down Knappen. They were checking house numbers for Richter's address. Almost at once they saw a small crowd gathered before the charred remains of two recently burned houses.

'Oh, no-o,' Clare groaned as Ryan slowed down. 'Don't tell me . . . Not after we've come all this way . . . ' But, even as she spoke, she and Ryan knew by the remaining numbers that one of the two destroyed houses had been Richter's.

'Now we know why the phone didn't ring,' Ryan said. He parked opposite, realizing now why his belly had acted up. 'And why Richter's daughter-in-law didn't say anything.'

'Granddaughter-in-law,' Clare said vaguely, not even aware that she was correcting him.

'Whatever,' Ryan said. 'Main thing is, this obviously only happened recently — yesterday some time — and that means — '

'We're either horribly unlucky . . . or someone's making sure we don't talk to Herr Richter.'

Ryan wasn't listening. He wondered if Richter had been burned with the house. It was possible that the old captain had been out at the time of the fire. Or got out safely. Or . . . 'C'mon,' he told Clare. 'Let's go find out what happened.'

They joined the small crowd. Clare, in

faltering German, asked about the fire and if Herr Richter had survived it. An old woman with soot-smudged, tear-stained cheeks said no. Both Herr Richter and Frau Richter had died. Also one of the Gutmann children, next door. A terrible tragedy.

'Ask her if she knows how the fire started,' Ryan said after Clare had translated the grim news.

Clare did so. The woman didn't know. Neither did any of the other neighbors. Nor anyone in the fire department, which had put out the blaze late yesterday afternoon. Clare listened as each neighbor offered his or her idea. She didn't understand some of what they said. But then, suddenly, she heard something that made her ask:

'Uh — excuse me. What was that about an American?'

Gerd Schmidt, the old man who'd been talking, was short and fat with red cheeks and huge white walrus mustaches. He repeated that yesterday afternoon, about two hours before the fire, he'd seen Herr Richter talking to a stranger outside his house. Later, after the stranger left, Herr Richter had told Gerd Schmidt that the man was an American.

'What'd he look like?' Clare interrupted.

'A short but big man,' Schmidt remembered. 'With gray hair.'

'Did he limp?' Clare asked. Schmidt didn't understand her. Clare limped a few steps, said, 'Limp,' as best she could in German, and at once Schmidt nodded. '*Ja, ja,*' he exclaimed, several times.

'I'll explain everything in a minute,' Clare told Ryan. 'But I'm almost sure Gray Hair was here.' Then to Schmidt: 'Did Herr Richter say what the American's name was?'

Schmidt didn't understand her. But another, younger man did. He repeated the question to Schmidt, who shook his white head.

'But he did limp and have gray hair?' Clare repeated.

Gerd Schmidt nodded vigorously. Clare turned back to Ryan and repeated everything.

'Bastard,' Ryan said. 'How'd he get here before us?'

'More than that, how'd he even know where Richter lived?'

'I don't know. I doubt if he was at the Navy Yards, or that archivist would've told us.' He added: 'I want you to ask the old guy if Richter told him anything else about the American.'

'Like what?'

'Anything. And while you're at it, find out if this is the first time Gray Hair's been here. Also, if the captain's had any other American visitors.'

Clare obeyed. It took a while, but with some help from the others, she finally had the answers Ryan wanted. 'Mr. Schmidt says that after Gray Hair left, Richter mentioned that the American had wanted to know if Richter could remember a spy called Falcon who'd transmitted messages to him from a place called Bogue Banks in North Carolina. Yes, he remembered. Why? The American wouldn't say. But he showed Richter a photo and asked him if this was Falcon. Richter said yes, and asked Gray Hair how he'd gotten hold of the picture. Again, Gray Hair wouldn't say. He just thanked Richter and drove away. Richter then said that all Americans must be spy-crazy, because this was the second one in six months who'd come over and asked him about Falcon.'

'Who was the first?' Ryan said.

'You'll never guess — our friend with the tattoos.'

'The big guy the archivist told us about?'

'The very same — Mr. Dean Callum.'

'Well, that clears up two problems: We now know that Richter could and did identify Falcon, and that Callum and Gray Hair aren't working together.'

'True. But we're still no closer to knowing who Falcon is. Damn,' Clare said suddenly. 'I feel like I'm partly responsible.'

'For what?'

'The death of three people.'

'Three?'

'Richter, his wife, and the little girl next door. I mean, it was my idea to take the morning flight out of Dulles. If we'd left the night before, we would've gotten here at the same time as Gray Hair, maybe sooner. Then the Richters and that poor little girl might be still alive.'

'An' if Richter had gone down with his U-boat,' Ryan said irritably, 'we wouldn't have had to come here at all, now, would we?' He scowled. 'So let's not waste time on assumptions or guilt trips, and start concentrating on things we can do something about.'

'Such as?'

'A phone call to Slater, for starters. Tell him the score. See if he'll put a man at Dulles — watch for Gray Hair, then tail him and see where he goes. He might lead us straight to Cassidy, an' then we got the makings of a connection — evidence that could link Cassidy to the death of the Richters.'

'Good idea,' Clare said. She felt considerably cheered. 'I'll call Karl soon as we get back to the hotel.' They headed back to the car.

During the ride back to the hotel some of Ryan's thoughts gelled. Gray Hair knew where Richter lived, because Clare's town house was bugged. It *had* to be. Otherwise, why would Richter have to die? And, more importantly, die yesterday? After all, he'd been allowed to live some forty years without apparently causing his killer or killers any concern. So why suddenly kill him now? Obviously, because he, Ryan, and Clare had been on their way to ask him the one question that could expose Falcon's true identity.

Satisfied that his conclusions made sense, Ryan wondered if he should tell Clare now that her house was probably bugged, or wait until they returned to the States. He decided on the latter.

21

It was nine twenty when they reached the Flensburger Hof. Because of the six-hour time difference between Flensburg and Washington, D.C., Clare decided against waking Slater in the middle of the night. Instead, she waited until she and Ryan had eaten breakfast and arrived at Frankfurt airport before calling the campaign manager. By then, as they stood at one of the terminal phones, the clock above the arrival and departure monitor showed it was 12:15.

'Six fifteen,' Clare said as she waited for the overseas operator to connect her with Slater's number. 'Karl should be awake by now.' But the phone rang and rang. Finally, Clare thanked the operator and hung up. 'He's probably off campaigning somewhere with Governor Fontaine,' she told Ryan.

'Who'd know where he was?'

'Ruth Livermore. But she's probably

with them. About the only thing we can do now is wait for another hour or so and then find out from somebody at campaign headquarters.'

At 7:35 A.M., Washington, D.C. time, the soft Southern voice of the switchboard operator, Mary Lu Hartley, told Clare that Mr. Slater was at the St. Regis Hotel in New York, and gave her the number. Clare thanked her and hung up. She had the operator connect her with the St. Regis. Ruth Livermore answered when Clare was put through to Slater's suite. She said that Mr. Slater was at a breakfast meeting with Governor Fontaine and some local fund raisers, and that she wasn't to disturb them unless it was an emergency. Was it? Clare said yes. Ruth told her to hang on.

Slater excused himself, followed Ruth back into his suite and picked up the receiver. 'Yes, Clare, what is it? Is something wrong?'

'Plenty,' she said. She then explained about the death of the Richters, adding that it appeared almost certain that the fire had been caused by the gray-haired man who worked for Senator Cassidy.

'Are you saying that you didn't get to talk to Richter at all?' Slater said, disappointed. 'Not even on the phone?'

'That's right. Ryan and I tried to call him last night, several times, but — '

'Then we're no closer to the truth about the photo than before?'

'Not as far as proving Cassidy's Falcon, no. But why else murder Richter — unless you know for sure that he can still identify you from a photograph?'

Slater digested this before asking: 'Is there another way of linking any of this directly to Cassidy?'

'There might be,' Clare said. 'Ryan thinks if you put a PI at Dulles and give him a description of the gray-haired man and have him tailed wherever he goes, it might lead us to Cassidy.'

'Why does Ryan think the gray-haired man will land at Dulles?'

'Just a guess. He's been one step ahead of us all the way, so it's pretty reasonable to assume that he left from Dulles on the flight the night before us. And if he did, then he probably bought a round-trip ticket which — '

'I agree,' Slater interrupted. He was anxious to return to his breakfast meeting. 'You give all the details and this man's description to Ruth, and I'll see everything's taken care of. Oh, and listen. Your flight stops in New York, right? I want you and Ryan to get off here, so Governor Fontaine can hear everything firsthand.'

'But, Karl,' Clare protested, 'our flight's booked through to Chicago.'

'So, you'll set up another flight out of New York later.' He handed the receiver to Ruth and hurried back to his meeting.

'Clare?' Ruth said into the phone. 'It's Ruth — you there?'

'I'm here,' Clare said. 'Guess we'll see you in New York.'

22

Due to the miracle of international time zones, Ryan and Clare arrived at Kennedy Airport in the evening of the same day they'd left Frankfurt. They had now been up for twenty-two hours straight. Both were groggy from jet lag and could feel no life in their leaden legs. Fortunately, Ruth Livermore had sent a limousine to pick them up. They sank wearily into the backseat and dozed while the car sped smoothly along the connecting expressways into the city.

At the St. Regis, on Fifth Avenue and Fifty-Fifth Street, a dignified uniformed doorman carried their bags inside and deposited them at the front desk. Ryan tipped him, while Clare verified their room reservations with the clerk. Ruth had handled everything with her usual efficiency. Soon they were registered in adjoining rooms and following the elderly bellhop across the quiet, plush, peach-colored lobby to the elevators.

Their rooms on the twelfth floor were decorated in the same subtle shades of peach and tastefully furnished like everything else in the lavishly elegant old hotel.

'I could get accustomed to this style of living very easily,' Clare said after the bellhop had left. 'I — ' She broke off as the phone rang. Ryan, stretched out on the bed in his own room, watched her through the open door that connected their rooms. He saw her speak briefly. Yawn. Yawn again and hang up. Sleepy as she was, he still found her very attractive.

'That was Ruth,' Clare said. 'Says she knows we must be exhausted, but Karl wants us to meet with the Governor as soon as possible.'

'Now soon enough?'

'Why not?' Clare yawned. 'That's if I don't fall asleep in the hall along the way.'

Governor Fontaine's suite was at the end of the hall. Two Secret Service agents ushered Ryan and Clare inside. Fontaine, his staff, Slater, and Ruth were discussing the speech the governor had to deliver at a labor union dinner that night. Slater told Ruth and the staff to leave, then introduced Ryan to the governor.

'A pleasure, Mr. Ryan.'

'Just Ryan, Governor.' Ryan admired the governor's strong handclasp. 'We'll save the 'Mr.' for when you become president.'

'Yes, well, uh — thank you, Ryan.' Governor Fontaine smiled, caught off guard by Ryan's remark. Slater at once rescued him.

'Excuse me, Henry. But since we're so pressed for time, why not let Clare brief you on everything that happened in Germany. That way you'll have facts to base your comments on.'

'Good idea, Karl.' Governor Fontaine sounded as tired as Ryan and Clare felt. 'Go ahead, Clare.'

'Thank you, sir. But if it's okay with you, I'll let Ryan explain. He invented the word *brief*.'

'Very well. Go ahead, Ryan.'

Ryan did so. Despite his weariness, he outlined everything briefly and accurately. When he was finished, Governor Fontaine crushed out his cigarette, sighed heavily, and shook his head.

'Incredible. Truly ... distressingly incredible.' Then, to Slater: 'But can we actually pin any of this on Senator Cassidy?'

'Unfortunately not. Not yet, anyway.'

'I guess that answers my next question,' Ryan said to Slater. 'You weren't able to tail the gray-haired man from Dulles?'

'Not so far, no.'

'So far?' Clare frowned. 'You saying he hasn't landed?'

'Not yet. At least the man I hired hasn't seen him.'

'I knew we should've followed him to Frankfurt,' Ryan grumbled.

'*If* that's where he went,' said Slater. 'Frankly, I have a hunch he either saw you in Hamburg or suspected he was being followed, and went to London — caught a flight from there to somewhere other than D.C.'

'I don't like it,' the governor said suddenly. 'All this foreign intrigue stuff, I mean. If any of our enemies ever discover what we're doing, they'll blast us higher than Watergate.'

'We can always drop the whole thing,'

253

Slater reminded. 'It's entirely up to you, Henry.'

'I'd sure like to ... ' Governor Fontaine lit another cigarette and inhaled deeply, flaring the end. 'The idea of accusing a man of Jim Cassidy's stature of being a Nazi spy bothers my integrity. It also borders on insanity, if you want to know the truth.'

The governor sighed wearily, exhaling smoke from his thin nostrils. 'We've gone this far, and all the evidence suggests the senator's involved, if not actually guilty, and, well, it would be foolish not to see it through to its inexorable conclusion. However,' he added, including everyone, 'not a word of this must leak out to the press before it's cleared by me. Not one single word, do you understand? Much as I want to be president — and there's nothing I want as much — I will not degrade myself in the eyes of my colleagues or the public and turn this — this fight into a mud-slinging smear campaign. Is that clear?'

'Perfectly,' Slater said. Then to Ryan and Clare: 'Agreed?'

They nodded. Clare fought not to yawn.

'Just one thing,' Ryan said to the governor. 'If by some freak chance we do prove that Cassidy was once a spy, what'll you do then?'

'What any loyal American would do — report it to the proper authorities.'

'And if they don't believe you? Or refuse to do anything about it?'

'Then I shall go right to the top — to the president himself.'

Ryan and Clare returned to their rooms. Before either had even started to undress, Clare's phone rang. It was Slater. He had just heard from the private investigator in Washington. The gray-haired man who limped had just landed at Dulles. He came in on a flight from Heathrow and was met by a tall, slender brunette in her late twenties who drove him into the capital. Unfortunately, due to street construction, the PI lost track of the woman's car near Thomas Circle. However, he was able to run a check on the car and discovered that it was registered to a Miss Nancy Shearer, Riverview Apartments, Taft Street, Mackey Hill.

'Is the PI going to check her out?' Clare asked.

'No. I've no idea where that would lead,' Slater said, 'and, as Governor Fontaine said, we don't want any premature leaks to the press.'

'Then it's up to us — Ryan and me, I mean — to see if there's any connection between the girl and Cassidy?'

'Exactly. The Governor and I are flying to Miami tomorrow. We'll be at the Fontainebleau. Call me there — day or night — as soon as you find out who this woman is.' Slater hung up.

Clare went to the door connecting her room to Ryan's and heard the water running in the shower.

It could wait, she realized. Nothing could change between now and tomorrow morning, anyway. So, quietly closing the door, she wearily undressed and went into the bathroom to take a long, luxurious hot shower.

23

It was surprisingly cold when Ryan and Clare landed at Washington National Airport. The early morning wind had Canadian teeth, and as they boarded the local shuttle bus they could feel it biting through their clothes.

'We should've s-stayed in Flensburg.' Clare shivered. 'It was only f-freezing there.'

They got off the shuttle bus near Franklin Square and hurried to the Porsche-Audi dealer. Clare greeted her car like a lost child. Then, after running it through a nearby car wash, they drove to Georgetown. On the way Ryan decided it was time to tell Clare that he thought her town house had been bugged. She was stunned and angry.

'But, how?' she demanded. 'When?'

'Who knows? Anytime. Main thing is, don't say anything about Falcon, Cassidy, Gray Hair, or this Nancy what's-her-name until we know for sure. Okay?'

'Okay.' She shivered, but not from the cold. 'Urgh. What an ugly thought. I mean people — strangers — listening to everything you say.'

There were few tourists about at that early wintry hour, and Clare found a parking space right outside her town house. Ryan carried the bags inside. As he did, he noticed a man sitting at the wheel of a blue sedan parked opposite. Ryan stored his image away for future reference. A small man. Early thirties. A stocking cap pulled low over reddish hair. Windbreaker collar pulled up to all but hide a small, pinched, cruel face.

'What's wrong?' Clare asked as Ryan moved to the upstairs bedroom window. He looked out without disturbing the curtains.

Ryan put his finger to his lips, signaled to remind her that the place might be bugged, and Said: 'I got a damn splinter in my thumb. Got any tweezers?'

'Just the ones I use on my eyebrows.'

'They'll do fine.'

Clare made a lot of noise opening one of the bags. Then she made more noise rummaging around inside. All the time she watched as Ryan moved quietly about the bedroom, looking under lamps, tables, chairs and behind the drapes, pictures, and the big antique mirror on top of the chest of drawers.

He found two bugging devices: one behind the bed headboard, the other under a table lamp. He left both where they were. Then he led Clare into the bathroom, closed the door, and turned on all the faucets, full force.

'I doubt if they put one in here,' he said quietly, 'but there're probably others downstairs.'

'What'll we do?' she asked. 'I mean, we can't live in the bathroom!'

'No need to. For now we'll just watch what we say — act like we don't know, nothing's going on.'

'All right.' Clare hesitated, anxiously biting her lower lip before adding: 'A few minutes ago, when you were at the window, did you see someone outside?'

Ryan didn't answer. 'I'll be more scared if you don't tell me,' she said.

Ryan shrugged. 'There's a guy across

the street in a blue Ford. Could be he's watching us, could be he's just sitting there. Hard to tell.'

'How'll we know?'

'When we leave here, see if he follows.'

'And if he does?'

'We'll ditch him. We don't want Cassidy or whoever's behind all this to know we've found out about Nancy Shearer — they'll just stash her somewhere. An' right now, remember, she's our only proof that Shining Jim's connected with Gray Hair.'

Clare was visibly shaken.

'Don't worry,' he said gently. Because of the noise of the running water, he had to speak into her ear. He smelled lilacs and for a moment forgot everything and was aware only of Clare's closeness. Moving his mouth across her cheek, he found her lips and kissed her hard. For a moment she was shocked. Then she responded, equally hard.

When they separated, Ryan looked into the face tilted up toward his, into the wide, sea-colored eyes. Neither spoke. Ryan then turned off the faucets, opened the door, and walked out.

Later, when they went outside, the man in the blue Ford sedan was gone. Ryan and Clare got into the Porsche and drove in the direction of Virginia. No one followed.

'Guess I was wrong,' Ryan said as they crossed the Key Bridge and entered Virginia. 'The guy wasn't watching us, after all.' They followed Lee Highway to the Mackey Hill district, got off, and drove along Scott Street to Taft. Between buildings the Potomac looked cold and gray in the steely morning light. Halfway along Taft was a small brown apartment complex: Riverview Villas. Ryan and Clare checked the mailbox. N. Shearer lived in Apt 203. They climbed to the second floor and rang the door bell, but no one answered. Ryan knocked, several times; there was still no answer. They decided to try the manager.

The elderly, balding manager lived on the ground floor. 'We got no vacancies,' he snapped before Ryan could speak. 'Didn't you see the sign?'

'We're not interested in moving in,' Clare said. 'We're with the IRS.' She flashed her billfold in the manager's startled face. 'Do you have a tenant named Nancy Shearer?'

'Yeah. Why? What's she done?'

'Nothing,' Ryan said, making it sound ominous. 'We're just interested in knowing where Miss Shearer works.'

'In the Capitol. But you guys must know that. She's — '

'Just answer the questions, please,' Clare told him. 'Now, what exactly does Miss Shearer do?'

'Well, I ain't sure what her title is,' the manager said, now anxious to be helpful, 'but she works in Senator Cassidy's campaign office.'

'You sure about that?' Ryan said.

'Real sure. Nancy's always tryin' to sell me a bill of goods on Senator Cassidy — '

'One other thing,' Ryan interrupted. 'Does Miss Shearer know a man with gray hair who limps? A man in his forties?'

The manager thought a moment. Then he shrugged his rounded shoulders. 'If she does, he don't come around here.'

'Thank you,' Clare said. 'We appreciate your cooperation.'

'Anytime,' the manager said ingratiatingly. 'Always glad to help you guys out.' He watched them walk out through the lobby, muttered, 'Nosy bastards,' and slammed his door shut.

'What was that you showed him?' Ryan asked Clare as they drove back to the capital.

'My research card for the National Archives.' Clare smiled. 'It looks impressive and I figured once I said IRS he wouldn't be looking anyway. At least, I know I wouldn't be.'

They drove on. Ryan kept checking the rearview mirror. No one was following, or, if they were, he couldn't detect them.

Presently, Clare said, 'Well, I guess there's no doubt now that Cassidy's our man.'

'Sure looks that way.'

'Do you think there's any point in trying to question the girl?'

'No. She'd only deny everything. Besides, as I said before, then Cassidy would know we're on to her and stash her somewhere — cut off our only link with Gray Hair . . . No,' Ryan said after a pause, 'the best thing we can do is, go to where she works an' try to follow her . . . keep following her and hope she leads us to either Cassidy or Gray Hair.'

'What if it's Gray Hair?'

'Then we'll tail him around the clock. See exactly what his connection with Cassidy is. When we know that, maybe we can lean on him a little — make him spill his guts about Cassidy. Then we're home free. If your Governor Fontaine's a man of his word, that is.'

'What d'you mean?'

'If he'll take the truth to the top — like he promised.'

'He will. I'd bet my life on it.'

★ ★ ★

It was eleven forty-five when Ryan parked on 16th Street across from Senator Cassidy's campaign headquarters. The wind had died down. But it was still cold enough to see the breath of the volunteer workers emerging from the ground-floor offices for an early lunch.

Leaving Clare in the car, Ryan entered

the spacious suite that was filled with campaign paraphernalia and paused before the reception desk. It was vacant. Ryan looked around him. None of the youthful, industrious campaign workers resembled Slater's description of Nancy Shearer.

'Can I help you?' Ryan turned. Smiling up at him was a bearded youth in rumpled clothes. He wore rimless glasses and smelled of coffee and cigarettes.

'I'm looking for Nancy Shearer,' Ryan said.

The youth looked at a desk in the corner, saw it was empty, and said, 'Hold on,' then shouted to the redhead typing beside Nancy's desk: 'Hey, Vera — where's Nance?'

'Lunch. Left 'bout twenty minutes ago.'

'Any idea where she went?' Ryan asked.

'Barney's, probably. Coffee shop on the corner.'

'I'll try there,' Ryan said, adding, 'Tall, slender, dark hair, right?'

The youth nodded and hurried away. Ryan left the office, crossed the street and joined Clare in the Porsche. 'She's gone to lunch,' he explained. 'May as well wait

265

till she gets back.'

Shortly, they heard a siren approaching. Moments later a paramedic ambulance sped past. They watched it weave in and out of stopped traffic. When it reached the corner, it braked hard, and skidded to a stop. Ryan got an uneasy feeling. 'C'mon,' he said suddenly. He got out of the car, waited for Clare to join him, and both of them hurried to the corner.

They were too late. Nancy Shearer was already dead. Ryan and Clare squeezed through the small, shocked crowd and saw the two young paramedics lifting the crushed, bleeding corpse into the ambulance. A Cassidy campaign button was pinned to her coat lapel. Campaign handbills were scattered over the street. Ryan heard a witness telling one of the paramedics that he'd seen the accident through the coffee shop window. The girl had been hit as she stepped off the sidewalk by a speeding car. 'She never had no chance,' he added grimly. 'This gray-haired guy who was driving didn't even try to swerve aside. I mean, hell, it almost looked like he done it deliberately.'

Ryan and Clare didn't talk during the drive to Georgetown.

Ryan realized as he turned onto Clare's now familiar tree-lined street and began looking for a parking space that someone at Cassidy's campaign headquarters had heard him inquiring about Nancy and, acting upon Cassidy's prior orders, had notified Gray Hair, who'd then killed her.

He found a space near the corner and parked. As Clare looked at him questioningly, he said gently, 'Maybe you should find yourself another place to stay for a while — least, till after the election?'

'No way,' she said. 'I'm scared sick, but nobody's going to drive me out of my own damn home.'

He said no more. As they walked to her town house, he saw that all the cars parked on both sides of the street were empty. He felt relieved, and wished there was something he could say or do to make her feel better.

But there wasn't. Fear was something you just had to live with, and accept. And do the best you could until it went away. And with Clare's kind of guts, Ryan figured that wouldn't take too long.

They reached the front door. Clare opened it with her key and entered ahead of Ryan. Then, a step inside the hall, she stopped — so abruptly that Ryan bumped into her.

'What's wrong?' he asked. When she didn't answer, or move, Ryan stepped around her.

Sitting in a living room chair beside the fireplace was a huge, balding man with tattoos on the backs of his hands. He wore a black suit that fitted too tightly, a white shirt with a black string tie, and highly polished black shoes. His left hand clasped an old Bible; the right, the one tattooed 'MJB,' a .38 revolver that was aimed at Clare.

'Come in,' Dean Callum ordered, rising. 'And shut the door behind you.'

24

Ryan obeyed Callum and closed the door. He'd already noticed the big man's tattoos, and guessed this must be the Dean Callum mentioned by the archivist. He also noticed Callum's dark, sunken eyes.

'Sit down,' Callum ordered. 'And do not try anything stupid,' he told Ryan. 'I am not a man of violence, but I'll do whatever I must to accomplish the Lord's bidding.'

'And just what is that?' Ryan said as he and Clare sat.

'That's 'tween the Lord and me.' Callum tucked the Bible away, leaned against the oaken mantelpiece, and trained the gun on Ryan. 'Now, why're you looking for the spy who killed Mary Jo Buffram?'

Ryan felt Clare trembling slightly beside him on the couch. He leaned back, the movement slow and easy so as not to alarm Callum, and casually put his arm about Clare's shoulders. Then: 'Who says we are?'

'I do.' Callum gestured toward the upstairs bedrooms. 'It's useless to deny it — either of you — because I've already read the documents you have hidden away. So, unless you want me to use this' — he wagged the gun — 'on the girl, you'd better tell me why you're after Falcon.'

Ryan realized that anything said in Clare's town house, due to 'bugs,' might be overheard. And since he didn't want whoever was listening to hear what he had to tell Callum, Ryan said calmly: 'If you'll let me smoke, I'll tell you.'

Callum hesitated, stared at Ryan with mad, distrustful eyes. Then he nodded, 'Go ahead,' and kept the gun trained on Ryan.

Ryan, moving very slowly, found pencil and paper in his jacket and Wrote something. He held the pad up, so Callum could read the message: 'This place is bugged. Talk outside.'

'Damn,' he said to Clare. 'I've left my

cigarettes in your car.' Then to Callum: 'Okay if I get 'em?' As he said 'I,' he motioned to show that he meant all of them.

Callum hesitated, still suspicious, then got up. 'We'll all get them,' he said. 'But I warn you, if this is a trick, I'll shoot you down in the street. Both of you!'

Outside, on the sidewalk, Callum indicated a brown station wagon across the street and said they would talk in there. He kept them both in front of him, gun in his coat pocket, and insisted that Clare sit in front and Ryan sit behind. Then Callum got in beside Clare, trained the gun on her, and said, 'Who would want to listen in on your conversation?'

'I've no idea,' she said. She tried hard not to show how frightened she was. 'For all I know, Mr. Callum, it might be you.'

Callum frowned, surprised. 'How do you know my name?'

Then, as neither of them answered: 'There's something you should know. My life means nothing to me. Nor do yours. If you don't answer my questions, I won't hesitate to kill you.'

'We saw your name on an information questionnaire,' Clare said, not wanting to get the archivist in trouble, 'at the Navy Yards.'

Dean Callum nodded, satisfied.

Ryan said, 'Why were *you* interested in that action report?'

'That's 'tween the Lord and me. Now, for the last time, why're you looking for Falcon?'

When they hesitated, Callum pushed the gun against Clare's side. She shut her eyes. Ryan realized they could hold back no longer. He said quickly, 'Put the gun away, Callum. I'll tell you all you want to know.'

'Then, tell me.'

'We're looking for Falcon,' Ryan said, 'because we think we know who he is.'

'Who?'

'Senator Cassidy.'

Callum flared. His eyes blazed in their sunken sockets. 'The Lord Christ will not tolerate lies!' he boomed.

'We're not lying,' Ryan said. 'You got to believe that! Hell, you've seen all the evidence we got — '

'I also know you went to Flensburg,' Callum interrupted. 'Spoke to *Kapitan* Richter. He would've told you that Falcon was not James Cassidy.'

'Richter told us nothing,' Ryan said. 'He and his wife were dead — killed in a fire before we could talk.'

Callum frowned, surprised. 'This wouldn't be hard to verify,' he warned, 'if you're lying.'

'Go ahead. Verify all you want. It won't bring back the Richters.'

For a long moment Dean Callum digested what Ryan had said. Then he removed the gun from Clare's side and tucked it in his pocket. But he kept his hand on it. And as Clare sagged with relief, he said, 'For the moment, I believe you. Now, you must believe me: the spy who killed Mary Jo Buffram, the man known as Falcon, is not Senator Cassidy.'

'H-How do you know?' Clare asked, finding her voice.

'Because Ernst Richter was given a picture of Falcon during the war, and he described to me what the man looked like.'

'We *have* that picture,' Ryan said. 'If you went through the U-boat documents, like you said, you must've seen it.'

'I did,' Callum said. 'But that is not the man *Kapitan* Richter described.'

'Then he lied to you,' Ryan said. ''cause a neighbor said Richter identified Falcon for the man who we think killed him. And also, we took that goddamn picture from the captain's security box itself!'

'There is no need for profanity,' Callum chided. Some of the religious fire had left his eyes. 'The Lord has given us sufficient words without our having to use His name in vain.'

'You can talk about the Lord while holding a gun?' Clare said, fear making her angry.

'Violence begets violence,' Callum said. He looked at Ryan, asking: 'For what purpose would Richter lie?'

'I don't know. Maybe if I'd talked to the guy myself, I could tell you.'

'I spoke to the good captain, at some length, and I don't believe he did lie.'

'One reason,' put in Clare, 'could've

been because Richter was still a hard-core Nazi and didn't want to betray Falcon's cover.'

'She's got a point,' Ryan said. 'Hell, you know how some of those old-timers are.'

Callum digested Ryan's words carefully. 'It's true,' he admitted, 'the *Kapitan* was a man of great pride and arrogance.'

'There's your answer, then,' Ryan said. 'Man of his mentality wouldn't identify a Nazi spy in Cassidy's position, now, would he?'

Callum didn't answer. He was obviously undecided and confused.

Ryan took advantage of it and said: 'Now you know our reason for going after Falcon — how about telling us yours?'

Callum shook his head. 'Only the Lord knows my mission,' he said. The mad fire returned to his eyes as he added: 'I do not believe that *Kapitan* Richter lied.'

'But — '

'I also believe you're trying to deceive me.'

'In what way?'

'All ways. No!' Callum boomed as

275

Ryan started to protest. 'I'll not listen to any more lies. First, you tell me that Kapitan Richter identified Falcon to a man who later killed him, and then you try to make me believe that he lied to me about the same thing. Well, it will not work. The Lord Jesus will not allow His disciple to be deceived. He has chosen me to deliver His vengeance and will not permit anything to stand in my way!'

'Vengeance for what?' Ryan said, losing his temper. 'Who the hell are you, anyway?'

Callum took the Bible from his pocket. Held it reverently. Spoke as if from the pulpit. 'Go now,' he told them. 'Get from my vehicle — both of you!'

Then, as Ryan and Clare started to get out: 'I warn you. If you don't stop interfering in this, I'll kill you as surely as they killed Him upon the cross.' He started the station wagon, waited for them to close the doors, and drove away.

Ryan put his arm about Clare. 'You okay?'

She nodded, her face still drained of color, her legs shaky.

'Let's get off the street,' he said. He started to lead her toward her town house, then stopped and said: 'Do you know somewhere we can talk? Someplace only you and me will be listening?'

'There's a bar just around the corner.'

They walked to the corner and entered a small bar that looked like an English pub: oaken beams, brass fittings, and a fire blazing in an open hearth. Ryan and Clare sat in a red leather booth by one of the stained-glass windows and ordered drinks from a plump-faced woman dressed like an English barmaid.

For a long time Clare seemed content to sip her double brandy and say nothing. Suddenly she said, 'What do you think Callum's connection with all this is?'

'I don't know. I've been trying to think. He mentioned vengeance, so maybe he lost his dad or brother at sea during the war and blames Falcon for it.'

'Makes sense.' She shivered, involuntarily. 'Frightening how much he knew about us, I mean.'

'HQ must've had someone following us. Must've been a real pro, too.'

'But how'd Callum know about us in the first place? That's what beats me. I mean, which of the people we've talked to, beginning, say, with that Coast Guard guy — what was his name?'

'Maynard.'

'Right. Beginning with him, which person along the way is the link to Dean Callum?' Before Ryan could reply, she added: 'Could Callum be the man on the phone who threatened us?'

'Uh-uh. No way. Their voices are nothing alike. Besides, that was Gray Hair. I'm sure of it . . . As for who put Callum on to us,' Ryan continued after a pause, 'I've been trying to hammer that one out ever since I saw him sitting in your living room, holding that gun on you. From Cassidy down, everybody's running scared. That's what makes this whole mess so goddamn dangerous.' He motioned to the waitress for another round. Then: 'I've been worrying some about that.'

'Go on.'

'Well, way it seems to me is — if we're going to nail Cassidy, *and* stay alive, we've got to become the aggressors.'

'Sounds like you have a plan.'

'Sort of.'

'What the hell's that supposed to mean?'

'Well . . . it's more like a hunch than a plan.'

'That's good enough for me.'

'Okay,' he said. 'The plan's this: You call Avery Brickland and set up that lunch he's so hot to have with you. Make it some off-the-track restaurant — you know, not one of the usual political watering holes — and I'll take your place.'

'And then what?'

'I'll try to get Avery to help us. Close as he is to Cassidy, he's probably the only one — other than Gray Hair, maybe — who can really sink Shining Jim.'

'Fair enough.'

'Questions?'

'Only one: Why should Avery Brickland help you? I mean, are you two friends or something?'

'Like I said: a hunch.'

'Which is based on what?'

'Patience,' Ryan said. 'I'll explain later.'

Frustrated, she chewed on her lip and then nodded. 'Okay. I'll go along with you — for now.'

'Thanks.'

'But I have to tell you, I resent the fact that you won't tell me what your hunch is. I thought we had no secrets.'

'We don't. It's just that if the hunch doesn't pay off I'll have egg on my face and I'm not anxious to have you see that. Now, will you call Avery — set up the luncheon?'

'Yes. When do you want me to make it for?'

'Tomorrow, if it's possible. Time's not exactly on our side.'

'True. Election's getting closer every day.'

Ryan wasn't thinking about the election. He was worried that Gray Hair's next target would be Clare or himself. And with them out of the way, and Fontaine and Slater fighting for their political lives, Cassidy would be in the White House before anyone could stop him. And the thought of a Nazi — even a former Nazi — at the helm of America sent an ugly chill through Ryan.

'Since we know your place is bugged,' he said, 'why don't you call Avery from here?'

Clare obliged. She was gone only a few minutes. When she returned and slid into the booth beside Ryan, she seemed to have gotten over her resentment and was smiling. 'All set,' she said. 'Noon tomorrow at *Jour et Nuit*. That's right here in Georgetown. I thought the closer to my place the safer it'd be for you.'

They finished their drinks. The bartender threw more logs on the fire. They blazed and crackled. Ryan and Clare could feel the heat on their faces. She suggested they return to her house. As they walked to the door, her thoughts made her smile. 'You know, Avery's going to be really disappointed when I don't show tomorrow.'

'He's gonna be more than disappointed,' Ryan said, visualizing Avery's shocked expression when they met, 'when he hears what I got to tell him.'

Outside, it was dusk: a violet-gray world of yellow-orbed streetlights. Ryan, anticipating trouble, kept close to Clare as they walked to her town house. And as they reached her front door, he paused long enough to be sure no one was visibly keeping them under surveillance. Then he told Clare that once they were inside, they would continue to act as if they didn't know the place was bugged. 'It might give us a few more days' breathing time, especially if we can feed them a little bait. You know, something that'll keep them on the hook. Something intriguing enough so that, until they know the answer, it will stop Gray Hair or whoever from trying to kill us.'

Clare had trouble falling asleep that night. As she lay there in bed in the dark, she was torn between feeling grateful that Ryan was asleep in the next room and hoping that having political people she knew seeing them apparently living together wouldn't somehow damage her chances of becoming press secretary.

She reminded herself that the move had been sanctioned — no, suggested — by Karl in the first place. But the governor might feel later — especially if his 'friends on The Hill' chose to pressure him not to select a woman by pointing out how 'indiscreet' Clare was with her love life — well, that pressure might be the difference between her getting and losing the job.

At the same time she couldn't help admitting that she genuinely liked having Ryan around. Under different circumstances, she had to admit that she'd probably feel quite strongly about him. But circumstances weren't different. And if by some freak chance Cassidy didn't become president, then Governor Fontaine was a sure bet for the White House and she'd be made press secretary!

That's if you don't end up like Nancy Shearer, a voice suddenly said in her mind.

25

At noon the next day Ryan entered the famous old Georgetown town house in which the *Jour et Nuit* restaurant was located and asked the maitre d' for Senator Brickland's table.

The maître d', who'd been expecting a lady, hid his surprise with admirable aplomb. He bowed slightly and asked Ryan please to follow him. He then led Ryan through the old, dignified dining room with its stone fireplace and white linen tablecloths, out onto a small, sheltered terrace where Avery Brickland sat with a tumbler of bourbon before him, eagerly awaiting Clare at a secluded corner table.

'My God,' Avery breathed, stunned, after Ryan sat down, 'is — is that really you, Kyle?'

'It's me, Ave . . . ' Ryan looked at his foster brother and felt the years of separation slip away. 'Been a while, huh?'

Avery still couldn't believe it. He sat there staring at Ryan, as if doubting his eyes. Then he leaned forward and gripped Ryan's forearm. Still shocked, he said, 'I — I just can't believe it. I mean . . . out of nowhere . . . all these years . . . never a word. Jesus, I thought you were dead!'

'I can't blame you for that,' Ryan said. He realized that too much alcohol had turned Avery's once-lean face fleshy. 'Been times — many times — over the years when I thought I was dead myself.'

'You could've at least kept in touch,' Avery said. 'You promised you would, and, well, God damn it, Kyle, I am your brother!'

'I know that, Ave. But, in case you've forgotten, I'm wanted for murder — a murder you committed and I took the blame for — '

'I know, I know — '

'And one little slip — by you or by anyone who knew where I was — could put me on the wrong end of a lethal injection.'

'I never would have let that happen,' Avery protested. 'You know that.'

Ryan didn't say anything.

'You believe that, don't you?'

'I'd like to.'

Avery went white and said angrily: 'Dammit, it was your idea to take the fall in the first place.'

'True. And I've never regretted it.'

'Well, I have,' Avery said, genuinely distressed. 'Daily — over the years. In fact it's eaten me up so badly I can't get through a day without this.' He held up the glass of bourbon and drained it.

'That's your choice, not mine.'

Avery gave an ugly laugh. 'Some choice! Jesus, Kyle, we both know I'm a gutless wonder. Why do you think my father fostered you in the first place — he hoped some of your guts and integrity might rub off onto me. When it didn't, he took it out on me rather than accept the fact that the great mighty Governor Brickland fucked up!'

'Everybody has faults,' Ryan said.

''Fault'? Is that what you call what he did to me?' Before Ryan could answer, Avery added: 'In other words, using me, his own son, as a whipping boy — literally

'— is okay with you?'

'You know better than that. I did everything I could to get him off your back.'

'Too bad it wasn't enough.' Avery signaled to the waiter to bring over another drink. 'Maybe then I wouldn't have become a lush.'

Ryan grimly studied his foster brother for a moment before saying: 'I'd say you got your revenge.'

Avery gave a disgusted grunt. 'You still think I deliberately pushed him down the stairs, don't you?'

'If I didn't, Ave, ask yourself: would I have taken off before the police and the coroner arrived?'

'I told you he fell.'

'After you hit him.'

'He was beating on me. I was just trying to defend myself.'

'Right.'

Avery said angrily: 'I didn't ask you to take off, or to be a fall guy.'

'Didn't have to. Knowing me like you did, you knew what I'd do almost before I knew myself.'

Avery reddened, hating himself at that moment. 'I never said you did it — not even when the detectives made me go over and over my story.'

The waiter came with Avery's drink. 'And for you, sir?' he asked Ryan.

'Nothing, thanks.' He waited for the waiter to leave before saying: 'Look, I didn't come to rehash the past. I did what I did for the Old Man, for all the years of kindness he showed me.'

'Yeah. You were always great at being a hero.' Avery gulped half of his bourbon, sighed deeply, and then looked toward the door.

'Clare Winslow isn't coming, Senator.'

Avery started to look surprised, recovered beautifully, and said cautiously, 'How do you know about Miss Winslow — this luncheon?'

'It's a long story,' Ryan said. 'So sit back and enjoy your drink, brother mine, while I try to explain it to you.'

'I'm all ears,' Avery said. He finished his drink and again signaled to the waiter to bring another.

As briefly as he could Ryan explained

that he and Clare were friends and that he'd asked her to set up this luncheon so he and Avery could talk about Senator Cassidy. 'I know you and he are close friends, but I have to know how close.'

'He trusts me . . . confides in me, if that's what you want to know?'

'Fair enough.' Ryan studied his brother. He'd lain awake all night trying to prepare himself for this meeting with Avery. The multitude of questions he'd asked himself, the answers he'd given, and the endless variations on both had churned unceasingly through his mind until they'd become a confusing blur and he'd had to stop — erase everything — and start afresh; accept that it all came down to two simple, basic facts: He needed Avery's help, and he had to know if he could trust him. In order to accomplish the latter, he knew he'd have to test his foster brother, then use his own judgment as to whether Avery still felt some loyalty toward him and, more importantly, loved his country enough to risk sacrificing his political career.

'So go ahead,' Avery said impatiently.

'What is it you want from me?'

'I need to know if I can trust four men,' Ryan said. 'They say you'll vouch for them, and, well, before I do business with them, I got to know if they're trustworthy.'

'Name them — and unless some kind of national security's involved, I'll tell you all I know about them.'

'Good. How about . . . Wells Beaman?'

'Wells Beaman?' Avery repeated the name slowly, thoughtfully, frowning all the time. 'Name doesn't sound familiar. You sure he said I know him?'

'Yeah. Says he spoke to you a couple of weeks ago.'

'About what? D'you know?'

'Uh-uh. Said it was private.' Ryan watched Avery's eyes every second as he added: 'He's editor of *The Carteret Observer* — a local paper in Morehead City, North Carolina — if that's any help.'

Avery frowned, genuinely puzzled. 'Sorry,' he said. 'The guy must have me mistaken for someone else. I swear I've never heard of him.'

Ryan shrugged, as if accepting that,

and said: 'What about a druggist named T. S. Murchinson . . . or a great big guy in his sixties, Dean Callum, who talks and dresses like a reverend?'

Avery started to laugh, checked himself, then studied Ryan, uncertain, as he said, 'Is this some kind of gag? I mean, so help me, Kyle, I've never heard of either of them.'

'It's no gag,' Ryan said tersely.

'Then, something crazy's going on . . . because, well, unless they're using aliases, I haven't spoken to any of those men.'

'They're obviously liars, then.'

'Sure sounds like it,' Avery said, adding, 'You know what's probably happened is, they used my name to help convince you to trust them, never thinking, of course, that you'd actually go to the trouble of checking their story out with me — personally.'

'Possible.'

'Probable's more like it. Assholes! You ought to nail their butts to the wall. By the way, now you've got me curious. Who's the fourth guy?'

Ryan studied Avery briefly, sensed he'd

been telling the truth, and decided it was time to trust him. Said quietly: 'You.'

'Me?' Avery sat up, shocked. 'What the hell're you talking about?'

'Just this,' said Ryan. 'You're one of the four men I've got to trust. In fact, Ave, you're the *only* one I can trust.'

'I don't get it.' Avery finished his drink, thoroughly confused. 'Trust me to do what?'

'I'll explain that later. First, there's something else I got to tell you . . . ' Before Avery could interrupt, Ryan told him everything that he and Clare had uncovered about Cassidy, Falcon, Mary Jo Buffram, Gray Hair, Richter — and anyone else who was connected to what he and Clare now collectively called the 'Falcon Conspiracy.' He also told Avery that he, Kyle, was the 'Mr. Ryan' whom Clare had asked Avery to persuade Cassidy to meet with in Wilmington; that the meeting had taken place; and that Clare had accompanied him. Cassidy had naturally denied their accusations. But then had sent his man, Gray Hair, to first buy the picture, and then, when that had failed, later to try to silence them permanently. And so on . . .

Avery, after ordering another bourbon, listened without any interruption. But his expression, as each piece of the story unfolded, ranged from shock to disbelief to incredulous dismay.

'Okay,' Ryan said when he'd finished. 'That's it, Senator. The whole nine yards.'

Avery tried to speak, drank some bourbon to wet the dryness constricting his throat, then said tensely: 'It — it isn't true. I don't care how bad it looks or — or how much goddamn proof you *think* you've got against Jim Cassidy. It just isn't true. He's as fine and honorable a man as there is in the whole Senate, on all of Capitol Hill, for that matter. And if he says he's innocent — that there's some kind of mix-up, however inexplicable — I believe him. What's more, Kyle, for the sake of this country — no, this entire goddamn world — you and Clare better believe him, too, and stop this whole, inane madness!'

'Sorry,' Ryan said softly. 'I can't do that, Ave.'

'But you've got to, Kyle! You've just *got* to! I mean, Jesus bloody Christ, you're trying to crucify an innocent man!'

That's only your opinion, pal. Clare and I think differently. Course,' Ryan added quickly, 'if you want to try to help *us* prove Cassidy's innocent, well, we might be willing to wait a few more days before turning everything over to the president.'

'How the hell am I supposed to do that?' Avery demanded.

'Get me Cassidy's service records. Coast Guard and Naval Intelligence, both.'

'*What?*'

'Don't 'what' me, Ave. Just do it.'

'But World War Two was forty years ago.'

'I don't care if it was *a hundred* years ago. The only way Clare and I will believe Cassidy is innocent — isn't Falcon — is if you can show me proof positive that he was somewhere else at the time of Mary Jo's murder an' the sinking of that U-boat. Otherwise' — Ryan shrugged — 'everything goes to the president.'

Avery paled, sagged in his chair, and Stared at Ryan like a trapped animal.

'You know what you're asking me to do, don't you?' he said finally. 'Betray my closest friend and the man I most respect.'

'Wrong,' Ryan said. 'All I'm asking you to do is — prove Cassidy's innocent. Hell, if he's all you say he is, then you got nothing to worry about. And if he isn't, well . . . '

Avery wasn't listening. 'I guess you know what something like this could do to my political career — if Jim finds out what I've done and goes on to become president, I mean? Shit, I couldn't run for office on an iceberg!'

'That's probably true,' Ryan agreed. 'But, look at it this way: If you prove Cassidy isn't a spy, you've given this country maybe a great president. And if it turns out that he *is* Falcon, you've stopped a potential Hitler from getting into the White House. I mean, what the hell? Either way, you're an instant winner.'

'Suddenly,' Avery said gloomily, 'that doesn't seem too goddamn important.'

'Reluctant heroes,' Ryan said without a trace of sarcasm. 'They're the best kind.'

26

Clare was elated that Avery had agreed to help, but suspicious of his motives. Unaware that Ryan was Avery's foster brother, she couldn't make herself believe that Avery would do anything that might alienate Senator Cassidy. That evening, while fixing dinner in the kitchen that earlier she and Ryan had made sure was 'clean of bugs,' she suggested that maybe if she knew how they met, or how well they knew each other, it would make her less suspicious.

Ryan was no help. 'Let's just say we were real tight once, and let it go at that. I'm sorry. Right now, that's all I can tell you.'

He watched her dicing the vegetables, trying to think of something to say. Then, as it hit him: 'You know, we've still got to think of some way to bait these guys — keep them guessing. Otherwise, pretty soon we're going to find ourselves targets again . . . ' He paused as the phone on the kitchen wall rang.

Clare answered it. It was Karl Slater. He was still in New York with Governor Fontaine. 'I just picked up your message from the hotel desk saying you called earlier. Anything special to report?' he asked.

'Plenty,' she said. She then explained about Dean Callum, Gray Hair, and Nancy Shearer's fatal 'accident,' and, missing Ryan's gesture, about his meeting with Senator Brickland. It was out before she realized, and even as she spoke she knew she'd made a mistake. Slater's long pause and Ryan's scowl only further convinced her that she'd blown it. She said hastily, 'In case you don't think that was too smart, Karl, you should know that Ryan knows Avery, and we both thought that since Cassidy knows what we're doing, anyway — and has already tried to have us killed — what difference does it make? After all, if, as Ryan believes, Avery isn't in on all this, his help could be invaluable. And if he is, well, like I say, we're not telling them anything they don't already know.'

'I suppose you're right,' Slater said in a voice that indicated he felt she was wrong. 'However, I did instruct you to clear everything with me first, so, in future, kindly do just that. Understood?'

'Understood.'

Slater thought a moment. Then: 'When is Senator Brickland supposed to contact you again?'

'Soon as he has all the info on Cassidy.'

'Did he give you any inkling as to when that might be?'

'No. But he knows we need it as soon as possible. With November eleventh closing in on us, every day counts.'

'Precisely,' Slater said. His enunciation of each word was so crisp and exact that it made most people who dealt with him inarticulate, some even inadequate, and, as a result, they did more listening than talking. This suited Karl Slater's martinet's ego beautifully. 'Well,' he continued, 'we shall just have to wait and see how Senator Brickland reacts. I, for one, think it was a tactical blunder to try to enlist his services, but . . . '

You had to say that, didn't you? Clare thought. She realized then that she was aiming her hurt and anger against Ryan at her boss, and mentally chiding herself, she heard Slater say, ' . . . meanwhile, until you hear from the senator, I want you and Ryan to stay put. I mean that, Clare. Other than a quick run to the market, you're not to venture outside the front door. Not for a moment. Understood?'

'Understood.'

'And call me the instant you hear from Senator Brickland.'

'Of course. Anything else?'

'Not if you've told me everything, no.'

'I have.'

'Very well, then. Good-bye.' He hung up before she could reply.

Clare replaced her own receiver, looked at Ryan, and shrugged.

'Sorry. I wasn't thinking.'

'Forget it,' Ryan said. 'No real harm done.'

'You sure? I mean, if I've put you in any kind of danger . . . '

'No. Course not. No danger at all. It's just that right now, the fewer people who know Avery an' I are friends, the better.' He returned to the crossword puzzle he was doing and hoped that Karl Slater wouldn't be intrigued to know how a low-profile marine salvage diver and a powerful United States senator were friends, and decide to investigate.

When Senator Avery Brickland said good-bye to Ryan outside the restaurant, he automatically looked around to see if anyone had recognized him. It was a nervous habit, acquired during his early months as a senator for two reasons: First, he loved the idea of his own importance and enjoyed catching people looking at him; and, second, he loved the company of beautiful young women and, since he was married and wanted to stay married, he needed to know just *who* those people looking at him were.

Today, however, even as he looked around he remembered that his luncheon had been with Kyle. He relaxed as he tipped the valet parking attendant who whisked up a taxi, got in, and told the driver to take him to the Senate.

During the ride Avery took several

deep breaths of the cool fresh air rushing in through the open window and tried to rid himself of the alcohol that was muddling his mind. He'd drunk too much at lunch. Besides, he still hadn't really gotten over the shock of seeing his foster brother again, and needed a clear head if he was going to figure out what his best middle-of-the-road position was in regard to Kyle's ultimatum.

The most important thing, he realized, was to make absolutely sure that Jim Cassidy never found out about his conversation with Kyle. He'd worked too goddamn hard, and had spent too much time 'stroking' Cassidy, to risk letting anything destroy their friendship now. Especially something as crazy as believing that Cassidy was a former Nazi spy! Just a little while longer and he'd have a heavyweight buddy sitting in the Oval Office. And from then on Senator Avery Brickland's status on The Hill would be firmly established. Not only that, he knew, but the innumerable favors and political sops that would come his way were too mind-boggling even to imagine.

Of course, he had no intention of helping Kyle. He'd decided that even before they had left the restaurant. Hell, even if it were true about Cassidy — and Avery knew goddamn well it wasn't — he still wouldn't have done anything. Nothing could stop the Cassidy political steamroller. It was destined to roll right down Pennsylvania Avenue to 1600, crushing all opposition, and anyone who thought differently didn't know anything about politics.

Unfortunately, though, it wasn't going to be that simple for him. He couldn't just ignore or avoid Kyle; his foster brother was too determined for that. And so, apparently, was Clare Winslow. Strange, Avery thought, he hadn't figured her for an idealist. Or a troublemaker. Neither lasted too long in the capital, and from everything he knew about her, she had every intention of staying. Rumor had it, in fact, that that cold-assed son of a bitch Karl Slater had persuaded Fontaine to make Clare the White House press secretary. Empty promises, of course, since Fontaine had little chance of becoming president.

But, still, it did show that Clare was capable, not just passing through.

It must have been Kyle's influence, Avery reasoned, that had made Clare change. Because if ever someone was perfectly suited to be an idealist, it was Kyle. It was his specialty. God, how he'd grown to hate his foster brother for his *beau geste*.

His mind returned to the past — to the night it happened. The sight of the Old Man lying in a crumpled heap, head twisted in an unnatural angle, at the bottom of the stairs had haunted Avery ever since. The guilt pains that followed had not lessened as the years passed, but increased. Now they were almost a part of him, as familiar as his own skin. Funny thing was he had pushed his father backward down the stairs, but he'd only meant to hurt him, maybe even cripple him so that he was bedridden. That way, Avery could escape the tongue-lashings and whippings that he faced on a daily basis.

But he'd never intended to kill him — at least, not consciously.

For a while drinking gave him some

peace. But gradually, drunk or sober, it made no difference — the nightmare continued unceasingly, driving him at times to the point of insanity.

Then Diana Cahill had entered his life. Diana's father, Brigadier General Alexander Cahill, had bought the ranch adjoining theirs. The retired general was a short, quiet, stern-faced man of sixty-four who'd been a widower for ten years. He never spoke of his dead wife, and lavished all his affection on his only child, Diana. She was not a particularly attractive girl, although she had beautiful, thick, dark gold hair, a boyishly slim body, and a farm freshness that made her appealing. But she knew how to laugh and exuded the kind of warmth and understanding that Avery needed and hadn't experienced since his mother died. The attraction between them was immediate and equally responsive, and they were married in a little Wyoming church within three months of the day the Cahills had moved in.

For the next few years Avery and Diana were as happy as any two human beings have a right to be. With Diana his constant companion and biggest booster, Avery stopped drinking, buried his guilt, and entered politics. He was an instant success! Helped by his late father's reputation and his own war-hero image, Avery shot into local prominence as Wyoming's youngest congressman. Then, when his term expired, he became nationally known by his surprising landslide victory over the incumbent senator, Tom Waverly.

Meanwhile, adding to their happiness, three children were born. Pudgy Alex came first; blond, brown-eyed Melanie next; and last, delicate, porcelain-skinned Caroline, named after Avery's gentle, beloved mother.

Life, it seemed, had nothing but smiles for the Bricklands. Then, tragically, fate's unavoidable 'balancing' occurred. First, Diana's father suffered a severe stroke that overnight turned him into a barely functioning vegetable and, a year later, mercifully took his life; then, two months later, Diana's car overturned, killing Caroline and crippling Alex so badly that he would always walk with a limp.

Diana blamed herself for the accident, although in truth it had been caused by a freak blowout on an icy highway, and retreated within herself. Years of psychiatry followed. Diana gradually came out of herself enough to answer when spoken to, and doctors were 'hopeful' that one day she'd fully recover. But they warned Avery not to expect any miracles.

Without Diana's love and support, Avery once more felt the pain of loneliness. He started hearing and seeing betrayed ghosts again, and soon sought sanctuary in the bottle.

Politically, however, the balance swung the other way. Due to the fact that James L. Cassidy had experienced similar withdrawal problems with his wife after their firstborn had died of Sudden Infant Death Syndrome, the two senators shared a common pain and became close friends. Once again Avery had 'strength' to cling to. Naturally, he had to absorb a lot of verbal abuse from his peers on The Hill, who accused him of ass-kissing and of being a Cassidy clone. But years of having to shut out his father's taunting had given Avery a 'tin ear,' and he was now blissfully immune to their mealy-mouthed slurs and accusations.

And now, finally, it had all paid off. Very shortly, Cassidy would be president, and Avery would be a voice to reckon with on The Hill.

Unless of course, Avery thought suddenly, Kyle and Clare's inane accusations somehow prevented Cassidy from becoming president. It couldn't happen, he knew. Hell, it was stupid even to think it might. But what if it did? What if it really did? He'd fall. Hard and fast. All the way to the bottom. He'd made numerous enemies while in the capital, enemies that, so long as he was a friend of Jim Cassidy, knew he was too strong to attack. But without Cassidy he was vulnerable. And those enemies would do everything they could to destroy him.

Feeling oppressed by a sense of impending political doom, Avery rode in the taxi along the Mall to the Senate Office Buildings with only one thought in mind: He must stop Kyle and Clare from causing Jim Cassidy any kind of problem. And he must stop them permanently.

But how could he do that? It wasn't sufficient just to say that Cassidy's service records weren't available; Kyle was resourceful enough to find some other way to acquire them. Nor could he risk turning Kyle over to Naval Intelligence, because his foster brother would undoubtedly guess who had betrayed him, and make goddamn fucking sure that Avery got smeared by the same charges of treason!

Admittedly, after all these years of apparent innocence, Avery doubted if any jury would be sufficiently swayed by a fugitive's testimony to convict a United States senator. But the bad publicity, fueled by his political enemies, would most likely destroy his career on The Hill.

And life without The Hill, Avery knew, would be no life at all.

27

Two days passed without a call from Avery. Ryan and Clare grudgingly obeyed Slater's instructions and remained inside her town house. But neither was happy about being 'grounded.' And on the morning of the third day Ryan, deciding that his foster brother might be stalling, had Clare call Avery at his Senate office. His secretary said that Senator Brickland was ill and wouldn't be in today. Clare promptly called a political columnist friend and got Avery's home phone number. Ryan then called Avery. The housekeeper answered. She said that the senator was resting and couldn't be disturbed.

'He'll talk to me,' Ryan said. 'Just tell him it's an old friend who's worried about Senator Cassidy's future.'

The housekeeper complied. Shortly, Avery came on the line. His voice was slurred and Ryan knew he'd been drinking. 'I'm still tryin' to get that information you want, Mr. Ryan. S'gonna take longer than I thought, though, so — '

'How much longer?'

'Dunno. 'nother day or so.'

'One day,' Ryan said. 'That's all you got, Ave. Then we go to another source.'

'Wha' other source?'

'One day,' Ryan repeated. 'No more. So you'd better get your act together, pal.' He hung up, looked across the kitchen table at Clare, and Shrugged. 'He's on the sauce.'

'Do you think maybe he's stalling?'

'Maybe. I'm not sure. Could be, he's just trying to get the info without causing too many waves.'

'If he is stalling,' Clare said, 'what do you think we should do then?'

'I've been thinking about that — trying to come up with an alternate plan if this one goes down the tubes.'

'So have I. I just hope you've been more successful than I have.'

Ryan shrugged. 'Only way out I can see, is to ask Slater or Fontaine to help us. One of them should have enough juice

310

to get us Cassidy's service records.'

'I'm sure they do. But I honestly doubt if either of them would risk getting involved in this — not without first being certain that Cassidy was guilty.'

'If we *knew* he was guilty,' Ryan snapped, angered by his confinement, 'we wouldn't be asking for their goddamn help in the first place.'

'True. But their position is: If we're wrong about Cassidy, it won't only give grounds for a massive libel suit, it'll destroy the governor's credibility and honor-above-all image.'

Great,' said Ryan, steamed. 'Then what it comes down to is your guys are willing to take all the glory . . . but not the fall.'

'That's it on the button. Politicians aren't exactly known for their bravery, you know.' Clare paused, mind working, then: 'We can always go to the press or TV. A story like this would send network ratings higher than the space shuttle.'

Ryan had been thinking. Remembering Fontaine's promise that he'd take any proof condemning Cassidy right to the top, Ryan said, 'Other than Fontaine or

Slater, do you know anybody with enough clout to get us into the Oval Office?'

'Probably. It'd mean pulling in a few outstanding favors, but I'm sure I could handle it. Why?'

Ryan wasn't listening. He'd grasped an idea out of all the facts, names, and alternatives that were punching around in his mind. 'That's it,' he said suddenly.

'It?'

'The bait we been looking for — to keep Gray Hair off our backs.'

'Going to the president, you mean?'

'Uh-uh. Listen,' he said, rising, 'in a moment we're going into the bedroom an' have an argument.'

'We are? Why — '

'Jus' listen, goddamn it!' He pulled her roughly toward him, kept his voice low, and said, 'You want to go to the press right now an' blow this story wide open. I don't. I want to wait until this Navy buddy of mine contacts me — gives me all the dope on Cassidy's service records.'

'Is Avery your Navy buddy?'

'No. Just in case he's in this with Cassidy, and they're making him stall,

312

we'll say this is some guy I know from 'nam who's now a brass hat at the Pentagon.'

'Okay. Then what?'

'You finally agree to wait until my buddy calls, which should be any day now. But for chrissake don't give in too easy,' Ryan added as they headed into the bedroom. 'cause if we don't make whoever's listening believe us, we're going to be considered bad risks for life insurance!'

Senator Brickland sat brooding in the paneled study of his stately white colonial home that stood on a quiet tree-lined street in Chevy Chase, Washington's most exclusive suburb. Dusk had fallen. The study drapes were pulled and the only light came from the fire dying in the hearth. Avery, slumped glumly in a big leather chair behind his desk, poured himself another bourbon. He stared fixedly at the flames flickering up the chimney, thinking: 'Being a man is . . . Is that all? If you think about it, son, it's more than enough.' Bullshit! Plain unadulterated fucking bullshit! An old man — no, a senile old man — just spouting off a bunch of rhetoric not worth listening to, not even worth remembering.

Avery drank deeply from the glass, barely tasting the bourbon as it went down. How can you fight a ghost? It has all the advantages. Invisible but always there. Lurking. Laughing. Taunting.

No escape.

God, how he hated Kyle. Just think how different, how easy life might've been if his parents hadn't died; if the governor and Avery's gentle, ever-compassionate mother hadn't taken Kyle in . . .

If. Some big fucking IF. They had. And Kyle was there. Always there. 'Why can't you be more like your brother, son?' Avery could hear the governor's 'theme song' even now. Mind sodden with booze. It still rang clear and pure. 'Mom, can I help it if I hate all the things the governor loves? And Kyle doesn't!'

Avery suddenly laughed. But only deep inside his head. No sound disturbed the quiet yellow pall in the study. What was it Kyle had said in 'nam — just before they took off on their mission? 'Remember, Ave, they can kill you but they can't eat you.' Whatever the fuck that meant.

Avery had wanted to deliver that same speech to Kyle on the phone, but hadn't. They'd spoken several hours ago. Long, depressing, unnerving hours in which Avery had struggled with his conscience, trying desperately not to accept what his mind had been telling him ever since he'd hung up: that he had to kill his brother. Probably Clare, too. Repugnant as the idea was, Avery realized it was the only solution to the problem facing him. And he had to do it immediately.

Avery looked at the glass-door gun cabinet that occupied the wall opposite his desk — the same cabinet that had been in his father's study at their ranch, Big Sky. Filled with his father's beloved guns; guns that Avery despised but kept on display because they gave his study the manly image that others expected the war-hero son of Governor 'Gus' Brickland to have.

He'd have to use one of those guns on Kyle and Clare, Avery realized. The short-barreled .38 Colt revolver, probably. It was small enough to hide in his coat pocket, big enough to do the —

Don't be a goddamned idiot! he thought suddenly. *You can't kill anyone! Jesus Christ, you couldn't even shoot a lousy stinking deer to please your father, so what makes you now think you can kill your own brother?*

'Because I have to,' he said, unaware that he'd spoken aloud. 'I must. I don't have any other fucking choice.'

Then, quit stalling, hero, and let's get it over with. Right now. Because the longer you wait, you poor dumb bastard, the harder, more impossible it's going to get. Can't you see that? Yes, he thought. He finished his drink, and Poured himself another, then picked up the phone and dialed Clare's number.

In the kitchen of her town house, Clare answered the phone on the second ring. She was in the middle of tossing a chef salad for dinner. She licked mayonnaise from her fingers and picked up the receiver. ''lo?'

'Clare?'

'Yes, Senator?'

'I'd like to speak to — uh — Ryan.'

'I'll get him for you, Senator.' Clare waved the phone at Ryan. He sat in the living room, working on a crossword puzzle. She mouthed the word 'Avery.' Ryan nodded, got up and entered the kitchen. 'This is Ryan,' he said into the receiver.

'I — uh — I've got what you want, Kyle. Friend of mine at the — uh — Pentagon just dropped it off.'

'Fine,' Ryan said. Avery sounded nervous. Ryan wondered if it was because his brother was lying, or just alarmed by what he was doing. 'When can I have it, Ave?'

'Soon as you want. Tonight, if you like. But I think you ought to know,' Avery added, 'these records only prove what I've said all along — the man in question is innocent.'

'Glad to hear that. I still want to see the records for myself, though.'

'All right. Just be a waste of time, however.' Avery rustled some papers on the desk, loud enough to be heard over the phone. 'Those dates you mentioned — when that girl was murdered and the sub was sunk — well, our friend couldn't have been involved in either incident,

317

Kyle, because he was at sea at the time.'
He rustled the papers again. 'I'm looking
at the records right now. May 'forty-two
you said, right?'

'Right. Eighth and ninth, to be exact.'

'Eighth and ninth, sure . . . ' Avery
pretended to be reading from the papers.
'Here you go. Says right here that our
man was pulling sub duty aboard a coast
guard cutter in the Atlantic on both those
days.'

Ryan stopped listening. According to
the facts he and Clare had gathered on
Cassidy, the senator had been transferred
to Naval Intelligence by May 10, and therefore wasn't on any Coast Guard vessel.
Sadly, Ryan realized Avery must be lying.
This meant he'd either seen Cassidy's service records and now knew the senator
was guilty, or had known all along Cassidy
was Falcon and was presently stalling in
the hope that he could convince Ryan that
Shining Jim was innocent.

' . . . so you see,' Avery concluded,
'there's absolutely no doubt that the man
is innocent. No doubt at all.'

'I'm glad,' Ryan said. 'I hated to think

he was in the first place. But I'm still going to need those records — '

'Why? Don't you believe me?'

'Sure. But I'm not the one you got to convince. Hell, after all the fuss Clare and I made, her people sure aren't going to take my word for it.'

'No, I guess not . . . ' Avery sagged in his chair. His last effort to avoid bloodshed had failed. He'd played his last ace. Now he had to kill Kyle and Clare. Right away. 'Well, no matter,' he said casually. 'I just thought I could save us both some wasted time, is all. But since I can't, why don't you and Clare meet me downtown at — uhm — uhm — Fifteenth and L. There's an underground parking garage on L, not far from the corner. I'll meet you both there at the lower level in, say, an hour?'

'We'll be there,' Ryan said. He hung up. 'I'm meeting him at Fifteenth an' L in an hour,' he told Clare.

'He's got the records then?'

'Sure,' Ryan lied. 'Everything we asked for.'

'Am I coming with you?'

'Nope.'

'Why'd you say, 'we,' then?'

'Did I?'

'Yes. You said 'we'll be there' just before hanging up.'

'If I did,' Ryan said, casually taking a piece of cheese out of the salad, 'I sure didn't mean to . . . 'cause the one thing Avery insisted on was that I come alone.'

The night had a wintry bite. But Ryan was oblivious to it as he drove along L Street, past Governor Fontaine's campaign headquarters, to the entrance ramp leading down to the basement of the multilevel subterranean parking garage. He was twenty minutes early, as planned, hoping to arrive first for this clandestine meeting with Avery. He guessed that Avery would come early, too. And he wanted this extra time to check out the area, to be ready for whatever Avery might be preparing for him. Of course, there was always the possibility that he was wrong, that Avery had Cassidy's records and intended to hand them over without any fuss. But hearing Avery's nervousness over the phone, knowing that he'd lied about Cassidy being at sea, well, odds were, Ryan told himself, Avery wasn't intending to play it straight.

As the Porsche descended the spiraling ramp to the basement, Ryan glanced instinctively in the rearview mirror. The mirror showed only the slanted wall of the level above. Satisfied that he was alone, Ryan listened to the low-pressure radials sweeping around the slick concrete curves past a big blue sign marked C, out onto the basement level.

At that late hour there were only a few cars parked in the neon-lighted spaces. Ryan looked around for Avery but couldn't see him. He parked alongside one of the large concrete stanchions near the exit ramp. Without the high-pitched whine of the Porsche engine, the garage was silent. Ryan got out and listened intently. The faint, muffled sounds of passing traffic drifted down from outside. Ryan hid himself behind the stanchion. He waited, calm yet keyed.

Shortly, he heard a car enter from the street and Start down the winding ramp. The sound of tires grew closer. Then a mist-green BMW sedan came around and down the ramp toward him. The overhead neon lighting reflected off the windshield and Ryan saw Avery at the wheel. He was alone. The sleek, high-performance sedan cleared the ramp, then slowed down as Avery looked around for Ryan.

He stepped out from behind the big round concrete post into the driveway so that Avery could see him.

The BMW pulled up softly beside Ryan. Avery turned off the engine and got out, carrying an expensive leather briefcase. Ryan noticed it was unzipped and he thought, *It's in there. The gun. The bastard's going to try to kill me. And he's smiling.*

Avery stopped in front of Ryan. Both were partly hidden from the rest of the garage by the stanchion. Avery's smile failed to hide his uneasiness. He looked past Ryan, ducking his head a little to see inside the Porsche. Then he frowned and, in a voice Ryan didn't recognize, said, 'Where's Clare?'

'With Governor Fontaine.'

For a moment Avery looked annoyed.

Then he shrugged it off and said, 'No matter,' and, with awkward casualness, reached into the briefcase. Out came a gun.

Ryan smiled.

Avery saw the smile and recognized it from the times he'd seen Kyle smile that way just before trouble started. It scared him. He gripped the gun tighter and tried not to sound afraid as he said: 'You knew I was lying, didn't you?'

Ryan shrugged.

'Yet you still showed. Why?'

'Curiosity?'

'Not you. You've never been curious about anything in your whole fucking life.'

'I had to make sure.'

'About what? That you're a fucking hero and I'm not?'

'You know better than that, Ave.'

'Do I? How? *How?*' Avery shouted the last word.

'We grew up together, remember?'

'Remember? *Remember? How* the fuck could I ever forget?'

Then, when Ryan didn't say anything:

'This is your own goddamn fault. You know that, don't you? I mean, shit, I gave you an out. All you had to do was pretend to believe me — tell Clare and her people that Jim Cassidy was innocent. Good Christ, was that so hard, so impossible to do?'

'Seemed like it — at the time.'

'Principles!' Avery spat out the word. 'That's what this all comes down to, doesn't it? You and your goddamn fucking principles! Well, what about those principles now, brother mine?'

''cause you're holding a gun, you mean?'

'Yes.'

'Depends on what conditions you're offering.'

'Your life — yours and Clare's — if you'll give me your word you'll drop all this shit about Cassidy right now ... tell your political wolves that you're wrong. That the two of you have seen actual proof that Jim Cassidy's innocent.'

Ryan frowned, surprised. 'That's all it'd take — my word?'

'Why not?' said Avery. He gave an ugly

laugh. 'If I can't trust you — after what you've done for me already — who the fuck can I trust?'

Ryan thought, carefully. The .38 short-barreled revolver in Avery's hand was aimed right at his chest. He recognized it as Governor Brickland's favorite handgun and thought, how ironic that in a few moments it might end his life. He also thought how simple it would be to lie to Avery; to give his word and then renege on it later.

'Well?' Avery said. He chewed his lip, anxious. 'How about it, brother mine? Do I have your word?'

Ryan wanted very badly to say yes. He even said it, several times, in his mind. But he found himself shaking his head, no.

'Shit!' Avery hissed. His gun hand twitched with rage. 'God damn it, Kyle, why not? Is it because you think I won't shoot you?' His voice shook as much as his gun hand. 'Well, you'd better think again, buddy boy, because I sure as fuck will. This thing you and Clare are fooling with is, well, it's too goddamn big to mess up now. And — and someone's got to stop you. You hear? Stop you. And, well, if it's got to be me, then that's okay, too, because . . . ' Avery simply ran out of words.

He tried to pull the trigger.

He couldn't do it.

And before he had another chance to try, Ryan grabbed the gun and twisted the barrel aside. The sudden wrenching movement jerked Avery's trigger finger, causing it to squeeze off a shot. The explosion in the confinement of the garage was deafening. Ryan momentarily lost all hearing as he grappled with Avery for the gun.

Suddenly, a second shot was triggered. The bullet burned through the fleshy part of Avery's right arm. He yelled with pain and dropped the gun. He staggered back against the concrete stanchion.

Ryan started toward him, concerned. 'You okay, Avery?'

'Get the fuck away from me!' his foster brother snarled. 'I don't want your goddamn sympathy!'

Ryan eyed Avery. He felt both revulsion

and compassion. Then, in a growled whisper, he said: 'Why didn't you shoot me when you had the chance?'

'I tried to.'

Ryan repeated: 'Why didn't you?'

'Who knows? Maybe I wanted to see you squirm.'

'Not you. That ain't your style.'

'Style?' Avery gave an ugly, painful laugh. 'How the hell would you know what my style is?'

'We're brothers, remember?'

'So were Cain and Abel!'

'That how you see us?'

Avery wasn't listening. 'Know how long I've hated you? *Really* hated you, I mean?'

Ryan shook his head.

'Ever since you took the blame for what I did. No,' he said as Ryan started to speak, 'don't interrupt. I've wanted to tell you this for a long time. Forever, it seems like. You took away my balls that day. I was ready to say it was only me who'd accidentally pushed my father down the stairs — I mean, I knew I'd done it, knew I was going to have to pay for it, and, well, for the first time I wasn't scared of admitting something. I was — was just ready to become responsible, a man. But you wouldn't let me. I started to tell you but you wouldn't listen. Had to be the fucking hero — '

Avery broke off as they heard a car roar in from the street and come racing down the ramp, tires squealing, toward them. Ryan and Avery looked at the ramp. Suddenly a blue and white police car, lights flashing, came speeding around an upper curve.

'Get out of here!' Avery told Ryan. 'They nail you, we all go down the tubes!'

Ryan realized he was right. He ran to the Porsche, got in, started the engine and gunned the car up the ramp. He passed the police car on the lower curve. The startled driver braked and tried to swerve into Ryan's path. He was moments too late. Ryan sped past, untouched, and shot up onto the second level. As he did, he saw a man limping hurriedly down the ramp to the basement.

'Gray Hair!' he said aloud. 'Sonofabitch, he must've followed me!'

28

Ryan was wrong. Robert 'Turk' Langley was not following him. He was following Avery and had been following him for the past two days. The word had come from the man who gave Langley all his orders — a man Langley respected, trusted, and would have obeyed no matter what was asked of him. 'Keep Senator Brickland under twenty-four-hour surveillance,' the man had ordered. Langley, working in shifts with men under him, had done just that.

Now, as he limped down the concrete ramp toward the two policemen talking with Senator Brickland, Langley knew that the tedious surveillance had paid off: he now knew the man who'd shot the young senator was Avery's brother, Kyle.

Langley, who had a complete file on Senator Brickland, knew Kyle was actually a foster brother. He was also a fugitive, long sought by the police for the murder of Governor Brickland. Obviously, Langley reasoned, this was why Kyle had changed his name and was operating a run-down marine salvage business in Morehead City. Langley smiled to himself. For a moment he forgot the ever-present pain in his right leg. The man he worked for would be able to make good use of this information.

Ahead the policemen had given Senator Brickland some hasty first aid and were now helping him into their patrol car. One of them was saying something about hearing gunshots as they passed the entrance to the garage, while the other seemed more concerned with the senator's injured right arm. Avery wasn't listening to either officer. And as Langley drew near, he heard Avery say, 'I'm sorry I can't give you a more accurate description, officer. But it all happened so fast, I didn't get a good look at him.'

'I did,' Langley said. He paused beside the patrol car and pointed to the top of the ramp. 'I saw the whole thing from up there. But for my regrettable slowness,' he added to Avery, 'I might've been about to prevent your injury, Senator.'

Avery tried to look pleased. 'Thanks. It

could've been worse.'

'What exactly did the suspect look like, sir?' the younger officer asked Langley.

'Tall, early to mid-thirties, dark hair — '

'I'm sorry,' Avery broke in, 'but you're mistaken there. The man who mugged me was kind of short, light-haired, and was fifty, at least.'

'I thought you said you didn't get a good look at him, Senator?' The older cop pinned Avery with a puzzled stare.

'I — uh — didn't. But I remember that much about him.'

Langley smiled. 'Forgive me, Senator . . . but perhaps in the excitement of everything you weren't able to see the assailant as clearly as I . . . '

'Happens, Senator,' the older cop said. 'Even trained police officers make mistakes in the heat of — '

'I'm sure they do,' Avery snapped. 'But, well, I am the man he shot. I ought to know what he looked like.'

'Of course, Senator, of course.' The older officer signaled with his eyes to his partner to talk to Langley, then said: 'I'll take the senator to Washington General,

Bryce — you bring his car along. Okay?'

'Will do,' said Bryce. He waited until his partner had driven off with Senator Brickland. Then he took out his notebook and grinned at Langley. 'If there's one thing you learn in Washington, sir, it's that you never argue with a senator. Now . . . why don't you give me your description of the suspect.'

Maybe it wasn't sob-story shit, Ryan thought suddenly, as he drove back to Georgetown. Maybe Avery was right? Maybe he did feel cheated because Ryan took the blame? Maybe — *Oh, for chrissake,* Ryan suddenly told himself. *How can you build a case or even make any sense out of a bunch of maybes?* Besides, if Avery had felt *that* bad about Ryan shouldering the blame, why had he kept quiet all these years? Ryan was grateful that he had. But he sure as hell would've understood it, if Avery couldn't have kept quiet. In fact, Ryan thought wryly, there were times during his self-imposed exile that he'd only wished to Christ that Avery *had* gotten him off the hook. Not that he truthfully had ever regretted taking the blame; he hadn't. But

Ryan did have to admit there'd been times when he'd had to quiet nagging voices in his mind that questioned his wisdom for turning himself into a perennial fugitive.

But this wasn't one of those times, Ryan convinced himself. He had more important problems to worry about, and to solve. Such as, how had Cassidy's people known he was meeting Avery in that garage? He was positive no one had tailed him from Clare's town house, so who'd told them? Avery? It was possible, Ryan realized. But unlikely. Why have Cassidy's top soldier around when Avery intended to do his own killing? And if Avery had brought Gray Hair along as a backup, then why hadn't his brother signaled to the crippled assassin to finish Ryan off?

Logic said because Avery, like Ryan, didn't know Gray Hair was hiding there. Logic also said that Avery, after keeping his fugitive brother's role of 'sacrificial goat' a secret for so many years, would not want Gray Hair or anyone else to know about the truth now.

No, Ryan reasoned, Avery had too much to lose to share his secret with anyone. Especially someone who could report everything to Cassidy! Still, if Avery wasn't responsible for Gray Hair being there, then who was? Clare and he had searched her kitchen thoroughly, and Ryan was convinced the 'leak' didn't come from there. But where? *Where?*

It was after eleven when Ryan entered Clare's town house. Clare was greatly relieved to see him — safe and uninjured. She led him into the kitchen and whispered that she'd seen a television news update that had reported the shooting of Senator Brickland in a downtown parking garage. The suspect, said the newscaster, had tried to rob the senator. Brickland had gotten shot during the brief struggle, though not seriously, while the mugger fled in a small white foreign sports car moments before the police arrived. Did they get the license number? Ryan wanted to know. Clare said no. But Ryan's description had been given to the police by an eyewitness, who had seen everything from the upper level. Ryan growled that the eyewitness was Gray Hair, and that he'd almost run over the cripple as he was driving out. Clare looked shaken. How could Gray Hair have known about — ?

Ryan cut her off. He hadn't the foggiest idea. He did have one suggestion, however: 'Better call your boss. Tell him what's happened. Let him decide what we do next.'

Clare obeyed. She called Slater at his condominium, explained everything and asked him what he thought they should do next. 'Hang up,' he told her.

'What?'

'Hang up the phone. I want to call someone.'

'Oh.' She hung up, then told Ryan what Slater had said. Ryan nodded to show he'd understood, then took a beer from the refrigerator and began working on a crossword puzzle.

An hour later the phone rang. It was Slater. He told Clare that he'd just spoken to the Secretary of State, Harold Royce. 'I told him that you and Ryan had discovered something about Senator Cassidy's past that involved national security and needed to talk to the president. He suggested that you talk to him first and wants both of you at his office at nine tomorrow morning. Clare?' Slater added when she didn't answer. 'Did you hear me?'

'Y-yes, Karl. I heard.' Clare collected herself. 'Nine o'clock. We'll be there.'

'Fine. Then call me right after you've spoken to Royce. I'm anxious to hear what he says.'

'I will.' Clare hung up. The idea of telling the Secretary of State that Senator Cassidy was a former Nazi spy made her uneasy. 'Ryan,' she said.

'What?' He looked up from his crossword puzzle.

'Tomorrow morning we go see Secretary Royce — tell him all we know about Cassidy and Falcon.'

'That Slater's or Fontaine's decision?'

'Both, I guess,' she said, disappointed by his lack of surprise. 'I didn't ask. Why?'

'No reason,' he said. 'Just glad they're keepin' their word about goin' to the top, is all.' He returned to his puzzle, irritatingly calm. But inside he had a knot growing in his stomach, as he wondered just how much longer he could possibly hope to keep his real identity a secret.

29

There was a thunderstorm during the night that made Clare turn over in her sleep. By morning the worst of the storm had blown on to Baltimore, but there was still rain in the air and Washington smelled like damp leaves.

Shortly before nine, while most of the capital's secretaries were settling into their desks, Ryan and Clare parked the car on 23rd Street, turned the corner, and walked along C Street to the Main State Building. Ryan carried the U-boat documents and all the other information they'd gathered on Senator Cassidy in Clare's briefcase. The actual weight of the briefcase was negligible, yet nothing Ryan had ever carried felt heavier. As they climbed the steps and entered the modern, block-long concrete building, Ryan had the distinct uneasy feeling that he was walking into a bucket of fishhooks.

Inside they crossed the spacious lobby

with its array of international flags and identified themselves to the federal security guards. One guard checked their IDs and the briefcase for weapons, while the other notified the Secretary of State's office that Ryan and Clare had arrived.

Shortly, a young woman dressed in chic clothes arrived. She introduced herself as Miss Fields. She led them up in the secretary's private elevator to the seventh floor. They walked along a hallway of offices that were occupied by the under secretary and the assistant secretaries, then entered a marble and wood-paneled waiting room outside the secretary's office. Here Miss Fields turned them over to the secretary's private secretary, Mrs. Adams, who said that Secretary Royce would see them shortly. She then offered them coffee or tea, which they declined, gave them magazines, made sure they were comfortable on the couch under the great seal of the United States, and returned to her desk.

They waited fifteen minutes. Then the meeting in the inner office broke up and the under secretary came hurrying out.

Mrs. Adams spoke briefly to him. Then she led Ryan and Clare in to meet the Secretary of State, Harold Royce.

Secretary Royce stood behind his large, militarily tidy desk, his back to the flag and the wall of photographs that showed him with past presidents and foreign dignitaries. The former brigadier general had a worldwide reputation for being tough, fair, and direct. Over the years his bluntness had caused some uneasy moments between the great powers, but he was dedicated and unafraid and believed America should bow to no one. Although fleshy and balding, he stood as stiffly erect as the day he'd graduated from West Point. Ryan guessed he was sixty, and admired the firm, crisp handshake and direct steel-blue gaze behind the rimless glasses.

'According to Mr. Slater,' Secretary Royce said after they were all seated, 'you two have an urgent matter of state to discuss.'

'Yes, we do, Mr. Secretary.' Clare took Falcon's photograph and all the documents and papers Ryan gave her from the briefcase and placed them on the desk.

'Everything that we're going to tell you is substantiated in here. These're copies, but naturally we have the originals and their authenticity can be easily verified.'

'Very well, Ms. Winslow. Please proceed . . . '

As briefly as possible, and with occasional help from Ryan, Clare described everything that they had uncovered about Senator Cassidy and Falcon. Secretary Royce didn't interrupt. But by his increasingly astounded and dubious expression, it was obvious that he couldn't bring himself to believe that the story was true.

'Forgive me if I'm blunt,' he said when Clare had finished. 'But my time is short and with a matter as potentially explosive as this, I can't afford to mince words.'

'Of course, sir. We understand.'

'Very well, then, let me say this — I personally cannot believe that so distinguished a man as Senator Cassidy could ever have been a Nazi spy. However, if, as you claim, these documents do substantiate your story, I would be very remiss in my duty if I did not report this to the president. So, let me do this — let me examine everything you've given me, and if I then feel that there is even the slightest chance that your accusations are valid, I will alert the president and make arrangements for you both to meet with him at his earliest convenience. How does that sound to you?'

'Fair,' Ryan said. 'We ask for no more.'

'Very well, then,' the secretary said, rising, 'if you'll tell my secretary where you both may be reached, I shall contact you as soon as I've made my decision.'

Satisfied, Ryan and Clare left the State Building and drove back to her town house. There, in the kitchen, she called Slater at campaign headquarters and told him what had transpired. He was pleased with their progress and instructed Clare to notify him immediately after they heard from the secretary. He then hung up with his usual abruptness, leaving Clare with an unuttered good-bye still on her lips.

The secretary did not call until late that afternoon. By then Clare was too nervous to sit still and even Ryan was finding it difficult to concentrate on his ever-present crossword.

'I've examined all the material,' Secretary Royce said, his voice brittle with tension, 'and although I am still of the opinion that Senator Cassidy's character is above reproach, I also felt there was sufficient evidence here to warrant alerting the president. I therefore went ahead and contacted the White House, and have been instructed to tell you that the president wishes to see you both at five thirty this afternoon. I take it that's convenient?' he added, in a voice that said it had better be.

'Yes, Mr. Secretary,' Clare said. 'Very convenient.'

'Good. Then enter through the appointments gate off Pennsylvania — the guard will be expecting you.'

Clare hung up. She realized she was trembling. Not too professional, she thought. Especially for someone who hoped to become White House Press Secretary. She looked out into the living room where Ryan had been listening on the extension. 'I don't know about you,' she told him, 'but I've got gooseflesh.'

'Relax,' Ryan said. He thought back to

his last White House visit and wondered if this time he was putting his head into a noose. 'Presidents are just people, like you 'n me. You'll do jus' fine.'

The Secretary of State was correct. The blue-uniformed federal officer at the appointments gate was expecting them. He stepped from behind the green-tinted window, verified their ID, then told them to go ahead. It wasn't until they'd driven through the gate and were heading up the stately driveway to the White House, that Clare realized in the excitement of everything she'd forgotten to call Karl.

Ryan and Clare didn't have to wait long outside the president's Oval Office. They'd barely gotten comfortable on the gold brocade couch, when the intercom on the secretary's desk buzzed. Mrs. Jennings answered it and spoke softly for a moment. Then she rose and smiled politely at Ryan and Clare.

'The president will see you now.'

She opened the door of the Oval Office, ushered them inside and silently withdrew. Secretary Royce, already on his feet, gave them a tight smile and led them toward the president. The chief executive rose behind his ornate, highly polished desk to greet them.

'Mr. President . . . this is Ms. Clare Winslow and Mr. Ryan.'

'A pleasure meeting you,' the president told them. He was a tall, slim man of sixty-three with slightly wavy gray hair, a reassuring smile, and a soft Southern accent. He had a certain calm confidence that eight years in office had given him, and Ryan thought that up close he looked gravely tired. Especially around his sincere pale blue eyes. But he moved and spoke with a gentle vigor and did not possess the harried look of persecution that Ryan remembered was so much a part of the president who'd pinned on his medal.

'Please, sit down, won't you . . . '

After everyone was seated, the president motioned to the documents piled before him on the desk.

'What you present here, Ms. Winslow . . . Mr. Ryan . . . are accusations of the gravest enormity.'

'We know that, sir,' Ryan said. 'If they

weren't, we wouldn't have troubled you with them.'

'Well, troubled me you have,' the president said. He toyed with a small, crystal, polar bear paperweight. 'However, despite the overwhelming evidence you've compiled here, I still cannot make myself believe that a man as highly esteemed as Senator Cassidy could possibly have committed treason in any way, shape, or form. I mean, good God, the Cassidys are one of America's most prestigious families . . . and to accuse their favorite son of being a Nazi spy is, well, almost treasonable itself.'

'We understand that,' Ryan said. He knew Cassidy and the president belonged to the same political party, and guessed the latter wouldn't be remembered too well if in his last weeks in office he pulled the plug on the man almost certain to succeed him. 'But we felt the possible alternative — a Nazi president — was equally treasonable . . . no matter *what* party you vote for.'

The president caught his meaning. He said hastily, 'Of course, of course. Politics must certainly never interfere with national security, I agree.' He turned to Secretary Royce. 'Whether we believe Senator Cassidy is innocent or not, Harold, we're still obligated as loyal Americans to investigate this matter thoroughly.'

'I agree, Mr. President. As Mr. Ryan pointed out, the alternative, if we are wrong, is too horrendous even to consider.'

The president turned to Ryan and Clare and indicated the documents before him. 'I will have everything here authenticated immediately. I'll also have my people make their own investigation of Senator Cassidy . . . ' He smiled his reassuring smile. 'Believe me, my friends, when both are complete, there will be no doubt as to the senator's innocence or guilt. We will know for sure!'

'And if he's guilty, Mr. President?'

'Then, rest assured, Ms. Winslow, the senator will be dealt with appropriately.'

As they drove away from the White House, Ryan instinctively glanced in the rearview mirror and saw a familiar face in one of the cars driving behind them.

'Don't turn around,' he told Clare. 'But

we've picked up a tail.'

'Who?'

'Gray Hair.'

'Damn.' Clare felt a moment of fear. Then anger and frustration took over. 'How the devil did he know we were at the White House?'

'It's got to be in your kitchen,' Ryan said. 'We must've overlooked a bug somewhere.'

'Can you lose him?'

'Sure. But I got a better idea.' Without her noticing, he reached under the seat. He found the gun he'd taken from Avery in the underground garage and slipped it into his pocket.

Ahead the rush-hour traffic had slowed to a crawl on Pennsylvania Avenue. Ryan changed lanes several times. He ignored the anger it invoked in the other drivers, and by the time they had reached the university there was half a block of cars separating them from Gray Hair. Ryan checked the rear-view mirror and saw Gray Hair trying to edge over into the same lane as the Porsche. Ryan grinned to himself. Then, as they stopped for the light at Washington Circle, he put on the hand brake, opened the door, said, 'Wait for me on the other side of the circle,' and was gone before she could protest.

Outside Ryan kept low as he ducked between the cars lined up behind the Porsche. He doubted if Gray Hair had seen him get out, and hoped he could reach the gimpy assassin before the latter realized he was missing.

Between cars he saw that Gray Hair was too busy trying to change lanes to notice that only Clare was in the Porsche. Ryan ran up to the cream-colored sedan, opened the passenger-side door, and jumped in before Turk Langley could stop him.

'What the hell — ?' Langley exclaimed, startled.

'Just making it easy on you,' Ryan said. 'This way, friend, you don't have to worry about losing me.'

'Losing you?' Langley raised his thick, bristly eyebrows as if puzzled. 'I'm afraid I don't know what you're talking about, sir.'

'Then know this,' Ryan said grimly. 'The gun in my pocket's aimed right at your guts. And for Nancy Shearer's sake, I'm praying you'll make me use it.'

Langley showed no fear. Despite his affected speech and mannerisms, it was obvious he was a steeled professional. He smiled, as if amused by Ryan, and said calmly: 'Then you're wasting your prayers, sir. Merely give me my orders, and like the good soldier I am, I'll obey them.'

'Keep driving,' Ryan told him. 'I'll say when to stop.'

Clare was parked at the curb near the corner of 25th Street. Ryan had Langley pull in behind her. She got out and came and looked in the passenger-side window. She shot Langley an unpleasant look, then asked Ryan: 'Where to now?'

'Somewhere nearby that's quiet. Not a lot of people around.'

'I know the perfect place. It's quiet and the only people around won't be listening.' She returned to the Porsche. They followed her along Pennsylvania to 28th, then turned and drove to where the street dead-ended at Oak Hill Cemetery. A misty rain was falling. It kept visitors away. In the gray of dusk the rows of headstones looked wet and lonely. Both cars parked under some trees just inside the cemetery entrance. Clare locked the Porsche and came and sat in the back of Langley's sedan. In front Ryan searched Langley but found no weapon. He then went through Langley's wallet. 'Robert T. Langley,' he read from the driver's license. '1501 Fairmont Street.'

'That's near Howard University,' Clare said. Then to Langley: 'How'd you know we were at the White House?'

'I didn't,' Langley said. 'I was merely driving along Pennsylvania Avenue, and — '

He broke off as Ryan grabbed his right hand, took hold of the little finger and bent it back enough to hurt. Then, as Clare looked away, unable to watch, Ryan warned Langley: 'If you don't want me to bust your goddamn finger — answer the lady.'

Langley stared at Ryan with heavy-lidded brown eyes. Then: 'There are sophisticated listening devices in Miss Winslow's town house. We — I know about everything you do.'

'Who planted those bugs?' Clare demanded.

'One of my men.'

'At whose orders?'

'Mine.'

'Who gave you the order?' Ryan said. When Langley hesitated, Ryan bent the little finger back harder.

Langley grimaced painfully. 'Senator Brickland?'

'Go higher. Who told Brickland?'

'I — I don't know,' Langley began. 'I — ' He suddenly moaned through gritted teeth as Ryan bent the finger almost to a breaking point.

'I swear I'll break the sonofabitch,' Ryan warned.

Langley gave a muted groan. Sweat beaded on his forehead. His eyes were squinted slits. 'Senator Cassidy,' he finally gasped. 'H-he gave the order.'

Ryan looked satisfied. But he still kept the pressure on the finger. And ignoring the fact that Clare was keeping her head turned away, he said, 'When you tried to buy that photo from us in Wilmington — that was for Cassidy too, wasn't it?'

'Yes.'

'Was it Cassidy who told you to shoot

us from the woods?'

'Yes.'

Clare, as if remembering that Langley was a professional murderer, suddenly looked at him and said angrily, 'That phony bomb under my tire — with the note — he tell you to do that, too?'

Langley nodded and blinked as sweat rolled into his eyes.

'How about torching the Richters?' Ryan said.

Again, Langley nodded.

'Because Richter could identify him from the photo?'

'Yes.'

'What about Nancy Shearer?' Clare demanded. 'Why'd she have to die?'

'I — I'm not sure,' Langley said. 'The senator never said. I think it was because she could link me to him and, therefore, both of us to the murder of the Richters.'

'And you do everything he tells you, right?' said Ryan.

'I'm a soldier,' said Langley. 'A soldier must obey orders.'

'Without question?'

'Without question.'

'Where's Cassidy now?' Ryan said.

'At his Senate office . . . or maybe his campaign headquarters . . . I'm not sure.'

'You soon will be,' Ryan said grimly. ''Cause you're going to take us to him.'

'But — '

'Now. Unless, of course,' Ryan added, 'you want me to bust this finger and the nine more!'

'I'll take you,' Langley said. 'But it won't do you any good. Senator Cassidy will merely deny he knows me.'

'That's all right,' Clare said. 'It'll be worth it, just to see the look on his face when he sees us all together.'

Ryan made Langley drive him back into the city. Most of the rush-hour traffic had completed its nightly exodus and was now jammed onto several parkways and beltways that, like concrete umbilical cords, linked the capital to the surrounding communities.

Clare followed in her Porsche. It was dark now and when Ryan looked back he could see the rain slanting across her headlights, and, with each sweep of the wipers, her face peering out through the glistening windshield.

As they started around Dupont Circle, passing Ford's Theater, Ryan asked Langley what made him so loyal to Cassidy.

'I believe in him.'

'What America needs is a Nazi president, right?'

'We could do worse.'

'I don't know how,' Ryan said. He saw the flashing red lights of a police car double-parked a short distance ahead and felt Langley instinctively slow down. 'Unless, of course, 'Tomorrow the World' is your plan — '

He broke off as Langley abruptly wrenched the wheel sideways, gunned the engine, and rammed the sedan into the back of the patrol car. The violent impact threw Langley against the steering wheel and Ryan into the dash, his head slamming against the windshield. Lights starred before his eyes. For several moments the sound of crunched metal and shattered glass seemed to come from far off. So did Langley's voice. Then Ryan's head started to clear. He realized he was alone in the car . . . that Langley had jumped out and was now staggering toward the two police-men who stood glaring at their battered car.

'H-Help me, Officer . . . help me . . . please . . . t-tried to kill me . . . he's a wanted man . . . saw him shoot Senator Brickland . . . '

Ryan heard snatches of Langley's shouting above the pouring rain and realized he had to get out of there. Scrambling from the car, he looked around for the Porsche and saw it had stopped a short distance behind. Clare was already getting out. Her face was filled with alarm. Ryan saw her silhouetted against the background of the oncoming rain-blurred headlights, waving to him.

'Ryan!' she shouted. 'Hurry! Get in . . . get in!'

He started toward her. Then he heard the police ordering him to stop and he knew he mustn't involve her. One of them had to be free, so they could reach the president and explain about Langley. With this in mind Ryan cut across in front of the accident-slowed traffic and ran toward an alley on the opposite side of the street.

Behind, the two policemen raised their guns to shoot Ryan. But there was too much traffic crossing before them. Frustrated, the policemen lowered their weapons and watched Ryan sprint into the alley. Then the taller policeman told his partner to call for a backup. 'I'll see if I can keep him pinned down in the alley!' He ran across the rain-slicked street after Ryan.

Clare, still beside her Porsche, watched the tall policeman disappear into the alley. Alarmed for Ryan's safety, she got back in behind the wheel and gunned the Porsche toward the intersection.

As she passed the damaged patrol car, she saw the shorter policeman talking on his radio. Langley had already disappeared into the morbidly curious, gathering crowd.

30

Arms pumping, Ryan sprinted along the dark empty alley. The backs of old industrial buildings rose up on either side of him. No lights showed in any of the barred windows, and all the doors were locked. At the end of the alley he was confronted with a high brick wall. He couldn't reach the top of it. Looking around, he saw a large trash bin outside a nearby loading dock. The bin had wheels and Ryan pushed it up against the wall. He climbed on top of the lid and started to pull himself up onto the wall.

Behind Ryan the tall policeman now entered the alley. He saw Ryan's silhouette atop the wall and shouted for him to stop. Ryan ignored him and continued to scramble over the wall. The policeman took quick aim and fired off two shots. Ryan, as he dropped to the ground, heard the bullets ricocheting off the bricks. The policeman swore savagely, holstered his gun, and ran toward the trash bin.

There was another alley on the other side of the wall; Ryan ran along it. He found himself on a lighted side street. Two cars passed. Ryan made sure neither of them was the Porsche, then sprinted to the corner. A sign said N Street. Traffic splashed across in front of him. Again he looked for the Porsche. It wasn't among the cars and Ryan wondered where Clare was. He hoped that she'd gone home. He could reach her later.

All thoughts of Clare vanished as Ryan saw a police car approaching. Above its rain-flared headlights, both officers were looking around.

Ryan ducked into the doorway of a closed antique store and pressed himself flat against the window. He waited, heart thudding, as he watched the patrol car splash past. Ryan gave it time to reach the next corner. Then he ran across the street and headed in the opposite direction.

Cassidy! That was where a loyal soldier like Langley would go. Or, at least he would contact him and report what had happened. After that, Ryan reasoned,

Cassidy would probably want Langley to disappear. If not for good, at least until after the senator became president.

No way, Ryan thought grimly. *Somehow I've got to grab Langley again. Get him to the White House. Force him to tell the president the truth.* With this in mind, Ryan headed for the only place he could think of where Langley and Cassidy might meet — the senator's campaign headquarters.

Ryan was soaked to the skin when he reached 16th Street. He paused outside the campaign offices and looked in through one of the windows. Inside, under the bright fluorescent lighting, there was lots of activity. Ryan couldn't see Langley or Cassidy, and guessed that *if* they were there, they'd be in one of the offices in back. About to go find a rear entrance, he paused as he saw a young woman get up from her desk, take a raincoat and umbrella from a nearby rack, and head for the door. It gave Ryan an idea. And as the woman stepped outside, popping open her umbrella, he confronted her. 'Uh — excuse me . . . '

The woman jumped back, startled. She peered suspiciously at Ryan. 'W-What d'you want?'

'I'm looking for a friend of mine — Robert Langley?'

'Sorry, I — '

'He works here. Kind of short and thickset, gray hair . . . has a limp.'

The woman thought a moment, then shook her dark head. 'Uh-uh. Sorry. Doesn't ring any bells.' She started to leave, then Paused. She pointed through the rain-streaked window and said: 'You might ask that old guy there — Sandy Fuller. He's been with the senator longer than anyone.'

'Thanks.' Ryan stepped aside so the woman could hurry off, then entered the campaign headquarters and squeezed his way through the mob of volunteer workers to Fuller's desk in back.

Fuller was on the phone: a small, wiry chain-smoker in a blue suit who motioned for Ryan to sit down. He also indicated that he wouldn't be long. But by the time he got off the phone, there was a puddle around Ryan's wet shoes.

'Scary, doctor — but when they're

giving away dough, it pays to listen.' He lit another cigarette from the butt already in his mouth, scribbled a reminder on a notepad, then grinned at Ryan. 'Okay — now what can I do for you?'

'A girl who just left said you might know Robert Langley.'

Fuller frowned. 'Only Langley I know calls himself Turk. Gray-haired guy who limps.'

'That's him,' Ryan said. 'Know where I'd find him?'

'No idea.'

'He's supposed to be with Senator Cassidy, if that'll help.'

'The senator's in St. Louis, pal. And believe me, Turk Langley ain't with him.'

Ryan frowned, puzzled. 'You sure about that? That the senator's in St. Louis, I mean?'

'Sure I'm sure. Just got through talking to him on the horn a few minutes ago.'

Ryan realized Langley had lied to him. He'd never intended to take Ryan to Cassidy; had just been stalling until he could find a chance to escape.

'You a friend of Turk's?' Fuller was asking.

'Not exactly.'

'Didn't think so. Else why would you come here looking for him, right?'

'Mean, he doesn't work here?'

'Uh-uh. Not for a camel's age.' He added: 'You a cop?'

'Nope.'

'Too bad.' Fuller picked his teeth with the edge of a business card. 'I was hoping the sonofabitch was in trouble.'

Ryan realized he might have an ally. Wiping a raindrop from the end of his nose, he said: 'I was told Langley and Senator Cassidy were good friends.'

'Two years ago, maybe. Not anymore.' Fuller rolled the cigarette to the other corner of his mouth and squinted as the smoke crawled up the left side of his face. 'What's your score in this, huh?'

Ryan took a chance. 'The woman I work for wants to see Langley in jail.'

Fuller broke into a grin that showed bad teeth. 'So you're a PI, huh? Figures.' He didn't elaborate, but added: 'Around here, pal, she'd have to wait in line.'

'He's that unpopular, huh?'

'You got it.'

'If I knew why, it might help me to find him.'

Fuller shrugged thin, rounded shoulders. 'Ain't no secret. Two years ago Turk and the senator were closer than Noah and his Ark. Did everything together. Then, about eighteen months ago, Jim Cassidy found out Turk was nothing more than a plant — '

'Plant?'

'Yeah. You know — a spy — put here by Fontaine's campaign manager, Karl Slater.'

Ryan felt as if something hard had hit him in the chest. Then, ignoring the trickle of water running down his forehead from his hairline, he leaned closer to Fuller and said quietly: 'Could you be mistaken about that?'

'What? That Turk was Slater's spy?'

'Yes.'

'No. No way, doctor.' Fuller removed the cigarette from his mouth for the first time and wagged it at Ryan as he said: 'See, there was kind of a stink about it. Not the kind that makes the papers or anything, but, well, among the Big Boys, the guys on The Hill who knew, it was considered pretty dirty pool. Even for Washington.'

When Ryan left the campaign headquarters, he hurried to the nearest phone booth and called Clare's town house. She answered on the first ring. 'Don't talk,' he told her. 'Just listen. Meet me at the place where you got the new windshield.'

It had stopped raining when the taxi let Ryan off outside the Porsche-Audi dealership. The place was closed. But lights were on in the showroom, making the display models gleam, and Ryan decided to wait in the shadows by the service department.

Thirty minutes passed. Then Clare drove up in a white Pinto. She was relieved to find him unhurt. As he climbed in the car beside her, she impulsively put her arms about his neck and kissed him. 'Thank God you're safe. When I drove around and couldn't find you, I thought — well, I didn't know what to think. You *are* okay, aren't you?'

'Sure. I'm fine.' He indicated the car. 'Where'd this come from?'

'Karl loaned it to me. When I told him

what had happened, he said the police were probably looking for the Porsche, and that we'd be able to get around a lot easier in this.'

'What else did you tell him?'

'Everything. He was real pleased about the president's reaction — oh, and he said he'd call a friend of his in the police department, have him take the heat off you. That reminds me,' she added, 'I promised to call Karl the moment I heard from you, so — '

'Before you do that,' Ryan said, 'there's something you ought to know.' He told her what Fuller had said about Langley working for Slater. She was stunned. She'd only joined Governor Fontaine's staff thirteen months ago, so she knew nothing about any political spy scandal. It didn't make sense, she said. Langley couldn't work for Karl. At least, not anymore. After all, what would Karl have to gain by stopping them from proving that Cassidy was once a Nazi spy? Surely, if anything, the very opposite would be true?

Ryan had to agree. Also, Clare went on, why would Langley — if he worked for

Karl — try to buy Falcon's picture from them? Again, wouldn't it be to Slater's and Governor Fontaine's advantage if they showed the picture to the press or the president? That way, the whole country would know about Cassidy's background. And it was certainly very doubtful they'd vote for him then.

Ryan had to agree with that, too. But it didn't stop him from thinking; trying to reason out alternatives that also might make sense.

'Another thing,' Clare continued, 'if Langley is Karl's boy, like that man says, why would he try to kill us? And, in the same vein, why'd he kill the Richters? The *Kapitan* could've identified Cassidy as Falcon, and faced with that sort of proof, Shining Jim would end up in jail, not the White House. Don't forget, too,' she added, 'that it was Karl who insisted we go see the Secretary of State. I mean, why do that if, at the same time, he was trying to kill us? No,' she said after a long pause, 'it just doesn't make any sense. Either Langley's working for Cassidy and that man you spoke to is a liar, or he just plain made a mistake.'

'Sure seems that way,' Ryan agreed. 'Course, it mightn't hurt to check it out. You know, see if there ever was any kind of 'spy' in Cassidy's camp.'

'Well, frankly, I think it's a waste of time. Besides, if there was some truth to it, I doubt if Karl would be too thrilled with me for reminding him of it.'

'I wasn't suggesting you call Karl,' Ryan said. 'I was thinking more like asking one of your reporter friends. You know, like the guy who gave you Avery's home number?'

Clare hesitated, obviously unhappy about the situation. 'I don't know,' she grumbled. 'I feel like I'm, well, stabbing poor Karl in the back.'

Better him than us, Ryan thought. Aloud, he said, 'Don't get me wrong. I'm not suggesting for one moment that Karl's behind all our problems. He couldn't be. But, you got to admit, it would take a lot of heat off Cassidy, if we knew for sure that Langley wasn't his boy, either. And after all, we've said all along, we don't want to ruin an innocent man

— be it Cassidy or anyone else.'

'You're right,' Clare said. 'For a moment there I was letting my emotions rule my head.' She started the car. 'Let's get to a phone. I'll call Jake Wyman right away. See if he knows anything about Langley once working for Karl.'

There was a phone booth in a service station on the next corner. While Clare called Wyman, Ryan remained in the car and tried to see if any of the things that had happened to them, bad or good, could possibly make sense if Langley still worked for Karl Slater.

Five minutes passed. Then Clare returned to the car. By her glum expression Ryan knew Wyman must have verified Fuller's story.

'Don't look like that,' he said, trying to cheer her up. 'Politics is a cut-throat business. Everybody knows that. An' besides, you can bet Cassidy has guys planted in your party. Only difference is, they haven't been caught yet.'

Clare hadn't been listening. 'It just doesn't fit,' she said, shaken. 'Karl's character, I mean.'

'Hey, he's just trying to win,' Ryan said. 'Americans demand that. I mean, who remembers second place?'

'But Karl's always stressed integrity . . . has been against any kind of smear campaigns or — or Watergate tactics . . . '

'So he made one mistake. Don't nail him to the cross for it. He's probably made up for it since, a hundred times.' When Clare didn't answer, Ryan added: 'Did Wyman happen to know who Langley worked for now?'

'No . . . '

'That sounds more like a yes.'

'Well . . . Jake said he didn't know if Langley still worked for Karl or not, but that the other day he saw them together in the National Archives. They acted like — well, you know, as if they weren't there together. But Jake says he'd already seen them talking to each other, earlier — and knew by their faces they were trying to hide something . . . and . . . ' She suddenly broke off and leaned her forehead on her arms on the steering wheel. 'Oh my God, Ryan,' she said hollowly. 'What in heaven's name does all this mean?'

'I don't know,' he said. 'But there is one way it'd all fit. And make sense.'

'How's that?'

'What if the photo we found in the U-boat wasn't Falcon?'

'But it is. Has to be. Otherwise, why kill Richter, who could verify it?'

'Because he *wouldn't have* verified it, that's why.'

'I don't understand.'

'Neither did I — till I remembered what Dean Callum said in your apartment. About Cassidy not fitting Richter's description of Falcon — remember?'

She said only, 'But we agreed Richter was lying.'

'I know. But I'm not so sure now that we weren't wrong. I've got a gut feeling that Richter would've told us the photo wasn't Falcon — just like Callum kept insisting.'

'But what about that neighbor? The old guy who said that Richter verified the picture of Falcon to Gray Hair?'

'Different picture.'

'What?'

'The picture Gray Hair had — or has

— is of Falcon. That's why he had to kill Richter. He went there to test him. And once he knew the old captain could still identify Falcon, and we were due to talk to him any day, Richter had to die.'

'It's possible, I guess,' Clare said, unconvinced. 'But if what you say is true — and I'm not sure it is — then how'd the photo we found get into Richter's secret files aboard the U-boat?'

'I'm not sure,' Ryan said. 'I've been trying to figure that one out myself. I guess the only logical way,' he added after a pause, 'is for someone to have planted it there.'

'B-But the sub went down in 1942!'

'I mean recently. I know, I know,' he said, seeing her look of disbelief, 'it sounds like something out of a goddamn James Bond movie. But . . . Jesus, right now it's the best I can do.'

Clare studied Ryan a moment. She could almost see the wheels turning in his mind; might've heard them, if her own wheels weren't clicking so loudly. Taking charge, she said, 'I don't know about you, but I could use a drink.'

They drove to the first bar they saw: the Blue Corral. It was on H Street, not far from the strip joints and massage parlors, and they sat in a back booth, close so they could hear themselves speak above the loud country-western music.

Over drinks, they repeated everything they'd discussed in the car. Clare still couldn't accept it, or wouldn't (she wasn't sure herself which was true), and when they once more got around to how the photo of Falcon — or Cassidy — got aboard the U-boat, Clare said that meant someone other than themselves, and Mitch, of course, must have known where the submarine went down. 'But who?' she said. Then, as it hit her: 'Langley?'

'Possible,' said Ryan. 'But I doubt if he did the diving — not with that leg of his. Besides,' he added, knowing she wasn't going to like this, 'Langley's only a soldier. Man we want is the general who gives the soldier his orders.'

There was a long pause as Clare forced herself to digest Ryan's statement and its implication. Then, as if wrenching out a tooth, she dragged the words out of herself and Said grimly: 'Mr. Karl Slater, right?'

Ryan nodded, Ignoring the loud foot-stomping music coming from a jukebox near the bar. 'I'm sorry,' he said. 'But, as best I can figure, right now it does seem to all point his way.' He then explained that Slater had known where the U-boat was; could've hired a diver to plant Cassidy's photo, waited awhile, then suggested to Fontaine that raising the U-boat and making it a war memorial would be a great vote-getter. Then, once Fontaine agreed, Slater put Clare in charge of the project, told her how vital to the campaign it was, then sat back knowing it was just a matter of time before someone found the photo and realized it was Senator Cassidy.

Clare didn't interrupt Ryan. But her pale, tight-lipped expression said she was still unwilling to believe a man she so respected could be this devious.

'That's all possible,' she agreed when Ryan had finished. 'But there's something you're forgetting: Karl was against my going after Cassidy right from the start.'

'Was he? I'm not so sure. Hell, he knows the kind of person you are — that you're no quitter. Could be, he used a little reverse psychology — you know, made it tough on you, so you'd be all the more determined to see it through. Prove Cassidy was guilty. Now, that's only a wild guess,' Ryan added before Clare could protest, 'and I could be way off base. But, like I said just now, it does seem to all point his way.'

Clare didn't answer. She was so unnerved by the idea that Fontaine or Slater could possibly resort to such ugly smear tactics, she couldn't sit still. She asked Ryan to take her out to the car. He understood. Once in the car, he made no attempt to press her into conversation but just sat there beside her, silent, motionless, trying to fit the rest of the pieces into this new and shocking puzzle.

'Could we just drive?' she said presently.

'Sure.' He started the car. 'Any place particular?'

'No . . . Yes. Along the Mall.'

Ryan obeyed. They drove up one side

374

of the Mall, and down the other. There was little traffic at that late hour. Again? he asked. Again, she said. Ryan obeyed. He wondered if she was trying to find some solace from the greatness all about them. When they made the turn in front of the Capitol Building, she suddenly asked him to pull over. There were NO PARKING and NO STOPPING signs all over the place. Ryan parked between two of them, killed the lights and engine, and waited.

'What about Wells Beaman and Murchinson?' she said suddenly. 'They in on it, too?'

'I don't know.' Ryan shrugged. 'I'm still stumbling around punching at shadows myself. I somehow doubt it, though. My guess'd be that Slater sent Langley to talk to them — say that he worked for Cassidy — so that, later, when we spoke to them, we'd think the senator was worried an' trying to cover his tracks.'

Again it made sense. Clare sighed. She then wanted to know if Ryan thought the threatening phone call, phony bomb under her tire, and the shooting from the woods were all more of the same: reverse psychology. Ryan didn't know. 'Sure is possible, though. In fact,' he said, thinking back on it, 'the shooting kind of chewed on me from the start. After all, if you want to shoot someone, why wait until they're going seventy miles an hour along a highway? Hell, there are plenty of places better than that. 'specially when your target isn't suspecting anything. And something else,' he added, 'an' this kind of itched at me, too — their always using Langley.'

'How do you mean?'

'Well, he's not exactly hard to identify. Instead of using some ordinary guy who would've probably gone unnoticed, Slater or Cassidy, or whoever's behind all this, kept using Langley. I mean, Jesus, now that I think about it, it's almost like they *wanted* us to know who was after us . . . doing the killing.'

'If these things bothered you so much,' Clare said, frowning, 'how come you never shared them with me?'

Ryan frowned himself. 'There's no real clear-cut answer to that,' he said. 'First off, they were just little naggings I got — you know, thoughts that came to me an' then passed on, . . . an' then, well, under the circumstances, they sounded pretty stupid . . . an' . . . an' anyway, you wouldn't have believed me . . . and I figured we had enough to argue about without me throwing sticks on the fire . . . '

She said quietly, 'I still wish you'd told me. I mean, we were — are — supposed to be a team.'

'Yes,' he said. 'I guess you're right. Trouble is, being a team is something I don't find too natural . . . or easy to fit to.'

Neither spoke for a while after that. Although it was dark, the lights illuminating the Capitol Building made everything in the area quite bright. Even inside the car. Now and then headlights flared over them as an occasional tourist took a late-evening look at the Capitol. Neither Ryan nor Clare seemed to notice them.

Presently, Clare said, 'Let's go home.'

Ryan started the car. They headed slowly along the Mall in the direction of Georgetown.

'I guess you could be right about Karl,' Clare said grudgingly. 'But right now I'm just not ready to accept it.' When Ryan didn't say anything, she added, 'For one thing there are too many loose ends, such as Dean Callum and Avery's behavior, and, for another, if Karl is involved, that means Governor Fontaine must be, too. And I just can't buy that. I mean, for years now everyone on The Hill — even his worst enemies — has agreed that Fontaine is a man of honor and integrity.'

'He still could be,' Ryan said. 'Hell, maybe he isn't involved in this at all. Could be Slater planned the whole scheme himself. We know he's capable of it. Having Langley spy on Cassidy proves that. And he sure as hell has plenty to gain. You said yourself that he was the power behind the throne. Well, a throne's no good unless there's a king on it. Or, in this case, a president. Only problem is,' Ryan continued, 'Slater knows goddamn well that Fontaine doesn't stand a rat's chance of getting elected. So could be he decided to give him a little help and devised this scheme to knock Cassidy out of the running.'

'But surely Karl would've known that sooner or later the truth about Cassidy would leak out?'

'Sure. But so what? By then Fontaine's in the White House and Slater's powerful enough to ride out any repercussions.'

Thinking aloud, Clare said bitterly, 'And I helped him.'

'We helped him,' Ryan corrected. 'Which is just what Slater counted on. He was smart enough not to get involved himself — even protested all along that he didn't believe any of it. But, meanwhile, he was getting us and other people to do his dirty work. What's more, the clever bastard mixed truth with fiction, so that the more facts we uncovered — like Cassidy's old man being pro-Nazi an' Mary Jo getting killed by Falcon — the more we believed everything else was true.'

Clare gave a troubled, disillusioned sigh. 'Just for the moment,' she said glumly, 'assuming you're right about all this, what do we do now? To stop Karl, I mean?'

'God only knows,' Ryan said. 'So far

I've come up with zilch. I'll tell you this much, though — it ain't going to be easy. We've done too good a job proving Cassidy's guilty for us now to be able to just stand up an' say, 'Hey, guys, time out. It's all been a big mistake. What we've been telling you is wrong. Shining Jim is innocent, Mr. President, and — ''

'The president!' Clare looked horrified. 'Oh my God, Ryan, I'd forgotten all about going to the president.'

'Well, you can believe he hasn't forgotten about us,' Ryan said grimly, 'that's for damn sure. Neither has Secretary Royce. So, if you've got any clever ideas tucked away, kiddo, now'd be one hell of a good time to dig 'em out.'

'I only wish I had,' Clare said, dismayed. 'But, truth is, I can't think of a thing.' What was more, she thought, with the election almost on them, and half the local police force breathing down Ryan's neck, it looked like they'd just about run out of time.

Ryan, who'd been thinking, too, realized what they needed most was concrete proof to show Slater was behind all this.

And as they drove past a campaign billboard showing Governor Fontaine smiling down at them, Ryan suddenly had an idea. 'What's the chance of getting a sample of Slater's handwriting?'

'Pretty good. Why?' Clare said, puzzled.

'How soon could you get it?'

'Tomorrow. Maybe even tonight. The campaign headquarters is still open. I can probably find a memo or something that Karl's written without too much trouble.'

'Great. Then let's get over there right now.'

'All right.' Clare bit back her curiosity and remained silent as they drove toward 14th and L.

31

The glowing red numerals of the digital clock on Karl Slater's desk at campaign headquarters showed 9:18 p.m. Slater eyed the time momentarily. He went to the small portable refrigerator and opened a bottle of Perrier. Pouring the sparkling water into a chilled glass, he returned to his desk.

Since early morning it had been a politically successful day. Funds were rolling in; the governor's speech last night to labor union leaders had been favorably received; and polls across the country continued to show that Fontaine was making steady if not spectacular gains on Senator Cassidy. Stimulating news indeed! And although no one on the governor's staff was yet bold enough to predict a November 11th victory, most were now confident that their man would at least make a race out of the election.

If only the poor stupid slobs knew what

was about to happen, Slater thought smugly. They'd be more than confident — they'd be ecstatic!

He'd had a violent urge to share his secret with the *Washington Post* reporter who had interviewed him that afternoon. 'Listen, you brainless simpering idiot,' he'd wanted to shout, 'Don't you realize that in a very short time I, Karl Slater, will be solely responsible for the biggest, most shocking voter turnaround in this country's political history! I, not Wall Street, not the union leaders, not the politicians, not even the voters, will have actually put a man in the White House! Single-handedly!'

But he'd said nothing. He'd merely answered the reporter's probing questions carefully and succinctly (never once allowing himself to be viewed as anything but Governor Fontaine's strong, silent, faithful shadow), then agreed to one picture and concluded the interview. Although it had been brief, the reporter hadn't protested. He, like all of Washington's press, knew how seldom Slater permitted interviews, and he had left the office happily impressed.

Now, as Slater sat there at his desk sipping the refreshingly cool Perrier water, he felt smugly pleased with himself. All was well in political heaven. Thanks to Ryan and Clare Winslow, and their visit to the president, a certain stumbling block known as Senator Cassidy would soon be removed from the path to his goal: the White House. Then, with Fontaine's election a foregone conclusion, he, Karl Slater, would become personal advisor and confidant to the new president. And after that? Well, it wouldn't be too difficult to ease more and more of his own men into powerful positions, and —

The jarring ring of the telephone interrupted his festering dreams of power. It was his private line. Slater guessed it was Langley reporting in. He was right. Langley explained about his run-in with Ryan and Clare and how he'd escaped from them by ramming a police car.

Although Clare had already told Slater about most of the trouble she and Ryan had had with Langley, Karl let Langley finish so he could see if the two stories conflicted in any way. When basically they didn't, Slater ordered Langley to continue keeping Ryan and Clare under twenty-four-hour surveillance. 'But I want you to hire all new men, Turk. That way there's less chance of anyone being spotted. Also, keep rotating them, no matter what it costs. Now that we're this close to victory, we can't afford any slipups, or — '

He broke off as through his office window he saw Clare enter from the alley. She looked concerned. She paused just inside the rear door, looked about her, saw there were no policemen around, then motioned at Karl, asking him if it was all right for her to see him. He nodded and gestured for her to come ahead.

On the phone he said, 'Clare's just walked in. I don't know if Ryan's with her or not. But if he is, I'll try to hold them here awhile, so you can get some men to tail them when they leave.' He hung up.

Across town in a street phone booth, Turk Langley dug out some dimes and started calling the men he knew he could trust.

In Slater's office Clare said that Ryan

was out in the car in the alley. He was waiting there until she found out if Karl had received word from the police that Ryan had been cleared. Slater explained that he hadn't heard anything yet. But his contact was most influential, and had assured Karl that he'd get everything straightened out shortly. 'In the meantime,' Slater added, 'I'm sure it's perfectly safe for Ryan to wait here with us. So, why don't you go out and get him — bring him in.'

When they were all comfortable in the office, Ryan thanked Karl for trying to help him. Slater shrugged it off as nothing. Then he mildly chided them for not remaining in Clare's town house as he'd instructed. Clare apologized, then said, 'But you also told me to let you know the moment I knew Ryan was safe. So, since we weren't that far from here when I picked him up, I thought we'd stop by and tell you personally. At the same time,' she added, 'find out if you'd heard from the police.'

The lie rolled out smoothly. Slater seemed to accept it without question.

Then he insisted that Ryan and Clare wait in the office until his police contact called. That way, he explained, there was no chance of Ryan being spotted or arrested. Before they could argue, he added that he'd have his secretary bring them some coffee and left the office.

Through the window Ryan and Clare saw Slater pause by Ruth Livermore's desk outside the door, speak briefly, then walk away.

'Maybe listening to you has made me paranoid,' Clare told Ryan as they watched Slater head into the restroom, 'but I sense he's up to something. I've no idea what. But, believe me, Karl's never been this polite or considerate since the day I met him.'

'Could be he's heard from Langley,' Ryan said, 'and is worried that we're getting too close to home.'

'If that's the case,' said Clare, concerned, 'maybe we should get out of here. I mean, perhaps he hasn't called his VIP police friend at all — is just keeping us here until the cops come and grab you.'

Ryan shook his head. 'I don't think so.

Slater doesn't want me — or you — arrested. Not yet, anyway. Not until we finish nailing down Cassidy's coffin with the president.' He went and stood by the window, adding: 'Take a look on his desk. See if you can find anything with his writing on it. I'll try an' screen you from Ruth an' the others.'

Clare moved to the desk and quickly went through the neatly stacked letters, reports, and memos. Ryan, meanwhile, remained by the window, trying to shield Clare with his body while he watched everyone working in the main office. He saw Ruth approaching with two cups of coffee.

'Watch it,' he told Clare. 'Here comes Ruth.'

Clare started away from the desk. Then she noticed a handwritten memo to Governor Fontaine that was signed 'K.S.' She deliberately knocked it and an envelope onto the floor behind the desk. Then she bent down, stuffed the memo inside her blouse, and straightened up with the envelope — just as Ryan opened the door for Ruth.

'Here you go, guys.' Ruth handed Ryan and Clare each a cup. ''fraid black's the best I can do, but — '

'Black's fine,' Clare said. She casually put the envelope on the desk. Then she indicated the varicolored flag pins on the wall map that reflected, through surveys, the governor's popularity throughout the different states. 'Looks like the governor's picking up the count in most places.'

'Yes, he is,' Ruth said. She sighed, weary and concerned. 'I just hope he hasn't made his charge too late. Gotta run.' She hurried out.

'Find something?' Ryan asked Clare.

'Yes. I'm not sure if Karl will miss it or not. But, even if he does, there's no reason for him to think either of us took it. Of course,' she said with a trace of sarcasm, 'since you never did say why you want it, I don't know if it'll be any good or — '

She broke off as the phone rang. It was Slater's private line. At her desk Ruth looked up as she heard the ringing but made no attempt to answer the call. Ryan looked out the window and saw Slater

389

hurrying toward his office. He opened the door for him. Slater entered, answered the phone, said, 'Just a moment,' and then to Ryan and Clare: 'Would you excuse me a minute . . . '

They left the office. Slater waited for the door to close. Then, into the phone, he said, 'What is it, Turk?'

'Everything's taken care of, sir. There's a man outside your building right now.'

'Excellent. Tell him their car's in the alley — a white Pinto. License number XXY-622.' He smiled as he hung up, then left the office.

Outside the door Ryan and Clare were talking to Ruth. Slater joined them. 'I'll walk you outside,' he told them. It was an order, not a request. They accompanied him to the rear door. 'The problem with the police has been cleared up,' he explained. 'However, I want both of you to remain in the house — until you hear from Secretary Royce or the president. Understood?'

Clare started to protest, but Ryan cut her off. 'Don't worry,' he said with uncharacteristic friendliness. 'We don't plan to go anywhere. Hey, an' — uhm — thanks for everything, huh?'

'My pleasure,' Slater said stiffly. 'Good night, Clare.'

'G'night, Karl.' Clare, realizing that Ryan must be up to something, allowed him to drag her out into the alley.

Slater watched as they crossed to the white Pinto. Then he closed the door and moved to the window overlooking the street. Shortly, Ryan and Clare drove out of the alley, turned, and headed toward Georgetown. A few moments passed. Then a black, late-model Oldsmobile pulled away from the curb and drove after the Pinto.

Slater smiled to himself and returned to his office where he made a call on his private line to the police department. He spoke softly for a few moments, then thanked the person and hung up. As he did, he noticed two things on his desk: An envelope was out of place, and a memo was missing. He called Ruth in.

'Did you take a memo addressed to the governor from my desk?'

'No, sir.'

'It's missing.' He sifted through the paperwork. 'It was here a few minutes ago, and — What're you doing?' he demanded as she bent down and looked behind his desk.

'I thought perhaps it might've fallen on the floor, sir. I saw Clare pick up an envelope earlier, and thought — '

'Envelope?'

'Yes, sir.' Ruth pointed to the unmarked envelope that she'd seen Clare put on the desk. 'That one.'

Slater picked up the envelope and noticed it had scuff marks on it. He frowned, always uneasy when unexpected things happened. Then, wanting to get rid of Ruth, he said: 'Of course! How foolish of me. I've already given that memo to the governor. I should've remembered.'

'The number of hours you work, Mr. Slater,' Ruth said admiringly, 'I'm surprised you remember anything.'

'Thank you, Ruth.' Slater smiled stiffly. 'That'll be all.' He watched her leave the office and return to her desk.

Then he sat there, absently sipping his Perrier, wondering why Clare would steal a memo that was merely a list of fund raisers that the governor needed to thank personally for their diligent efforts.

It was all very puzzling and very disturbing indeed.

32

At that same moment, across town in the quiet fire-lit study of his elegant Chevy Chase home, Senator Avery Brickland was also finding life more than a little disturbing.

He was finding it impossible.

Depressingly impossible.

He sat in a big, high-backed leather armchair in front of the dying fire, a near-empty bottle of bourbon on the table beside him. He felt confused. Ashamed. It was bad enough that he'd been cowardly enough to let Kyle take the blame for his own murderous act . . . but to then try to kill his brother when all Kyle had asked for was help — well, Avery knew he'd now reached bottom.

His own private hell.

Self-inflicted, solitary agony.

Inescapable.

Well, he sure as hell knew how to beat that one. Mind muddled with alcohol, he sat trying to find that special nerve it takes for a man to shoot himself with his dead father's favorite shotgun. The gun was a beautiful over-under Italian-made Baretta Silver Snipe with a well-oiled, hand-checkered, tiger-grained stock.

Avery hated that gun more than any other in the collection: partly because it had been the governor's favorite; partly because it had knocked him sprawling the first, and only, time he'd fired it; and partly because the governor bragged that the gun had been a gift from an Italian countess whom he'd 'screwed for six hours straight' during a post-World War II visit to Venice.

Avery held the beautifully balanced shotgun with the stock between his knees, the cold muzzle only inches from his sweating face, his uninjured left arm outstretched so that the thumb rested on the front of the curved, single trigger. The gun was loaded. All he had to do was push down with his thumb.

An hour earlier Avery, after eating very little dinner, had sat with his wife, Diana, and the children in the little rosewood room off the kitchen that they called 'TV Corner.' He was sober then. He'd surprised everyone with his unusually good humor and awful jokes until, finally, his eight-year-old son, Alex, had given him a worried look and asked him if he felt okay.

'Sure. I'm fine. Why do you ask?'

'No reason,' said Alex. He went on watching TV. 'Just wondered, is all.'

'Did you hear that, Mouse?' Avery said to Diana. 'A man can't even joke around in his own home without everyone thinking he's sick or crazy or something.'

'Not everyone,' Melanie said. She spoke without taking her eyes from the TV. 'I didn't say you were sick. Or crazy.'

'You didn't laugh at my jokes, either.'

'That's because they weren't funny,' Melanie said without malice. At seven she already had her mother's beautiful dark-gold hair and dark eyes, but her father's features. 'Did you think they were funny, Mom?'

Diana, with great effort, stopped watching television and slowly looked at her daughter. There was recognition in her eyes, something the doctors found encouraging. After a long moment, she said distantly: 'No, dear. Not very.'

'Well, thanks a lot,' Avery said. He pretended to be hurt. 'You guys are going to be sorry when you see me on Johnny Carson.'

'Not as sorry as Johnny,' said Alex.

Avery ignored him. Rising, he kissed Diana on the forehead. 'I love you, Mouse,' he whispered. 'Always remember that.'

She gave a faint smile. Avery moved up behind his children, who were sprawled in a tangled heap on the couch. He leaned down and kissed Melanie on the cheek. 'Love you, sweetheart.'

'Oh, Daddy . . . ' she protested.

He kissed his son. 'You too, pal.'

'Hey, don't, Dad. I'm trying to watch something.'

Avery straightened up, forced himself to smile and left the room. As he started along the hall to the study, he heard Alex say: 'Boy, Dad's really acting weird tonight.'

Now, as Avery sat in the quiet, warm

study, the twin holes of the over-under muzzle gaping up at him, he glanced toward the desk and saw the letter propped against the snapshot of his family. In it he'd told his wife and children that he was sorry to leave them but that he was unable to face a life of disgrace and imprisonment. He then exonerated his foster brother, Kyle Lane, of all guilt or responsibility for the death of his father, Governor Brickland. He, and he alone, was responsible.

It had not been easy to write that letter. He'd drunk most of the bourbon by the time he was finished. Then he had folded the letter about his Navy Cross and sealed everything in an envelope and addressed it to his wife and to the president of the United States.

'Being a man is being responsible,' he said, suddenly remembering his father's words. He then looked into the black gaping holes staring up at him. 'Did you hear that, Kyle?' he said. 'Being a man is being re — '

He pressed down on the trigger with his thumb.

His shotgun roared.

Deafeningly loud in the quiet study.

What remained of Avery slumped over the arm of the big leather chair.

Moments later Melanie burst in. Alex limped in behind her. Their eyes bulged at the grisly sight. Their minds froze and no sound came from their gaping mouths. Then, almost before they could truly grasp what had happened, the housekeeper rushed in. She took one look at the decapitated corpse and the blood-spattered walls, gasped with horror and then dragged the horror-stricken children from the room.

'Don't go in there, Mrs. Brickland!' she begged as she saw Diana approaching along the hall. 'Please . . . please don't!'

Diana ignored her. She entered the study and closed the door behind her. The housekeeper herded Alex and Melanie upstairs to her room.

In the study, Diana stood with her back to the door and looked at the lifeless body of her husband.

Her brains vomited.

Her mind screamed.

But her blank expression never changed.

Then she saw the letter. Numbly, she approached the desk. She picked up the letter, saw the envelope addressed to her and to the president, and put it into her housecoat pocket. Leaving the study, she went upstairs, past the room in which the housekeeper was trying to calm the hysterical children, and into her bedroom.

She calmly closed the door. Sitting on the bed, she read the letter. Again. She understood its contents but refused to accept them. She tried to push reality deeper into the writhing, black maw of her mind. But it rebelled; and the mental retching continued, increased, until she could no longer control it. Rising, she put Avery's medal into her jewelry box, entered the bathroom, tore up the letter and flushed each little piece down the toilet.

Diana Brickland had deliberately destroyed the last remaining evidence that could have cleared Kyle Lane of treason.

She returned to the bedroom. The roaring continued in her mind. She discounted it. She called her doctor. As calmly as if she were ordering aspirin, she told him

Avery had just killed himself with a shotgun. The doctor, shocked by the news and by the fact that Diana sounded so normal, said he would call the police and be right over.

Later, after the police had come, asked their questions, then left with the ambulance containing Avery's remains, the doctor gave Diana and the children a sedative. Diana took it, because the doctor insisted. But she didn't need it. Quietly, peacefully, she went to sleep. It was, the doctor told the gathering news media, the most remarkable and courageous reaction he'd ever witnessed.

33

As they drove away from Governor Fontaine's campaign headquarters, Clare took Slater's memo from under her blouse and gave it to Ryan.

He scanned it briefly under the dome light. As he did he missed seeing the black Oldsmobile that pulled out behind them and followed them at a discreet distance. Without a word he returned the memo to Clare.

Losing her temper, she exclaimed: 'You'd better start filling me in on what's going on in that mind of yours.'

Ryan ignored her for another moment. Then he gave a snarly chuckle and said: 'I thought you'd gotten over being curious?'

'Never mind what you thought. Just tell me why you wanted to look at Karl's handwriting?'

'To compare it with that memo we found in the U-boat.'

'The one from German Intelligence?'

'Right.'

'Why?'

''cause I think he might've written both of them.' Ryan looked in the rearview mirror, memorized what cars were behind them, then said: 'It's another long shot. But if we can get a handwriting expert to prove he did, we got Mr. Slater by the short hairs.'

'Then you think he planted the memo along with the photo?'

'It not only added a touch of authenticity, but it also verified who the guy was in the picture: Falcon.' He added: 'I never would've thought of it, but, well, when we were parked outside the Capitol Building a while back, I remembered something that'd puzzled me when Louise Klammer told us what the memo said — '

'What was that?'

'I can't remember her exact words, but basically she said the memo identified the person in the attached picture as Falcon. Of course, she never knew we had that picture. But I remember thinking then how risky it was for an intelligence outfit to identify — in writing — one of their spies. 'specially when there was no reason to. Hell, all German Intelligence had to do was tell Richter that it was a photo of Falcon. Then, if the U-boat's ever captured before he can destroy his files, at least no one would know they were looking at a spy.'

'That makes sense,' Clare admitted. Although annoyed that once again he hadn't shared his thoughts with her, she bit back her temper and said: 'I know where there's a graphologist, too — in Alexandria. I saw the sign one day while I was shopping on King Street. It's probably too late to go see her now, but first thing tomorrow I'll give her a call — see how early we can get an appointment.'

'Better than that,' Ryan said. 'Let's just drive over there. That way we know for sure no one's overheard our plan.' As he spoke, he looked in the rearview mirror again and saw that none of the cars following them were familiar.

★ ★ ★

At exactly one minute after nine the next morning, Mrs. Jennings ushered Senator James L. Cassidy into the president's Oval Office.

The president, already on his feet, came from behind his desk to greet the senator. The two men shook hands firmly in the center of the room.

'Hello, James . . . come in . . . come in . . .'

'Thank you, sir.'

'Some coffee or — or hot tea?'

'No — nothing, thanks.'

'Well, then, sit down . . . sit down.' The president sat behind his polished hand-carved desk, picked up the crystal polar bear paperweight and hefted it in his hands as Senator Cassidy got comfortable across from him. The chief executive seemed lost in thought for several moments. Then, looking up, he said, 'Shocking news about young Senator Brickland, isn't it?'

'Yes. Shocking.' Cassidy noticed an edge to the president's voice and wondered if Brickland's death was why he'd been summoned. 'Man his age, so much to live for — it's truly a great tragedy.'

'I agree. Not only to his family and friends on The Hill, but to the whole country.' He paused. Then, almost too casually: 'He left no note or explanation, you know.'

'I know, sir. I called his house as soon as I heard. The doctor there told me he hadn't.'

'Apparently, the senator had been drinking pretty heavily,' the president said. Again, casually.

Cassidy shrugged noncommittally.

'You two were friends, weren't you?'

'Yes. Good friends.'

'I'm sorry, James. Something as inexplicable as this . . . ' The president paused and let the words hang a moment before saying: 'I don't suppose you'd have any idea why he'd want to commit suicide?'

'No. None. In fact, when I spoke to Avery last week, he seemed in excellent spirits.'

'Oh? I heard he's been sick the last few days — hadn't come into his office or the Senate.'

'That's possible,' Cassidy said. 'Truthfully, I've been so swamped with campaign matters lately, I — '

'Of course, of course, I understand.' The president gently sat the polar bear on top of a file folder on his desk. Then he said: 'Tell me something, James — is there anything that you and Senator Brickland were currently involved in that might've prompted his suicide?'

'Involved in? I don't understand, Mr. President.'

'You know, some kind of personal problem . . . where the pressure finally got too much for him?'

Cassidy looked at the president. The face, gravely calm on the outside, seemed to be seething inside. Puzzled, Cassidy said: 'No, sir. Certainly nothing that I know of.'

'Are you absolutely sure about that, Senator?'

'Yes, Mr. President. Absolutely . . . ' Cassidy could almost feel the tension boiling inside the man facing him. He wondered what the hell was causing it. 'If you know something, sir, and think it concerns me, I'd appreciate it if you'd tell me what it is.'

The president gave a deep, troubled

sigh. 'Very well, Senator, I will.' He removed the little crystal bear from atop the file folder and carefully set it on the gleaming desk. He then opened the folder, took out the photograph that was presumably Falcon, and Showed it to Cassidy. He said that the CIA and Naval Intelligence had verified that it was a picture of the senator taken when he was in his early twenties. 'Do you deny that, Senator?'

'No, Mr. President.' Cassidy tried to hide the shock and dismay he felt. 'That's my picture, all right.'

'Then, perhaps you can explain why it was found among classified documents aboard a German U-boat that was sunk in 1942 off the North Carolina coast?'

'No, sir. I can't.'

'Can't? Or won't?'

'Can't.' Realizing now why he'd been summoned, Cassidy added quickly: 'As I explained to the man and woman who first showed me the picture, I gave it to a young woman that I was seeing at the time — '

'Mary Jo Buffram?' The president read

the name from the file.

'Correct. As I'm sure you're now aware, she was found murdered on Bogue Banks. And it's my belief, Mr. President, that the man responsible for her death — a spy whose code name was Falcon — took the photograph from her purse and carried it aboard the submarine.'

'Why would he do that, Senator?'

'I don't know, sir. Since I wasn't present at the time — '

'According to your service records,' the president broke in, 'you were in the process of being transferred from the Coast Guard to Naval Intelligence — ciphers, to be more exact.'

'Yes, sir.'

The president looked at the file another moment, reading briefly, turning pages, nodding, and then closed the folder and replaced the crystal polar bear on top of it.

'Unfortunately,' he said in his gravest Mount Rushmore voice, 'it seems that on the actual day or night of the murder, May ninth, you were at neither base but were, in fact, in transit from Wilmington,

North Carolina, to Roanoke, Virginia. Isn't that true, Senator?'

'I believe so, Mr. President.'

'Records don't lie, Senator. And *your* records state that you had forty-eight hours in which to report to your destination. What did you do during those forty-eight hours, Senator? What exactly did you do?'

'Mr. President, that was forty years ago . . . '

'Are you saying you don't remember?'

Cassidy looked into the tired, lined face of the man across from him and saw nothing but mounting contempt. He let all his breath out in a long, deep sigh. 'Driving,' he said. 'That's what I was doing, Mr. President. Driving a new car I'd just bought from Wilmington to Roanoke.'

'Alone, Senator?'

'Yes, sir. Alone.'

'Then there are no witnesses to substantiate the fact that you were not on Bogue Banks.'

'No, Mr. President. None that I can recall, anyway. And even if there were, after forty years . . . ' He shrugged. 'I doubt if they'd be too reliable. However,' he added, his tone mildly defiant, 'nor are there any witnesses to indicate that I was there, either.'

'No witnesses, perhaps, Senator. But certainly a lot of incriminating evidence that supports the fact that you were.'

Senator Cassidy grew angry. 'Mr. President, are you accusing me — a United States senator — of treason? I would very much like to hear you come right out and say those exact words . . . '

The president hesitated. He was well aware of the enormity and the repercussions of such an accusation. He was also aware of what his legal advisors had warned: namely, that the 'evidence' was highly incriminating but not necessarily conclusive enough to have Cassidy arrested or charged with treason. And yet, the president had integrity and felt a genuine obligation to his country. So, on his own authority, and believing that what he was doing was right, he cleared his throat and said very carefully, 'What I am saying, Senator, is this: Soon this country will be going to the polls to elect their next president. The man chosen will represent the voters' faith, hope, and trust, the man they feel is most capable of being their leader as well as the leader of the greatest nation in the world. And because of those things, I believe it is only fair that these same voters be given the chance to know all about the man they intend to elect — to know about him, and then decide whether or not he is their rightful choice. Don't you agree, Senator?'

Cassidy said only: 'What exactly are you getting at, Mr. President?'

'Simply this, Senator. You may be that man, James Cassidy. In fact, it's almost a certainty that you will be. Therefore, I believe the voters have a right to know about the contents of this file — '

'I disagree, Mr. President. Emphatically! Why, you know as well as I do, sir, that such an accusation coming at this late a date — giving no one enough time to judge carefully or weigh any evidence in my favor — would politically crucify me . . . *and* our party.'

'I'm inclined to agree,' the president said. He picked up the crystal polar bear, leaned back in his chair, and studied the paperweight. 'And if there were more time — less urgency due to the immediacy of the election — then I might resort to other methods. But there is no time. And the voters *must* know of your background. Therefore, what I say must be done. And you, Senator, must be the one to do it.'

'Never,' Cassidy said. He stood up, enraged and tugged his fingers violently through his gray-blond hair. 'Unlike Senator Brickland, sir, I do not believe in suicide!'

'Very well,' said the president. 'Under such grave circumstances, you then leave me no choice but to address the nation myself.'

Cassidy sagged, but remained standing. He cleared his throat. 'But, sir, I urge you to first consider the consequences — dire, condemning consequences that will follow both of us for the rest of our political and non-political lives — should you charge me falsely of treason.'

For a long, hard moment the two men locked gazes. Then the president returned

the polar bear to the desk. Sighed. Almost
regretfully, he said: 'I mentioned something similar to the man and woman who
brought these charges to my attention
. . . do you know what the man said,
Senator?'

'No, Mr. President.'

'In essence, Senator, he said that the
alternative — a Nazi president — made
any other decision equally treasonable.'

34

Shortly before ten o'clock that same morning Ryan and Clare left the town house and drove to the graphologist's office in Alexandria.

They drove in silence. Both were still in a state of shock from the news of Avery Brickland's death, which had been announced earlier on the radio. The announcer explained that although no suicide note had been found, the police were of the opinion that the senator had taken his own life.

Despite Avery's attempt to kill him in the parking garage, Ryan still felt that irrational filial love for his foster brother. If only Avery hadn't pushed the governor down the stairs, he thought, things might have been so different between them.

But Avery had. And despite Avery's denials, Ryan believed his foster brother had intentionally meant to kill the governor. And that was unforgivable. And even though he, Ryan, had decided to take the fall for the murder — in some strange way repaying the governor for all his kindness and affection — he couldn't forgive Avery for ruining any chance Ryan had for a future.

As he and Clare drove across the Key Bridge, over the cold, flat, wintry-gray Potomac, Ryan realized there was now no one alive who could clear him of murder. And although he'd never given much thought to the possibility of clearing himself, the possibility had always been there. But now it wasn't. It was gone. Lost forever. And the idea of never being able to prove he wasn't a murderer — whether he'd wanted to or not in the past — made him suddenly and desperately want to clear himself.

But how?

The drive along the George Washington Parkway provided its usual magnificent river view of Washington. Although both were too deep in thought to care, or notice, they drove past Arlington Cemetery, the Pentagon, Crystal City . . . and alongside the noisy waterfowl sanctuary and vast railroad yards.

The graphologist's office was in Old Town. It was a narrow building tucked between an antique store and an ice cream parlor on King Street. Ryan parked outside. He and Clare got out of the Pinto and entered the brick-fronted, bay-windowed office. They hadn't noticed the short, squat, balding man who had followed them from Georgetown — Kurt Wharburton, one of Langley's men. Once he saw Ryan and Clare enter the graphologist's office, he used his mobile phone to report in to Langley.

In his Washington apartment Langley told Wharburton to maintain surveillance. Then he called Karl Slater on his private line at campaign headquarters.

'Graphologist?' Slater repeated, puzzled. 'What could they possibly want with a handwriting expert?' He turned things over in his mind a moment. 'When they leave the office, Turk, have your man go in there and find out exactly what they were after. Then get back to me — immediately. Understood?' He hung up.

Langley then called Wharburton and

gave him his instructions.

Inside the small, quiet, stiflingly warm office, Ryan and Clare introduced themselves to the graphologist, Ms. Sandra Bonjour. Ms. Bonjour was about Clare's age but there all resemblance ended. She was round, with short, squat legs, and in her bright orange shift resembled, Ryan thought, a blonde, frizzy-haired pumpkin. And despite beaded curtains and the sickly sweet fragrance of incense, there was nothing gypsy-like about her actual approach to graphology. She sat at her desk under a bright fluorescent light, and compared the writing on both memos through a powerful magnifying glass. She was extremely methodical and meticulous. After thirty minutes of silence, she gave a satisfied 'Uh-huh,' swung the magnifying glass aside, and turned to Ryan and Clare.

'Oh, yes,' she told them, in her cultured Boston accent. 'Definitely. Quite definitely. Even though one is in German, the other English, both memos were written by the same person. Who, incidentally — and I'd stake my reputation on this — is a man.'

Thanking her, they left.

Outside, after the intense and stifling heat, Ryan and Clare felt the cold air shoot into their lungs like a shot of adrenaline.

'Well,' Clare said as they got in the Pinto, 'that settles it, doesn't it? Whether I want to face it or not, this whole thing is nothing but one big insidious smear set up by Karl or Governor Fontaine or both.'

'Sure looks that way,' Ryan said. 'I'm sorry, Clare. Real sorry.'

'Thanks. I . . . ' She couldn't find any words. She felt angry, betrayed, disillusioned, bitter, and, perhaps more than anything else, foolish. But she masked it all behind a look of tight-lipped determination, and without a word got into the car with Ryan.

Across the street Kurt Wharburton remained at the wheel of his Oldsmobile until the Pinto had driven away. Then he got out, crossed the narrow street with its wintry trees and brick-paved sidewalks, and entered the graphologist's office. The front door had a bolt as well as a key lock. As Wharburton slid the bolt in place,

Sandra Bonjour swayed out of the rear office, hanging beads clicking behind her, and demanded to know what he was doing.

'Lady,' he said simply, 'I'm gonna make this easy for you. You tell me what them two people who just left wanted, an' I'll be gone outta here quicker'n you can spit. Otherwise' — he knocked over a small antique glass cabinet containing porcelain figurines; everything smashing to the floor — 'I'm gonna make this painful for you.'

Sandra, afraid and completely bewildered, explained everything.

'Don't move,' Wharburton warned her. He got on the phone and passed the information on to Langley.

The gray-haired cripple, still nursing his swollen, tender finger, gave a low, surprised whistle. 'Return to Winslow's town house,' he told Wharburton. 'Maintain surveillance.' He next called his men in the field and instructed them to watch all the bridges back to Washington. There was a possibility that Ryan and Clare had not yet crossed the Potomac, he explained, and whoever spotted them was to notify him immediately and then tail them wherever they went. Lastly, he called Slater on his private line at campaign headquarters.

The silence that followed lasted so long, Langley wondered for a moment if he'd been cut off.

'You're quite certain this information is absolutely correct?' Slater said, quietly seething.

'Yes, sir. Wharburton called from the graphologist's office.'

'Very well,' Slater said. Time had run out, he realized. 'Then I want Ryan and Clare picked up immediately. Immediately, Turk. Understood?'

'Consider it done, sir.' Langley hung up. Then he started making the necessary calls.

It was almost noon when Dean Callum finished writing up a proposal bid for a new janitorial job. It had taken him most of the morning to decide on a Christian and yet profitable price. Now, stiff from leaning his huge frame over the cluttered desk, he straightened up in the chair and began rubbing the ache from his massive shoulders.

Shortly, his secretary entered with a

newspaper and his lunch — a cold roast-beef sandwich and a carton of milk from the cafe across the street.

'The president's going to speak on TV at five o'clock,' she told Callum.

'About what?'

'I don't know. Radio didn't say. Just said it concerned all Americans.' She indicated the proposal. 'Want me to type that up before I go to lunch?'

'Bless you, child, no. I want to read it one more time. Run along now,' Callum said, smiling. 'Enjoy your lunch with God.'

Alone, Callum pushed the paperwork aside and placed his lunch before him. Then he clasped his big, tattooed hands together, bowed his head, and humbly said grace. Afterward, as he ate his lunch, he turned to the personal want ads in the newspaper. Among them his own ad read:

REWARD OFFERED for any unpublished information concerning the 1942 murder of Mrs. Mary Jo Buffram.

Under that was listed the telephone number of the local answering service that Callum had hired to take messages. He had placed the ad in the newspaper in April, right after two old friends, Wells Beaman and T. S. Murchinson, had called him and said that they'd received a visit from a gray-haired man who limped. Both added that the man wouldn't give his name, but mentioned that he worked for Senator Cassidy and asked a lot of questions about Mary Jo and the Nazi spy supposedly responsible for her death.

Callum had visited the senator's campaign headquarters in the capital, as well as in Virginia and Maryland, and tried to locate the gray-haired cripple. But no one knew anyone who fitted the description. Frustrated, Callum decided against revealing himself to Senator Cassidy and instead ran the reward ad. He'd had several crank calls during the first couple of months, then all response stopped. During that time Callum visited the Washington Navy Yards, and because of the information given him by the archivist, had flown to Germany and spoken to Ernst Richter. The ex-U-boat captain gave him Falcon's description, which Callum sketched into a picture that Richter said was an excellent likeness of the spy.

Callum then returned to Washington. Months of silence passed. He had all but given up hope when he'd received Beaman's second call concerning Ryan and Clare Winslow's interest in Mary Jo and Falcon. That had revived Callum's hopes, until the day that he'd spoken to them in his station wagon outside Clare's town house and realized that they didn't know who Falcon was, either. Crushed, Callum decided to run the ad until the end of the year, promising himself then that if he'd uncovered no further information regarding Mary Jo's murderer, he would give up the search altogether.

Now, as he turned from the personal want-ad section and began looking through the paper for some mention of why the president was addressing the nation, Callum suddenly saw it. There, under a political cartoon showing Governor Fontaine emerging from the looming shadow of Senator Cassidy, was a photograph of Fontaine's campaign manager, Karl Slater. The caption under the photograph called Slater the quiet, guiding strength behind Governor Fontaine.

But Callum didn't read the interview itself. He barely realized it was even there. All he could see was the photograph. He stared fixedly at it, mind whirling, blood thudding in his ears, his thoughts and emotions a mixture of hope and disbelief.

'It's him!' he said, not realizing he was thinking aloud. 'Older, grayer, more lined, of course . . . but still him. *Him*.'

He pushed away from the desk and dropped to his knees, bowed his head, clasped his big-knuckled, tattooed hands together before him, and prayed: 'Oh please, please dear Lord, do not tease my eyes with this miracle unless it's true, I beg of you, Lord. Hear me. I am your servant, O Lord . . . Guide me . . . tell me what it is that you want me to do.'

35

Clare said little as she and Ryan drove away from the graphologist's office in the direction of Georgetown. The bitter realization that Karl Slater, and possibly Governor Fontaine, too, had plotted such a vile and devious smear campaign against Senator Cassidy — and had made her and Ryan a party to it — so disillusioned her that she considered quitting politics forever.

Beside Clare, Ryan saw her tears and respected her need for silence. He didn't feel like talking either. Instead, he used the time to figure out what their next move should be. Obviously, they had to notify the president and the Secretary of State of their findings, so that all action against Cassidy could be stopped and Slater and Fontaine — if the latter was involved — be held accountable for their part in at least three murders.

Equally obvious, Ryan realized, was the need for protection for Clare once Slater knew they were on to him. Any bastard capable of ordering three murders to hide a secret would sure as hell not mind adding another to the list. Especially after he discovered that Clare was responsible for revealing his secret!

'We must call Secretary Royce when we get inside,' he said as they stood on the doorstep and she dug out her key. 'Tell him what we've found out an' then get him to give you around-the-clock protection until the guys behind all this are picked up.'

'Protection?' she said. 'Against what?'

'Never mind,' Ryan said. 'Just open the door so we can get off the street.'

Clare numbly obeyed. Her mind was still too occupied to argue. They stepped inside. She paused to put the key in her purse, while Ryan turned to close the door. For a moment his back was to her, and then he heard her scream.

Whirling around, Ryan saw she was struggling in the grasp of two men. He started for them, then stopped as he noticed a third man standing by the window.

'Go ahead,' Langley urged. The gun in his left hand was aimed at Ryan's belly. 'I'd just love an excuse to maim you — permanently.'

Ryan froze where he stood. 'It won't do you any good to kill us,' he said softly. 'The president already knows the whole story.'

'Wonderful,' Langley said. He smiled, as if he knew Ryan was lying. 'In that case, sir, I'm sure you both won't mind coming with us to listen to his speech. Will you?'

'Speech?'

'Yes. It's been announced that the president will address the nation on television tonight.' Langley's smile widened. 'Apparently, the gentleman has something of great importance to share with us.'

Ryan and Clare exchanged uneasy glances. But before they could say anything, Langley ordered them outside at gun point. They crossed the street and got into Langley's car. Ryan sat in front with the driver, a large, muscular man of forty named Prince, while Langley sat in back with his gun pressed against Clare's ribs.

The third man waited until he was sure there wasn't going to be any trouble, then got in his own car and took off.

They drove to Karl Slater's condominium on Massachusetts Avenue. Slater hadn't arrived yet. Langley had Prince keep Ryan and Clare in the bedroom while he called campaign headquarters and notified Slater that everything was under control.

Slater gave a faint sigh of relief. Then, his emotions disciplined, he said: 'I've just spoken to a friend at the White House, Turk. He says only the Secretary of State knows exactly what the president's speech is about . . . but that there's a rumor it concerns Senator Cassidy.'

'Have you told Governor Fontaine yet, sir?'

'No. Nor do I intend to. He called me a few minutes ago and said he planned to watch the president at home. I'd much prefer he heard about Cassidy that way. It will have greater impact on him.'

'I wish I could be there with him,' Langley said. 'See the look on his stupid face when the president announces that

Senator Cassidy was once a Nazi spy.'

Slater laughed, something that Langley had never heard him do. 'Nothing can stop us now, Turk. Within a very short time, we will be safely ensconced in the White House. The *White House*, do you hear?'

'I hear, sir,' Langley said. He closed his eyes, visualizing it, then added: 'Exactly where a soldier and his general should be.'

'Yes,' Slater said crisply. 'It is most fitting, Turk. Most fitting indeed.'

36

Ryan sat in a comfortable chair in the plush green and gold bedroom of Slater's condominium and tried to figure out how he and Clare could escape. The odds were against them, he knew, and unless he could think of something before the president spoke on television, their chances of remaining alive were pretty goddamn remote!

The room itself offered no solution. The only window was big but it overlooked the street, five stories below. And the door into the living room was blocked by Prince. The large, sullen-faced enforcer sat facing them in a chair outside the bedroom, gun in hand, the door open so he could watch their every move.

Ryan glanced about him. The door leading into the elegant bathroom with its marble walls and gold fixtures offered no solution, either. The window was too high and too small to crawl through, and again there was that five-story drop to consider.

Clare, stretched out on the huge, round, gold-colored bed, saw Ryan looking about and read his thoughts. 'Forget it,' she said softly, so only he could hear. 'I've already given myself a headache wondering how to get out of here. There's just no way.'

'There's always a way,' he said. 'The hard part is not giving up before you find it.'

'I wish I had your confidence. It might stop me from feeling so scared.' She folded her hands behind her head then, and nervously chewed her lower lip as she stared at the ceiling.

Ryan realized again how much he cared for her. He knew the only thing that mattered to him right now was getting her safely out of there, no matter what the cost.

Slater arrived shortly after four. He and Langley spoke briefly in the living room. Then Slater came and stood in the bedroom door and smiled stiffly at Ryan and Clare.

'I wonder,' he said smugly, 'if you'd do

me the honor of joining us.'

'Go fuck yourself,' Clare told him. 'Lousy two-faced bastard, you've given me your last order.'

But Ryan was already rising. Clare saw the faint nod he gave her, indicating she should obey, and without another word accompanied him out into the living room.

'Just don't expect me to be entertaining,' she snapped as she passed Slater.

'I won't,' he said. He stepped back, allowing Prince to keep Ryan and Clare covered. 'I'll leave that up to the president of the United States.'

His big living room had an antique-gold mirror on one wall, rare paintings on another, and a sliding glass door leading out onto a balcony overlooking the street. Ryan noted the distance to the front door as he and Clare were escorted by Prince to the couch. It was roughly twenty feet, and he knew he'd have to cause one hell of a diversion if Clare were ever going to reach the door and get outside without getting shot.

'What makes you think the president

will be so entertaining?' Clare asked Slater once they were all seated before the big-screen television.

'Because, my dear, thanks to you and Ryan, here, our noble patriarch will be pronouncing the political death of one James L. Cassidy. This, naturally, will open the way for the man we all admire most, Henry Fontaine, to have clear sailing right into the White House. And if you don't find that entertaining, Ms. Winslow, then I'm afraid you've been working for the wrong party.'

'I have,' she said bitterly. 'Or, at least, the bunch of slimy low-lives running it. Tell me something, Karl,' she added, 'How come I've never noticed you coil when you sit down?'

Slater smiled thinly, amused by her rage. 'Perhaps because you've been too busy dreaming about becoming the first female press secretary.'

'Yes, I think you're right,' she admitted. 'In fact, I know you are. Otherwise, how else could I have mistaken you and Governor Fontaine for human beings?'

Again Slater gave a thin, tight-lipped

smile. 'Don't *give* the governor any credit for this, Ms. Winslow. I assure you, he's quite unaware of what is going on.'

She sensed he was telling the truth. 'You saying that he doesn't know you've been smearing Cassidy?'

'Of course he doesn't. Unfortunately, our dear honorable governor is the kind of idiotic purist who would withdraw from the nomination if he so much as smelled the word *smear.*'

'Well, that makes me feel a *little* better,' Clare said. 'All I hope now is, I live long enough to see you and Langley, here, get yours.'

'Somehow, I rather doubt that you will,' Slater said. 'Either of you.'

'If that's true,' Ryan put in, 'then maybe you wouldn't mind answering a couple of questions.'

'Such as?'

'Was Senator Brickland ever involved in any of this?'

'No.'

'How about Wells Beaman or T. S. Murchinson?'

'No. Neither. I merely had Turk visit

435

both of them to make Clare — and whomever she enlisted to help her — *think* that Senator Cassidy was trying to cover up his past. To help convince her of that, Turk always mentioned that he worked for the senator. I knew that would start you wondering,' Slater continued, looking at Clare, 'and along with all the other intrigue — like Falcon's picture, Mary Jo's murder, Murchinson's jealous, crazy accusations, Cassidy's pro-Nazi father — it was merely a matter of my sitting back and waiting . . . watching . . . letting your dogged determination gradually weed out what you thought was the truth . . . '

'Sweet of you,' Clare said. She was quietly raging. 'And I, perfect pupil that I am, didn't let you down, did I?'

'Not once, my dear.' Slater's smile grew taunting.

Ryan saw Clare, unable to control her frustration and loathing, start to move as if to attack Slater. He quickly caught her by the arm, used his weight to make sure she couldn't go anywhere, and said to Slater, 'Something that's always puzzled me is, where Dean Callum fits in.'

'Dean Callum?' Slater frowned. 'I don't know any Dean Callum.' Then to Langley: 'Is he one of your men?'

'No, sir.'

'You don't expect us to believe that, do you?' Clare put in. 'Or anything else you say.'

'What you believe,' Slater snapped, 'is of no interest to me. At this juncture, I — '

Ryan stopped him. Long ago he'd decided that Callum wasn't working for Slater or Langley; he'd just wanted to see if either of them had any idea who the 'fanatical reverend' was. Guessing now that they didn't, he said: 'Forget Callum. He's probably just some religious crank, anyway. What I want to know is, why did you kill Nancy Shearer? I mean, soldier boy, here' — he nodded at Langley — 'torched the Richters because the old captain would've said the Falcon photo was a phony, right?'

'Yes.'

'Okay. But why then kill the girl? What did Nancy Shearer have to do with all this foreign intrigue bullshit?'

'Very little,' Slater said loftily. 'She was merely a pawn, sacrificed for the greater cause. I needed one of Cassidy's employees to actually be at Dulles Airport, so you would believe that Turk was working for the senator. I therefore chose Miss Shearer. She generally met all the visiting VIPs, anyway, so she was a natural for the task. When no one showed, she believed she'd been the victim of a prank phone call and returned home.'

Ryan gave Slater a hard stare. 'Then the only reason you killed her was because if we'd spoken to her, she would've told us what really happened?'

'Exactly. You might not have believed her — not with all the evidence you'd already compiled against Cassidy — but I wasn't prepared to take that risk.'

'Why, you cold-blooded bastard!' Clare exclaimed. 'Murdering innocent people for . . . for . . . '

'Please,' Slater said, unruffled, 'let's not get unduly emotional. A plan as complicated and vitally important as this had to be perfect right down to the minutest detail. Absolutely nothing could be left to chance. And believe me, my dear, nothing was.'

'Including 'bugging' my town house,' Clare said.

Ryan saw Slater and Langley exchange faint smirks. For a moment he wondered why. Then, as it hit him, he guessed: 'Bugs that weren't even hooked up, right?'

'Correct,' Slater said. He shot Ryan a look of surprised respect. Then said: 'Since Ms. Winslow reported every move you two made directly to me, I didn't see any need to eavesdrop.'

'Then why put them there?'

'To confuse us,' Ryan said. It was all beginning to fit. He felt only one or two pieces still remained missing. 'Keep us off his tail. Without those fake bugs — us thinking that Cassidy had put them there — sooner or later we would've gotten suspicious; wondered how the hell the enemy always knew our every move.'

'Again, absolutely correct,' said Slater. 'Ryan, you're a smart man.'

'Wrong. A *smart* man would've figured

all this out while it still could've done him some good.'

'Perhaps.' Slater smiled. 'Anyway, as I said, nothing was left to chance. Like pieces of a giant mosaic, each tiny clue was fit precisely in place before my plan was put into operation. That way, nothing unexpected could happen. Because it's the unexpected — that infinitely minute yet overlooked detail — that so often causes the ruination of an otherwise perfect plan. And I was determined not to let that happen — '

'Aren't you forgetting something called luck?' Clare reminded him, interrupting. 'After all, if you hadn't been lucky enough to find that old photo of Cassidy, the rest of your little scheme would've been worthless. Incidentally,' she said, curious, 'where did you find that picture? I mean, everyone seems to think it was in Mary Jo's purse, so — '

'It was,' Slater said. He paused, quietly triumphant, then: 'In her purse, along with some snapshots of her friends.'

'Then how'd you get hold of it?'

'Because,' Ryan said, gritting, 'he's

Falcon. Aren't you, Karl?'

'Yes,' said Slater. He sat stiffly erect. 'I congratulate you on your astuteness, Ryan.'

Ryan didn't say anything. Angry with himself, he looked at Clare, who was still stunned, and shrugged as if to say sorry.

'Now, now,' Slater said smugly, 'there's no need to be so hard on yourselves.'

'Tell them, sir,' Langley urged. 'Tell them how you did it. Let them see how really ingenious you are.'

'It was simple,' Slater said. 'But, then, most truly brilliant plans are. As a Coast Guard officer in those early months of World War Two, I knew of Cassidy's relationship with Mary Jo Buffram. Therefore it was easy for me to plant all the clues which I knew would entice you and Miss Winslow into believing the senator was both Falcon and Mary Jo's murderer.'

'Th-then it was *you* who killed her?' Clare said, finally finding her voice.

'With these very hands.' Slater held them up for Ryan and Clare to see.

'Murchinson was wrong, then?' Ryan

said. 'It was you, not Cassidy, that Mary Jo was seeing on the side?'

'Correct. She was perfect for my needs.'

'Until she caught you using that transmitter?'

'Curiosity,' Slater said, shaking his graying blond head. 'A very dangerous affliction. Just think,' he added with a tight grim smile, 'none of this would've been possible if a certain young girl hadn't gotten bored and decided to find out what I was doing.'

'It wouldn't have mattered,' put in Langley. 'You would've still found a way to win this election, sir. I'm sure of it.'

'You still haven't said why you took Cassidy's picture,' Ryan said.

'I didn't. At least, not just the picture. I took Mary Jo's billfold. The picture just happened to be tucked inside.'

'For the money, you mean?'

'No, of course not. At the time, my family had plenty of money.'

'Then why?' asked Clare.

'Because I thought it would make it more difficult for the police to trace her identity should they find the body. I intended to throw the billfold away later. But then, when I saw Cassidy's photo, something — some inner sense — made me hang on to it.'

'And when the murder hit the papers,' Ryan said, 'and the cops found the transmitter and started talking spies, you figured things were getting too hot for you and went underground, right?'

'Eventually, yes.' Slater paused, his expression sneeringly arrogant as he reflected upon the past. Then: 'You see, Senator Cassidy was not the only one whose family had influence. My own father, who regrettably did not live to witness my success, had certain powerful friends who arranged for my medical discharge. After that, of course, it was simple for me just to disappear.'

'Until after the war was over?'

'Yes. Then, in the late forties, again with my father's help, I began a career in politics with one goal in mind: the presidency. Unfortunately, it gradually became apparent that I lacked the necessary social charm for the position, so — '

'You decided to become a king-maker instead.'

'Precisely. And, as the record shows, it is a role I am ideally suited for. The only problem in the beginning was to make sure that I attached myself to the right 'king.''

'Then, along came Fontaine — '

'Exactly. I knew immediately he was the right candidate. All he needed was the right person behind him to give him that extra ingredient — drive — which he so obviously lacked.'

'He lacked more than drive,' Ryan needled, 'or you wouldn't have needed to smear Cassidy.'

'Ah, yes, that indefinable magic . . .' Slater sighed and shrugged his thick shoulders. 'When I first became Fontaine's campaign manager, Senator Cassidy had announced that he had no intention of running for the presidency. And against all his other opponents, the governor seemed clearly the winner. But, unfortunately, Cassidy was just playing a waiting game. And within a few weeks he made his move and gave his little 'I have been persuaded to run'

444

speech.' Slater paused, his deep-set blue eyes narrowed in anger, then added: 'When the announcement came, I knew Fontaine didn't stand a chance of defeating Cassidy, and what we needed was a quick assassination . . .'

'Very pretty,' Clare said.

Slater ignored her. 'That was when I sent for my dear friend, Turk.' He looked at Langley as a father looks at his favorite son. 'Injured war hero, disillusioned veteran, impoverished cripple cheated by the VA out of his pension — who could do the job better?'

'Sounds like a marriage made in heaven,' Ryan said sarcastically. 'Tell me, guys, what stopped you from burying Cassidy?'

'The fickleness of the public,' said Slater. 'I realized that even with the senator dead, there was no guarantee that Henry Fontaine would be elected. Whereas, if his opponent were smeared only days before the election, the public would have no choice but to vote for the remaining nominee. So, once Cassidy announced he would run, I hired a diver to help me find the U-boat, exchanged photos, planted the fake memo from German Intelligence, then killed the diver and — '

He broke off as with alarming suddenness the front door was kicked open.

Ryan, along with everyone else, turned and looked, startled, as Dean Callum staggered into the room.

He was an awesome, wrathful sight.

Larger than life.

He held an old service revolver in one hand, while the tattooed knuckles of the other were bleeding from his fight with the lobby security guard. His clothes were torn. His face was bruised and swollen. But he seemed oblivious of it. He paused a few steps into the room and glared at the faces before him, sunken eyes raging with religious fanaticism, and then aimed his gun at Slater.

'Murderer!' he shouted. 'At long last God has delivered you to me!'

Ryan hurled himself at Prince, who was already reaching for his gun. Langley, an instant later, tried to protect Slater by throwing his body in the line of fire.

Callum fired. The gunshot rang deafeningly in the confined space. The bullet hit

Langley in the back. It slammed him against Slater, sending them both sprawling to the floor.

Callum fired wildly again. He missed everyone but shattered one of the mirrored walls. Glass flew everywhere, driving Clare down behind the couch. Langley, meanwhile, rolled over, pulled his gun, and shot Callum neatly in the belly. The balding giant dropped his revolver, grunted with pain, but still came stumbling toward Slater.

Ryan saw none of this. He was too busy fighting Prince on the gold-carpeted floor. They rolled over and over, Ryan trying desperately to keep the muscular enforcer from shooting him. Both struggled for possession of the gun. Ryan finally forced the barrel upward, into the side of Prince's neck. Prince tried to twist the gun away. But Ryan was too strong for him and in the struggle Prince inadvertently pulled the trigger.

The bullet smashed into Prince's jaw, up through his head, and blew off the top of his skull. He died instantly.

Ryan scrambled up. He saw Clare

ducked behind the couch; Prince dead on the gold carpet; Langley, on his knees in front of Slater, arms outstretched, both hands holding the gun with which he now shot the onrushing Callum in the chest. The huge man staggered, as if punched, but continued to lunge for Slater. And before Langley could fire again, Ryan kicked the gun out of his hands. It flew across the room, hit the arm of the couch, and slid under an end table.

'Get that!' Ryan shouted at Clare. As she scrambled for the gun, he grabbed Langley and kneed him in the throat. The gray-haired cripple collapsed, choking. Ryan knocked him senseless with a swift, chopping blow across the back of the neck.

Slater, meanwhile, tried to get away from Callum. He scrambled up. Realized Callum was blocking his path to the front door. Whirled around, fearful. Saw the balcony. Ran to it and tried with fumbling fingers to open the door.

He had it partly open and was trying to squeeze himself through — when Callum caught him. The insane-eyed giant in black seemed unaffected by his wounds. He grabbed the panicked campaign manager in his massive arms, lifted him effortlessly overhead, and hurled him through the sliding glass door.

The door shattered. Broken pieces of glass flew everywhere. Slater, bleeding profusely, fell sprawling onto the balcony. He lay where he fell, momentarily stunned, ears roaring.

Callum lumbered through the broken glass door after Slater. More glass showered onto the balcony. Callum crunched over it, mindless of the blood coming from his glass-inflicted cuts and the bullet wounds in his chest and belly.

Slater saw him coming. As if in a daze, he scrambled away, crablike. Then, trapped in the corner of the balcony, he raised his hands to protect himself.

'W-wait!' he begged as Callum reached for him. 'Stop-p! I don't know you! Who — ?'

'I'm the Lord's disciple,' Callum boomed. Blood came from between his foam-flecked lips. 'Chosen by Him to avenge the death of my wife!'

'Death of your — ?' Slater's voice was

choked off as Callum picked him up and crushed him in a bear hug. Slater struggled frantically, eyes searching the sweat-soaked, blood-flecked, deranged face glaring at him.

'Who . . . are . . . y-you?' he finally gasped.

'Buffram,' said Dean Callum. 'Marine Sergeant Alvin Buffram!'

Behind them, in the living room, Ryan and Clare heard the name and looked at each other. Shocked.

Ryan saw Callum lift Slater high overhead and ran outside to stop him.

He was too late. Dean Callum threw himself and Slater off the balcony.

37

Ryan ran to the railing and looked over. Slater's prolonged, fading scream floated up to him. Then the two still-clasped bodies hit the sidewalk, bounced floppily apart, and landed in separate, mangled heaps. Passersby stopped and looked up at the balcony, then back at the lifeless bodies in stunned, horrified silence.

Ryan bounded back into the living room. 'Call the secretary,' he told Clare. 'Have him stop the president from making his speech.'

Clare picked up the receiver, dialed the State Department, and asked to speak to Secretary Royce. Then, as his secretary came on the line: 'This is Clare Winslow. I must speak to Secretary Royce at once. It's an emergency.'

'I'm sorry, Ms. Winslow. Secretary Royce isn't here. He's on his way to the White House.'

'Then call him in his car,' Clare

insisted. 'Tell him that Ryan and I have positive proof that Senator Cassidy is innocent, and he's to stop the president from making his speech.'

'But — '

'Just do it!' Clare shouted. 'And tell him that we'll get to the White House as fast as we can.' She hung up. Then, checking her watch, she added to Ryan: 'We've got fifteen minutes to get to the White House.'

They ran from the condominium, along the hall to the elevator. The down button was alight, indicating the car was already in use. Ryan grabbed Clare's hand and pulled her on along the hallway. 'C'mon. Stairs'll be quicker!'

They ran down the four flights of stairs, Clare kicking off her high heels. There wasn't time to talk. Both doubted that the secretary would act upon receiving their message. Nor did it seem likely that they would reach the White House in time to convince the president not to address the nation. But they had to try. Because of them, and Slater's plan, Cassidy was about to be falsely accused of treason and

452

politically ruined. As he'd told them that day in Wilmington, it would be on their consciences forever if they destroyed an innocent man.

Downstairs the lobby was crowded with residents gathered about the battered security guard. Ryan and Clare turned outside, unseen. Another mob had collected on the sidewalk about the mangled corpses. Drivers of passing cars had stopped to gawk. Massachusetts Avenue was jammed with honking rush-hour traffic.

'We'll never get a cab in this mess,' Ryan said. 'We'd be better off on the corner.' They ran down the block, looking around for a taxi. Ryan saw one in the cross traffic that was stopped at the light. Grabbing Clare's hand, they ran between cars and across the street. The taxi driver saw them coming and waved them off. 'Can't take you,' he shouted. 'I'm on my way to pick up another fare.'

'Not anymore,' Ryan said. He opened the rear door, pushed Clare inside and scrambled in after her. 'Right now,' he added, 'all you got to do is get us to the

White House — fast as you can!'

'Sorry, mister, I can't — '

Ryan reached over the seat and grabbed the startled driver. 'This is an emergency,' he hissed. 'Either *you* drive — or I do. Take your goddamn pick.'

'I'll drive,' the driver said grudgingly. 'But I warn you, this is kidnapping.'

'Tell that to the president,' Clare said.

The driver drove off, grumbling. But in traffic his competitive spirit rose. He drove recklessly fast, cutting in and out of the rush-hour traffic with accustomed ease, and pulled up at the appointments gate at exactly five minutes to five.

Ryan pushed extra money in his hand. The two of them scrambled out of the taxi. Both had their ID ready. But before Clare could get out more than 'This is an emergency,' the guard had glanced at their ID and was leading them through the gate to an awaiting limousine.

'The secretary's expecting you,' he told them. He then slammed the door and motioned for the driver to go. The limo sped smoothly up the driveway.

38

Two solemn-faced, gray-suited Secret Servicemen hurried Ryan and Clare down the long burgundy-carpeted hall that led to the White House Communications Center.

The president and Secretary Royce were already in the small TV studio, talking in quiet, urgent tones by the door. The press secretary and several White House staff members stood nearby. Behind them, camera and lighting crews gave their equipment a final check, while soundmen tested the microphone on the president's desk, which sat center stage before a wall bearing the great seal of the United States.

'Four minutes, Mr. President,' the press secretary reminded him.

'Thanks, Bill.'

A makeup man hovered nearby, anxiously sponging away the perspiration that glistened on the president's pancake-tanned forehead. The Secret Servicemen escorted Ryan and Clare into the studio, then withdrew at the president's nod.

'What the hell's this all about?' the president said before Ryan or Clare could speak. 'First, you bring me evidence to prove Senator Cassidy's guilt, and now you tell Secretary Royce, here, that the man's innocent. What kind of game are you two playing?'

'No game, Mr. President,' Ryan said quietly. 'Simple truth is, we made a mistake.'

'A mistake?' began the secretary.

The president cut him off. 'What kind of a mistake?'

'Mr. President,' Clare said, 'we know who Falcon is now. It's Karl Slater, Governor Fontaine's campaign manager.'

'Slater . . . ?' The president exchanged dubious frowns with the secretary. 'How do you know that?'

'He told us,' Ryan said. 'Just before he was killed.'

'Karl Slater's dead?' The president and the secretary looked shocked.

Ryan nodded. 'Few minutes ago.'

'He'd planned to kill us,' Clare put in, 'right after your speech. But Alvin Buffram — husband of that girl Falcon

456

murdered on Bogue Banks — broke in . . . '

'Two minutes, Mr. President.'

'Be right there, Bill.'

'Mr. President,' said Clare, 'please, you can't make that speech.'

'Young lady, do you know what you're asking?'

'Yes, sir. But Senator Cassidy's innocent, and — '

'How *can* he be?' demanded the president. 'All the documents from the U-boat have been authenticated, and even the senator himself admits the picture you found is his — '

'It *is* his,' Ryan said. 'But it was planted there — by Slater. Since he was the spy, he knew exactly where to put it.'

'He also wrote that memo himself,' Clare added. 'The one that was supposed to be from German Intelligence. We had a graphologist compare it with an office memo Slater had written — she verified both were done by the same hand.'

The president frowned, uncertain now, and looked questioningly at Secretary Royce.

'It wouldn't hurt to check it out, sir,' the secretary said.

'Cancel the speech, you mean?'

'I was thinking more along the lines of postponing it,' Secretary Royce said. 'At least, till after you have either a CIA or FBI graphologist examine samples of Slater's handwriting. That shouldn't take long. And depending on their findings, you can either reschedule your address or cancel it altogether.'

The president nodded. He carefully considered what the secretary advised, while Ryan and Clare waited tensely for his decision.

'One minute, Mr. President . . . ' The press secretary now approached within a step or two, adding: 'You really should get seated, sir.'

The president motioned with his impeccably groomed hand, 'Yes, yes, all right, Bill,' and sighed heavily, 'If I cancel my speech,' he told Ryan and Clare, 'there's going to be millions of Americans out there in front of their television sets . . . wondering what the hell's going on.'

'I know that,' Ryan said. He looked the

president respectfully in the eyes. 'And I don't mean to be rude, sir, but, well, better they wonder than remember, later, that you misinformed them.'

There was silence. No one in the studio moved. For a moment, as he and the president remained eye-to-eye, Ryan wondered if he'd trumped an ace. Then: 'Mr. President, *please* . . . ' the press secretary urged.

'That's okay, Bill,' the president said. He stood erect. Taller than anyone present could ever remember. 'I've decided not to address the nation tonight, after all.'

If the studio had been quiet before, now it resembled a morgue. Ryan and Clare looked terribly relieved.

'B-But what shall I tell them?' the press secretary stammered. 'The networks . . . and the press, I mean?' The president looked directly at Ryan. There was nothing but respect in his grave blue eyes.

'What would *you* tell them?'

'The truth,' Ryan said.

The president smiled, then laughed softly. 'Thank you, son,' he said quietly. 'I might never have thought of that.' He then turned to the press secretary and told him to issue a statement to the networks and the press that the president was postponing his address until some last-minute information that was critical to the content of his speech had been carefully analyzed.

39

By eight fifteen that night the police had arrested Robert 'Turk' Langley, and two FBI graphologists had confirmed that the now-deceased Karl Slater had written the memo found aboard the sunken U-boat.

Greatly relieved, the president canceled his speech and issued a brief press release that blamed a 'heretofore unknown national security risk' as the reason. Most of the country shrugged this off as political 'gobbledygook,' and went on about their business. But the smart minds in Washington realized that, translated, this meant that something was going on at the White House . . . and promptly jammed the phone lines trying to discover who knew the truth.

The president, meanwhile, notified Senator Cassidy that he'd been exonerated of all spy accusations and apologized for the harsh and undue stress he'd been put through.

Cassidy was so relieved at being cleared, he merely accepted the apology courteously and agreed solemnly that the president had been acting within his rights.

Both men were only too pleased to get off the phone.

The president next notified a stunned Governor Fontaine about Slater and his attempt to discredit Senator Cassidy, adding that due to the efforts of Mr. Ryan and Ms. Winslow, this near miscarriage of justice had been averted literally at the last moment.

It was another phone call that both men were eager to end.

Ryan and Clare had been 'uneasy guests' of the president ever since the halted telecast; now, as they joined the president and Secretary Royce in the Oval Office, they were unable to tell by the grave expression on both faces whether the news was good or bad.

'Sit down, please,' the president told them. Then, as they did so: 'I have received the graphologists' reports on Karl Slater's handwriting, and . . . ' He paused, letting them hang there for a final moment as he and Secretary Royce continued to frown, and then added: 'Everything is as you both stated.'

Ryan felt something heavy slip from his shoulders. He smiled, and by looking at Clare knew she had experienced the same relief.

'Thank you, Mr. President . . . Mr. Secretary,' Clare said.

'Thank *you*,' the president replied. 'I just wish there was some way in which I could reward you both for the great service that you've done this office . . . and your country.'

The president looked at the secretary. At Clare. Then at Ryan. Then, 'You're an unusual man,' he said. 'Brief as our relationship has been, I feel I've gained something just by knowing you. You, too, Ms. Winslow. Please accept my deepest and warmest thanks.'

'Mine also,' said Secretary Royce. 'And please remember, if my office can ever be of service to either of you, don't hesitate to call me personally.'

It was time to go. The president insisted

Ryan and Clare be taken home in a White House limousine. Good-byes were said. Then they were escorted out to the car by Secret Servicemen.

Alone with the secretary, the president poured them both a drink and the two old friends sat there talking for a while. 'It hasn't been such a bad eight years,' the president reflected. 'There's been a few times when I wondered what the hell made me crazy enough to accept this job, but, well, like I say, Harold, it hasn't been such a bad eight years.' He paused as the intercom buzzed, and Mrs. Jennings's voice — cheerful despite the late hour — told him that Senator Brickland's widow was on the phone.

'She apologizes for calling this late,' Mrs. Jennings added, 'but what she has to tell you is of the utmost urgency.'

'Put her on, Mrs. J,' the president said. 'Stay,' he then said as the secretary respectfully started to leave. 'I've no secrets from you.' Then he picked up the phone and spoke to Mrs. Brickland.

Diana was calmer than he'd expected. specially when he heard what she had to say. Her husband had indeed left a suicide note, she explained, and after reading its contents, she had wrongfully destroyed it. But now her conscience insisted that she not keep his confession a secret any longer. Then, in a quiet, slightly faltering voice, she revealed the entire contents of the letter.

The president listened without interrupting, although inside he was shocked and dismayed by Avery's confession. When Diana was finished, he said gently: 'Thank you, Mrs. Brickland. I know how awfully difficult this call must have been for you, and I cannot tell you how much I admire your courage and integrity for sharing this regrettable news with me. At this moment,' he added, 'I am not sure what should be done next, but I shall discuss it with my advisors and try to do whatever is least painful for you and your family.'

After the chief executive had hung up, he finished his drink and poured himself another. Then he picked up the little crystal polar bear and toyed with it for a few moments before telling Secretary

Royce the gist of the phone call.

The secretary was stunned to hear the news of Senator Brickland's guilt. He was also greatly concerned about Kyle Lane, and the injustice he'd suffered unnecessarily all these years.

The president was equally disturbed. 'We must do all we can to find this man, Harold. I wouldn't want my term to end knowing someone of his character and courage is still forced to live in hiding.'

'I agree,' said the secretary. 'I just hope he's still alive.'

40

The White House limousine sped smoothly through the well-lit streets of the nation's capital. In the quiet, dark comfort of the backseat, Ryan and Clare sat deep in thought as they relived the day.

They were starting to unwind. As they did, both felt a strange mixture of relief and sorrow as they realized the grand adventure was over. From now on there'd be no more Falcon or probing into Senator Cassidy's past; no more diving on the U-boat; no more threat of being followed or killed; no more traveling together; no more even being together.

In fact, Clare thought regretfully, with her once more handling Governor Fontaine's PR campaign, and Ryan back at his salvage business in Morehead City, there really would be no reason for them to ever see each other again.

The depressing thought prompted her to break the lengthy silence. 'Well, I don't know about you,' she told Ryan, 'but after all that's happened in the past few weeks — especially today — I doubt if anything's ever going to shock me again.'

He smiled, but didn't say anything. He just sat there looking into her large, dark-lashed green eyes and forced himself to admit how much she meant to him. As he did, somewhere inside him he felt a key turn: a decision made. 'That right?' he said quietly. 'I'm glad to hear that.'

Something in his tone worried her and made her feel uneasy. She said only: 'Why?'

''cause I'm going to tell you something,' he said. 'Something that I've never told anyone before.'

She should've been pleased. Hell, she'd been after him long enough to share his thoughts. Himself. But instead her uneasiness increased. She felt gooseflesh rise all over her. And without knowing why, she sensed she didn't want to hear whatever it was that he intended to say. But before she could stop him, he told her who he really was.

She was surprised, although all along she'd guessed he was a man with a secret.

But while she listened, knowing as she did how hard it was for him to talk about himself, she realized that for once something other than her career mattered to her. She cared for Ryan and didn't want to lose him.

She didn't know how deeply she cared; only time could answer that. Nor did she know how much *he* cared, or whether she could keep him and still keep her career. Or whether after the election, she'd even want a career. None of those things mattered right now. All that mattered was that she did not lose Ryan.

'Why're you telling me all this now?'

''Cause I've decided to turn myself in — face whatever the law has to throw at me — and I wanted you to know before I did.'

'Terrific,' she said, almost angrily. 'Your timing's lousy. You know that, don't you?'

'What d'you mean?'

'I *mean*, Ryan, why the devil must you turn yourself in now?'

''cause I'm tired of living a lie — always wondering if the next guy along has handcuffs.'

'I see.' She paused, wondering how she could stop him. Then: 'I don't suppose there's anything I can say, or do, to make you change your mind?'

'No. Nothing.'

'I didn't think so.'

'I'm sorry. It's nothing personal or anything. It's just that, well, I know now I've got to be free — no matter what the cost.'

'Even if that cost is us?' It was out before she realized. Immediately embarrassed, she added quickly: 'Listen, I know this is going to come as a shock to you — it did to me, too — but, well, I . . . I've gotten used to having you around, and . . . well, I like it. Like it a lot . . . and . . . well, I — oh, damn,' she said suddenly, 'what's the use? You're not going to change your mind. And this whole thing's absurd, anyway.'

He studied her, surprised to learn that he meant something to her, too. Then, 'I never knew,' he said gently, 'that it was the same for you, I mean.'

'Well, now you do,' she said, adding, 'Does it make any difference? No,' she said when he didn't answer, 'of course it doesn't. Not with you. It should, though — especially now.'

''cause we both feel something, you mean?'

'No. Though that's important, too. No, what I meant was, surely you've more than repaid society for Avery's deception and Governor Brickland's death. So, why risk almost certain imprisonment, if not death itself, when it'll serve no real practical purpose?'

He shrugged, wishing he was better with words so that he could explain exactly how he felt. He said: 'I'm sorry, Clare. This is something I got to do.'

She sighed, knowing now that she'd lost him. 'Very well,' she said. 'If I can't change your mind, how about one favor?'

'It's yours.'

'Turn yourself in tomorrow. That way, we can at least spend tonight together.'

Ryan looked at her a moment, his yellow-gray eyes expressionless. Then he cupped her face in his hands and kissed her for an answer.

It was a searching, passionate kiss.

471

When they finally separated, Clare said:
'Was that a yes or a no kiss?'

'Couldn't you tell?'

'Uh-uh.'

'In that case,' Ryan said, 'we'd better try it again. And keep on trying it . . . until you find out.'

They did.

Outside, the faces of Senator James L. Cassidy and Governor Henry Fontaine smiled down at them from campaign billboards.

THE END

We do hope that you have enjoyed reading this large print book.

Did you know that all of our titles are available for purchase?

We publish a wide range of high quality large print books including:
Romances, Mysteries, Classics
General Fiction
Non Fiction and Westerns

Special interest titles available in large print are:
The Little Oxford Dictionary
Music Book, Song Book
Hymn Book, Service Book

Also available from us courtesy of Oxford University Press:
Young Readers' Dictionary
(large print edition)
Young Readers' Thesaurus
(large print edition)

For further information or a free brochure, please contact us at:
Ulverscroft Large Print Books Ltd.,
The Green, Bradgate Road, Anstey,
Leicester, LE7 7FU, England.
Tel: (00 44) 0116 236 4325
Fax: (00 44) 0116 234 0205

MYSTERY IN MOON LANE

A. A. Glynn

What could be the explanation for that strange affair of the corpse in old-fashioned clothing, taken from a burning building in Moon Lane by rescuers during the Blitz, Christmas 1940? Who is the mysterious young woman who models for young artist Jevons as he paints in a haze? What is the myth of the seal woman, and should Dan and his wife Leonora be afraid? Ghosts, myths and ancient curses are the subjects of six stories from the pen of A.A. Glynn.